THE
COOTER
FARM

THE
COOTER
FARM

A NOVEL BY

Matthew F. Jones

HYPERION

New York

Library of Congress Cataloging-in-Publication Data

Jones, Matthew F.
    The Cooter farm : a novel / by Matthew F. Jones. — 1st ed.
      p. cm.
    ISBN 1-56282-991-2 : $18.95 ($23.95 Can.)
    I. Title.
  PS3560.052244C66   1991
813′.54—dc20   91-28419
                                                                CIP

Design by Irva Mandelbaum

First Edition

10 9 8 7 6 5 4 3 2 1

Very special thanks to:

Judith Riven, for her guidance, insight and kindness in the editing and publishing of this book.

My agent, Michael Carlisle, for his support, perserverance and abiding belief in me and my work.

The staff and writers at Squaw Valley, for providing me with the opportunity.

Reuben Jones, for coming along when he did.

To Charles W. Jones (1919–1991)
"The point then, was not words,
  but deeds, right?"
And to Karen,
For everything, thanks.

Behold, I shew you a mystery; We shall not all sleep,
but we shall all be changed,
In a moment, in the twinkling of an eye, at the last trump.

—I Corinthians 15:51–52.

THE
COOTER
FARM

1

"**Y**ou can't work in shit all day long and expect to walk away smelling like a rose." My Uncle Hooter Cooter gave me that advice when I was ten years old. In the years since I have been the recipient of countless pearls of wisdom, both solicited and unsolicited, but none have endured with the strength of that simple, untouched statement.

His real name was Stewart Cooter, the oldest of the three Cooter children, but everyone called him Hooter Cooter on account of his laugh. It started out slow and low in volume—"Hoo, Hoo, Hoo"—and steadily built in intensity like a steam engine gathering speed until it could be heard by everyone remotely within hearing distance. Finally, when Uncle Hooter was all out of breath—having literally laughed himself into exhaustion—he would roll his head way back so that his eyes were pointed toward the sky and exhale one final long-drawn-out "Hoooooo," as if he were contemplating what it was that was so funny in the first place.

Shit, cowshit in particular, was a weighty subject within the Cooter family, and my Uncle Hooter was the self-acknowledged expert among us. He was a dairy farmer. He farmed the same piece of land his father had farmed and his father's father before that. Two hundred and fifty acres in Devon County, New York. It was not considered prime farmland. The terrain was hilly and rocky—"the consistency of chicken and dumplings" my uncle used to say—but the Cooters were stubborn people, firmly entrenched in their own tradition, and they steadfastly refused to give the farm up.

Devon County is located in the Sanasaw River Valley. Of my time there I remember pockmarked hills bunched around the valley like storm clouds and the river itself, lazy in summer, hard in winter, and savage in the springtime, moving constantly through the valley like a determined gypsy. Then there were the hollows, running like veins throughout the hills of Devon. It was here, up the hollows—far removed from the river and the prime flatlands that ran adjacent to it—that a farmer had to work like hell just to eke out a living. And even then there were no guarantees.

The Cooter farm was located half-way up Shenker Hollow. Shenker was considered a "rich hollow" on account of its population, which, in the local vernacular, was predominantly "city folk." This simply meant that, aside from the Cooters and the Bateses, the heads of the five remaining Shenker Hollow families were something other than farmers by birth and were, more than likely, conceived someplace outside of Devon County. By contrast, the "poor" or native hollows throughout the county, such as Slide and Dead Creek, were inhabited solely by large extended families, in which all of the members looked uniquely similar, with their large heads, vacuous gazes, and varying numbers of teeth.

There were approximately eighty head of cattle on the Cooter farm during its best years. Of this number, around sixty were milkers and the rest calves and unfreshened heifers, depending on the time of year. Despite the terrain and its composition it was, all things considered, probably one of the most prosperous of the hollow farms—which is somewhat analogous to saying that Marv Throneberry was one of the better ballplayers of the original Mets. There was a vast difference between tilling the lush flatlands down by the river and trying to make things grow on the side of a rock-infested hill. Down there, my uncle often pointed out, anyone could prosper. Up in the hollows there was an art to it.

The first twelve years of my life were spent on the Cooter farm. My father was the second oldest of the Cooter children. He was christened Harold Cooter, but was given the nickname Scooter in the ninth grade after he set a new record for the one-hundred-yard dash in the Sanasaw Valley Athletic Conference. The name stuck.

He married Nora Anne Sasser the day after their high school graduation in 1956. After a week-long honeymoon at Niagara Falls, they set up house in a mobile home about two hundred yards distant from the Cooter residence. My brother Craig was born ten months later. Nora Anne wanted to have another child right away—"In this godforsaken country the worst curse that can befall a person is to be raised an only child"—but shortly after Craig's birth, Scooter became convinced that he had developed cancer of the testicles and refused to engage in any further sexual activity.

The diagnosis took place in the shower the day before my mother returned home from the hospital with Craig. While "soaping himself"—this was Scooter's phrase; my Aunt Mary Jean claimed that my father was actually "flogging the dolphin" when the discovery occurred—he happened upon a bump at the base of his testicles. He immediately diagnosed cancer, refused to see a doctor, and prescribed cold ice packs and total sexual abstinence until the offensive growth disappeared. Upon my mother's attempts to arouse him during this period my father would leap out of bed, charge into the kitchen like a prefight boxer, and pour a tray of ice down his shorts. Sexual excitement of any kind, he explained, would send blood rushing to the inflamed area, causing his balls to swell and to eventually drop off like overripe acorns in the fall.

This course of treatment continued for almost a full year, with Scooter arriving home from work in the evening and flopping immediately onto the couch, where he would remain for an hour with a bag of ice applied to his balls. Thereafter he would spend twenty minutes with his legs spread apart in front of a mirror, groping at the affected area as if it were bread dough, massaging it all the while with Barlow's udder balm.

According to Nora Anne and much to my father's credit, I suppose, he was an excellent parent to Craig throughout his ordeal and never missed a day of work as a result of his illness. He was, in fact, the perfect father and husband with the one exception that he failed to fulfill his connubial duties, and that one shortcoming, to my mother's way of thinking, removed him from the umbrella of protection provided for in their wedding vows.

Nora Anne finally issued an ultimatum. She threatened to take Craig and move into Anton if Scooter would not agree to see Dr. Lerner, the Sasser family physician. My father at first protested—the fact that the bump had not gotten any larger in nearly a year was proof that his treatments were working and besides he didn't want another man to "fondle his privates"—but he finally gave in when Nora Anne met him at the door one Friday evening with her coat on, her suitcase in hand.

When the fateful day arrived, Dr. Lerner conducted a thorough physical examination and announced that, number one, what Scooter was feeling was his epididymis and that he, Dr. Lerner, also possessed one, as did every other normal male of the species, and number two, that if Scooter continued to apply ice to his balls he was in danger of incurring permanent nerve damage in the area.

Scooter, much relieved, went home to make up for lost time. I was born nine months later.

Scooter loved to farm. He loved to get up in the morning before the sun and he loved to come home at night, remove his shit-laden shoes, fill his pipe, and go out on the porch to gaze out over the fields of his workplace. This information is relayed by me secondhand. My father's days as a farmer ended shortly after I was born. For me, personally, it is hard to picture my father as a contented farmer who loved to sweat in the fields during the day and to squeeze cow teats at night. It is difficult for me to envision him sitting out on the back porch of the Cooter house, smoking, drinking, and discussing butterfat content until past midnight. All of that occurred before any time that I have the slightest memory of. I mention it by way of background, as information relayed to me by people who do remember.

The problem was that Nora Anne didn't like the smell of cowshit. Everything about farming bothered my mother. She said that she couldn't sleep with a man who smelled like a heifer. It made her feel that she was doing something "vulgar and immoral." Her father, who managed a hardware store in Anton, had wanted her to marry a nine-to-fiver—a businessman like himself. She threatened to leave Scooter unless he found another job. Three years after they were married, Scooter took a job as an artificial inseminator with Century Semen, Incorporated. He thus became the first Cooter male in three generations to forsake farming for a "workaday job."

The rest of the Cooters wouldn't let Scooter forget that he had abandoned the family farm. They lost respect for him and saw him as a weakling. A man who didn't have the backbone to stand up to his wife. When Uncle Hooter spoke, the rest of the family would listen intently and nod their heads in silent agreement, appearing like blind disciples fawning over a holy man. Indeed, at the dinner table, my uncle seemed often to be regarded as some type of Shenker Hollow guru. But whenever Scooter began to speak, the rest of the family would look down at their plates, greatly intrigued suddenly with what they were eating, and Uncle Hooter would go "Hoo Hoo Hoo" as if whatever it was that Scooter had to say was very funny indeed.

My father never complained, but Nora Anne did. Once, when the entire clan was together at the big house for Sunday dinner, she screamed at the assembly: "What is the matter with you people? Why don't you give Scooter a chance to speak?"

"What did she say?" asked my grandfather, who was very old at the time and had lost most of his hearing.

"She wants to know why we don't listen to Scooter," said my grandmother, who, as the diplomat of the family, did her best to appear fair in these situations.

"I guess I know all I need to know about bull semen," said Father Cooter. Uncle Hooter went, "Hoo Hoo Hoo," and then everyone else, even my father, joined in the laughter.

That evening, I heard my parents talking in their bedroom. Nora Anne was crying and my father was trying his best to console her.

"Why do you let them do it?" my mother sobbed.

"They're my family. They don't mean nothing," said Scooter.

"They laugh at you. They don't respect you. It's humiliating to me and to the kids. How do you think they feel seeing their father laughed at?"

"They're just children. They don't understand."

"Let's move away, Harold. Start fresh someplace where you can be your own man."

"A man doesn't leave his roots," said Scooter.

My mother must have buried her head in the pillow then. I heard her crying once more. This time in low gasping sounds as if she were having trouble getting air. Scooter mumbled something and walked out of the room.

My father was on the road most of the week selling bull semen. He had a briefcase filled with literature extolling the virtues of Century Semen. It contained hundreds of pamphlets, each one adorned with pictures of jet-black bulls in four-point stances, staring with glassy eyes and flared nostrils, their tremendous balls hanging like honeydew melons inches from the ground. Underneath each picture, in large black print, was the bull's name, qualifications, and the cost of its semen.

SURE SHOT
Dam-RAMSDEL
Sire-SHARPSHOOTER
$1,500

Century sold its semen mostly to the richer, purebred farms downstate. The Cooters, like most of the farmers in Devon County, had their own scrub bulls for breeding purposes. I once overheard Hooter tell my father that he could buy half a herd of heifers for the price of "one shot of that jism that you sell."

My father's goal was to save up enough money to buy a few quality bulls of his own. He dreamed of the day when he would own his own mail-order insemination service so that he could sit at home, jerk his bulls off, and sell their semen to rich farmers all over the county without ever having to leave Shenker Hollow.

Being on the road as much as he was took its toll on Scooter. If he was home more than two days in a row he would grow restless, as if he couldn't find enough to occupy him. Or perhaps it was just the opposite and he was bombarded with possibilities too multitudinous to choose from. At times his mind seemed to be a depository into which ideas settled like nuclear fallout. Occasionally one of these ideas would fester and grow, appearing to obliterate all others as if it were some cancerous cell suddenly run amok. He loved us, of that I am quite certain—although there was a time when I was not so strongly convinced of it. For years I simply believed that my father was weird.

He has been convinced that he is dying ever since I have known him. Of course science will bear him out. It is an established fact that once the human body completes puberty the dying process begins. This I can state without reservation since Scooter not only informed both Craig and me that it was so on numerous occasions throughout our childhood, but also periodically provided us with medical treatises on the subject, the pertinent passages always carefully underlined.

Several times a year my father would contract some type of major, debilitating disease and then, much to the consternation of all of us, find it necessary to immediately announce its onset to the entire family. The discovery of his symptoms and his subsequent self-diagnosis could arrive at any time and would manifest themselves in most unexpected ways. When I was six years old he lost his favorite pipe. He searched the entire trailer only to come up empty-handed. He then instructed Craig and me to help him look again, but to no avail. Finally he gave up and accused his younger sister, Mary Jean, of stealing the pipe on one of her frequent visits. After he had enlightened us all with a fifteen-minute dissertation on the irresponsibility of youth and on how little crimes lead to bigger crimes, my mother suggested that he take a look in his back pocket. When he did, there the pipe was, right where he had left it.

Holding the offending instrument in his hand, my father

collapsed onto the couch as if he had been punched in the solar plexus. He was silent as he turned the pipe over in his palm, examining it as if it were the smoking gun that would send him to the electric chair. At long last, he looked up, holding his hand out for the rest of us to see.

"Kids," he said barely above a whisper. "Your daddy has something very important to tell you."

The sound of his voice caused my stomach to twist into a fist and I instinctively reached for Nora Anne's leg to hold on to.

"You're both big boys and I am very proud of you, but . . . you're going to have to take on even more responsibility soon."

"For Christ sake, Harold." Nora Anne only called my father Harold when she was mad or disgusted.

"Please, let me finish, Nora Anne." My father's voice was still low, but steady.

"You're scaring them for the love of Pete."

"I don't want to frighten any of you. But I think it is better to tell you all now than . . . later."

"Tell us what, Daddy?"

"Your mother knows what I am talking about. She just loves us too much to want to think about it, but it can't be hidden any longer. The symptoms are as plain as the nose on your face," said Scooter, gazing up at my mother as if he had just noticed her presence in the room.

Nora Anne, hands on hips, curled her lower lip over the upper one taking on the appearance of one of those aborigine women with the pegged noses and deflated breasts whose pictures often decorate the pages of *National Geographic* and who, in succeeding years, would serve as kindling for my smoldering adolescent libido.

"Harold, what in God's name are you talking about?"

"It's called Alzheimer's disease. I've been watching it progress for weeks."

"Once more, Harold. I'm afraid you have lost me."

"I didn't want to upset anyone until I was absolutely sure."

"You're out of your mind."

"It's part of the disease," his voice was starting to rise and to take on the indignant tremor of logic. "Presenility, loss of memory, dementia . . . Honey, you've seen it happening as well as I."

"Is Daddy losing his mind?" sniffled Craig, who had been born with a postnasal drip that caused his nose to run like a water faucet when he was excited. As a child, my brother never simply talked. He either sniffled, wailed, or whined when communicating. Sometime between adolescence and adulthood he added an indignant stammer and a sort of high-pitched bellow to the above repertoire.

"Your father apparently has already lost his mind, by his own admission, and now he is causing me to lose mine." Jesus. Did it spread? Like the flu maybe? One member of the family gets it and the next thing you know everyone else is afflicted, running around like blithering idiots with their brains leaking out of their ears? Even to a six-year-old this possibility was terribly frightening.

Nora Anne turned and walked from the room, dragging me behind as I clung stubbornly to her leg like someone's oversexed dog. In the kitchen she took out a cutting board and a large knife and began chopping up vegetables as if they alone were to blame for the heartaches of womanhood. The more fervently she attacked her quarry the more difficult it became for me to maintain my death grip upon her leg, yet somehow I managed, refusing to let go until long after I had heard the sound of the front door opening and my father's pickup truck as it pulled noisily out of the driveway and rambled off down the hollow road.

2

Other than Craig, who was very strange and seldom spoke to me while we were growing up, Mary Jean Cooter was the only person living on the farm who was at all close to me in age.

Bradford Cooter was the next to the youngest of Mother and Father Cooter's four children and he was eleven years older than Mary Jean. Bradford—most folks called him Looter Cooter on account of the fact that he had been arrested on numerous occasions for petty larceny and had once spent six months in the county jail—lived and worked on the farm and spoke in what, to a ten-year-old child at least, were mostly indecipherable phrases. Once, after I had accidentally knocked over a pail of milk during evening chores, Looter turned to me and said, "Fucking kids, fucking cows. I don't know what's worse, fucking kids or fucking cows."

Mary Jean, who was three years older than me, was my closest friend and only confidant. We worked together in the barn, morning and night, sat together every day on the school bus, and spent the majority of our free time with one another.

13

We were drawn even closer together by our common belief that we were both somehow misplaced. Neither of us felt as though we actually belonged on the Cooter farm—I on account of the way in which my father was ostracized, and Mary Jean because she was convinced that she was never intended to be. The thing that stuck in her craw wasn't so much the age of her parents when she came into being—her father being sixty-two and Mother Cooter being fifty-three at the time. Rather it was the fact that she was conceived sometime after the great tractor accident in which my grandfather's brains were scrambled beyond repair.

He was baling hay on the side of a hill when the John Deere 10-40 that he was driving hit a rut and tipped over. Father Cooter landed on his head in the pasture and was lying unconscious beside the overturned machine—its engine still growling and giant wheels spinning in wasted effort—when Uncle Hooter found him. For over two weeks following the accident, he remained in a coma in the Devon County Hospital. After he woke up it was several more months before he was able to recognize anyone. Most of his days were spent gazing out the big kitchen window in the breakfast room of the Cooter house, blowing tiny spit bubbles and occasionally blurting out largely incoherent phrases about the "big war" or "the enemy." My grandfather had served in World War I and, according to his doctor, the accident had somehow triggered his long-repressed memories of the period.

Eventually much of his memory returned, but he never did recover the "full package" as Mary Jean so artfully described it. Working on the farm was impossible. Even the smallest tasks became jumbled in his simple mind. The rest of the family unanimously agreed to retire Father Cooter from day-to-day operations in the barn the day that he sat down beside a perfectly healthy breed bull and nearly castrated the poor animal by yanking on its distended testicles as if they were milk-filled teats.

It was close to two years following this terrible misfortune when, much to everyone's surprise I am sure, my grandmother discovered that she was pregnant with Mary Jean.

According to Mary Jean there was a simple explanation for her being. "After the accident Mother figured the farm'd never survive without another man to take Papa's place in the barn. She kept her eye peeled and when she seen her chance she took it, by which I mean the first time she caught the old man with a hard-on she hiked up her skirt, showed him where to stick it, and prayed she'd get a man like what she wanted. Only it didn't happen that way. She got me instead."

"I was nothing but a wild hare," she was fond of saying. Whatever the motive behind her existence, wild hare or no, I for one was thankful for her company. In a childhood of uncertainties and swaying emotions there was never a doubt about where Mary Jean stood in my heart. I loved her unabashedly. And if I was never quite as certain about her unwavering devotion to me, at least she was always around in the rough times.

To my admittedly naïve mind she was a wealth of knowledge and seemingly possessed a degree of information on every conceivable subject, particularly the serious ones—such as basketball and ice hockey—and the more mysterious ones— like sex. My aunt was not only a tremendous athlete—once she had established position under the basket her hook shot was virtually unstoppable—but a natural behind the mike as well. She could do a running play-by-play during our fiercest backyard confrontations without missing a beat. "Greer into Chamberlain—Chamberlain spins on Counts—the big guy fakes. Pumps. Shoots. Yes! and a foul!—The Dipper with a chance for three."

But perhaps as important as any of her other qualities was her ability to make me laugh. And laughs, in the hip-deep quagmire of the Cooter farm, were a rare commodity throughout my youth.

3

F ollowing my grandfather's accident, Hooter, as the oldest
son, assumed command of the farm. If the Cooter farm
had been a ranch, then my Uncle Hooter, short and squat
with a chaw in one cheek and his John Deere cap pulled tight
to his razed head, would have been its foreman. He laid down
the law for the rest of us and his finger alone pushed the
buttons that made us go.

He patrolled the barn like a prison yard commandant—
"Looter, you're a half hour late, damn it! Out larcenizing again
last night? Big fucking crook, going around stealing Frito-Lays
and six-packs of beer! That ain't no way to learn farming."

One thing you had to say about Hooter was that he was
nondiscriminating. No one escaped his watchful eye or was
exempt from his periodic outbursts. He worked harder and
longer than anyone else in the family and often told us that
he would have been satisfied if any of the rest of us would
accomplish even half of what he did in a day. The truth was,
and everyone knew it, that none of us could, and that without
Hooter the farm, like so many others scattered throughout

16

Devon County, would stumble along into irretrievable poverty.

Few people argued with Uncle Hooter. Looter once tried to stand up to him and got knocked into the manure spreader for his effort. Dripping with shit and bellowing like a heifer in heat, he charged at Hooter—"I'll kill you, you lousy bastard!"—only to be tripped up by his snarling brother, who easily sidestepped his younger sibling.

"You ain't got balls big enough," growled Hooter, turning away in disgust. "You're just a small-town punk."

Mother Cooter generally sided with Hooter in everything. "It ain't easy running this place and I just thank the good Lord that I got one son that grew up to be a man."

"But how come he's so mean to everybody?" I asked.

"If he weren't giving the orders, Ollie, nothing would ever get done around here. Your father, bless his wandering soul, is too busy thinking he's dying to keep an eye on things, and Looter ain't worth a tinker's damn for nothing but thievin'. Since your grandfather had his accident that leaves nobody but Hooter to see to things."

"Maybe someday I'll run the farm, Grandma."

"That'd be just fine, Ollie. Somebody has to to take over, and your Uncle Hooter sees something special in you all right. That's for sure."

In truth, I believe I did receive less of my uncle's wrath than most anyone else. I guess he just felt sorry for me sometimes on account of Scooter, whom he viewed as a pathetic although harmless enough creature.

"Ollie," he would say, "you got the right makings to be a good farmer. Just don't shy away from the shit and don't let no woman tie a string to your balls." I wasn't exactly sure what he was talking about, but I was reasonably certain that his words were somehow intended as a putdown of my father.

Uncle Hooter never married. He claimed that he didn't have

time for a wife. Besides, a woman wouldn't add anything to the life he already had except for maybe a few additional headaches, and those, he continuously reminded the rest of us, he already had plenty of, mostly as a result of his thankless efforts in trying to keep the farm afloat. He had been born in the Cooter house—my grandmother gave birth in her bedroom on a Friday afternoon and was back in the barn to help with the chores on Monday morning—and God willing he would die there.

Every Friday evening after dinner he took a shower, put his best pair of coveralls on, and drove into Anton. Friday afternoon chores were always a little easier on the rest of us as a result of Hooter's change in attitude as the evening drew closer. All throughout milking he would whistle and exchange pleasantries with the rest of us, something virtually unheard of during the rest of the week. Even the cows seemed more relaxed, as if the lack of tension in the barn made them more willing to surrender their nutritious gifts.

Mary Jean was the one who told me what it was that Hooter did on his trips into town. "First he goes to the Moonrunner and gets piss drunk. Then he goes over to Martha Wadkins' house and gets his gun off."

"His gun off?" Mary Jean was very worldly for a girl of her age, and many of her expressions required interpretation.

"Yeah. You know, they screw."

"What do they screw?"

"Each other, dummy. He sticks his thing in her thing and they screw."

"How do you know?"

"I seen 'em."

"When did you see 'em?"

"Last year. One night when I slept over at Karen Bristle's house. She lives right next door to Mrs. Wadkins, and this one night we seen Hooter go in through her backdoor and then the bedroom light went off. So we snuck over and looked through the window. They looked just like a bull and a heifer going at it, only they weren't standin' up."

"I don't believe you." I was only ten years old and couldn't picture Hooter humping like a bull or imagine why he would want to. I had seen cows doing it lots of times and it didn't appear to be a very enjoyable experience. A lot of grunting and groaning, with the bull trying to get the heifer in position and her acting as if she weren't at all interested. Then, after it was all over, the two of them would look at each other like the whole thing had been a big mistake before walking off in opposite directions. To imagine Uncle Hooter, who was built somewhat like a sumo wrestler, attempting such a thing with Mrs. Wadkins was nothing short of ludicrous. He would crush her to death. Martha Wadkins sang in the church choir every Sunday. She had a milky complexion and, from where I sat, appeared to be fragile as a twig.

"Believe it or not, it's true," said Mary Jean, "and someday I'll prove it to you."

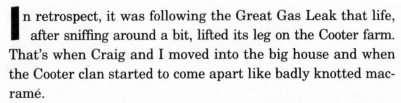

4

In retrospect, it was following the Great Gas Leak that life, after sniffing around a bit, lifted its leg on the Cooter farm. That's when Craig and I moved into the big house and when the Cooter clan started to come apart like badly knotted macramé.

It was a Saturday morning in May. Sun shone through the slats in the window shades of my room, splashing across my bed like golden liquid. Voices woke me, soft and muffled, coming from the kitchen.

"Then you have noticed changes?" I eased quietly out of bed and tiptoed over to the bedroom door.

"Harold, for Christ sake, will you leave it alone." My mother's voice was like somebody's favorite record after it has been played to death. I pressed my ear up next to the door and tried not to breathe.

"I just can't think anymore, babe. Something is destroying my mind. Maybe there's a gas leak in the stove."

"Harold, I'm leaving."

"Our bedroom is right next to the kitchen and it's a well-known fact that inhaling natural gas kills brain cells."

"I have had it."

"What?"

"I said I'm leaving."

"Where are you going?"

"I don't know. Anyplace. I can't take it anymore." I heard footsteps, light and quick like a deer on ice, and the front door opened and shut.

The station wagon started up, followed by the sound of wheels spinning through loose gravel and a momentary flash of blue paint as the car passed by my window on its way out the driveway. There was to be no slaughter of helpless vegetables this time. My mother was gone and the trailer was left in silence, the kind that traps you like an armed guard. I didn't dare move away from the door for fear that the noise would summon some new explosion within the trailer. At long last a kitchen chair scraped across the linoleum floor. The sound was like an owl's screech. Footsteps, this time heavy and deliberate, moved across the room. Someone was dialing the telephone.

Then I heard Scooter's voice, quiet but firm: "Yes, is this the service number? I'm calling to make a complaint.

"This is Harold Cooter from up in Shenker Hollow. We've got a gas leak out here and I would like someone to get out here right away to look at it." Pause. "Uh huh. Yes, well, this is an emergency. My wife has already left on account of it and I won't sleep in the trailer until it has been repaired." Pause. "Thank you."

The phone clicked back into its cradle. I heard Scooter walk over and knock on Craig's bedroom door. "Come on, Son, get up right away. We're going over to the big house for breakfast."

Then he was at my door, knocking and delivering the same message as if he were some kind of hotel wakeup service, while I scrambled away from the door and hurried to get into my clothes.

My two uncles and Mary Jean had just come in from the morning chores. Mother Cooter was making breakfast, and my grandfather was sitting at the kitchen table piling sugar cubes on top of one another and making gurgling sounds.

The smell of cowshit and warm silage mingled with that of sausage and pancakes. The screen door slammed behind us as we entered the kitchen, set apart by our lack of essence.

"Hoo! Hoo! Hoo!" crowed Hooter. "Look who's here. The big-shot business executive and his family. I'll bet they just got up."

"Well, kids, there's plenty of fixin's. Just pull up some chairs and we'll start beefing you up," said Mother Cooter.

"Where's Nora Anne?"

"She left," said Scooter.

"Huh? Left where?" Hooter grunted. He had just forked a huge pile of pancakes onto his plate and was in the process of rolling one up with cinnamon and butter.

"Gone. I don't know where," said Scooter as he calmly reached for a cup of coffee.

"You ain't making sense, boy. She run off or what?" Hooter had just crammed an entire rolled-up pancake into his mouth. Melted butter and cinnamon oozed from the corners of his lips as he spoke.

"I guess. That ain't why I'm here, though. I come asking for a favor."

"Mary Jean, you go on and take Craig and Ollie out back on the porch. Here, kids, pile your plates up and skedaddle." Mother Cooter spoke in the tone of a drill sergeant. We did as she said without protest. Obviously an adult conversation was about to occur, which meant that we weren't welcome and that more than likely it had something to do with us.

Mary Jean and I immediately removed two lawn chairs from the back porch and ran quickly around the outside of the house to the kitchen window. Placing the chairs down, we stood up in them just high enough so that our heads came to a spot directly below the windowsill. Craig quietly watched the entire proceeding with a bemused look upon his face, as if bored with such juvenile antics, before sniffing in disgust and returning to the porch to finish eating his pancakes.

The words from inside the kitchen floated through the open window and reached Mary Jean and me in muffled snatches, where we crouched silent and unmoving on our unsteady platforms.

"I want to leave the kids here," my father's voice was sharp and clear as a gunshot.

"Here? What on earth for?"

"There's a gas leak in the trailer."

"Gas leak! Jesus Christ! He's dying again, Ma. Hoo! Hoo! Hoo!"

"I don't see nothing funny about it."

"What did he say?" asked Father Cooter, who had lost his hearing around ten years prior to losing his mind.

"He's got a gas leak."

"Probably been eating too many cucumbers," said my grandfather.

"Hoo! Hoo! Hoo!"

"Son, why don't you just call the gas company and get the leak fixed?"

"I did. They're coming out this afternoon."

"So?"

"So I'm going away for a few days," he took a deep breath and spit it out as if it tasted bad, "and since Nora Anne ain't goin' to be here I want to leave the kids with you."

"Boy, you always been a little unraveled but now I swear the whole coil come undone. What in blue blazes are you talking about?"

"My trailer has a gas leak. My wife run off and left me with two kids even though she sees me getting worse every day and knows I ain't got much time left. Everybody knows I'm dying but they act like nothing is happening and I got to get away and think the whole thing out." He spoke very slowly, enunciating each word as if he were explaining simple logic to a young child.

"But, Son, you can't just leave your boys, especially with Nora Anne gone. We'll get the gas leak fixed."

"Gas leak my ass! Ma, the man is talking about leaving his kids and you're talking about fuckin' gas leaks!"

"Gotta change your diet. Eat different. Yes sir. Stay away from the Guddamn garden. . . ."

"Dad, just eat your breakfast. Hooter, raising your voice and cussing never did nobody a lick a' good."

"A man that would run off and leave his own kids ain't worth a hell of a lot if'n you ask me. Course I knowed that about him the day he decided to leave the farm and put on a salesman's suit," said Hooter, going on as if my father wasn't even in the room.

"They're better off without me. I'm slipping. Slipping fast, and they can see it plain as anybody else. It pains me to have to look at their faces everytime I can't remember something or I start stumbling over my words as if I'm drunk."

"Son, you need a rest, that's all. Nora Anne is just blowin' off steam. She'll be back. A mother never strays far from her children. Just leave the boys here with us and pick them up when you're ready." My grandmother spoke as if Craig and I were a pair of shoes that were being dropped off at the cobbler's.

"I love 'em, Ma, but they'll be better off here. Ollie loves the farm and Craig was always his mother's boy anyhow. I reckon she'll be by to pick 'em up if I ain't."

And that was all I heard because just at that moment the chair I was standing on slipped out from underneath me and I came crashing down on top of Mary Jean. Mother Cooter yelled for us to get away from the window and my grandfather started screaming, "Get the guns! Get the fucking guns! The lousy bastards are coming through the windows!" And somewhere amid all that confusion my father slipped out the front door, got into the truck, and drove away. And that's how I ended up at the big house.

5

I had difficulty sleeping those first few weeks at my grandparents' house. Most nights I would wake up alone and in
the dark to the sound of hushed and anxious voices—"Tiny
gremlins," said Mother Cooter, "dancing a soft shoe amongst
your gray matter." By the moon's light, I would study the
webbed cracks in the ceiling above my bed, shamelessly
pledging all manner of promises to God—until the first ray of
sun chased the gremlins away. If my grandmother was right
about the source of those nocturnal voices, then they were
surely dancing to a tune of longing and guilt; longing for my
parents and the safety of the trailer and guilt as thick as
honey for the self-perceived certainty that I was somehow responsible for their departure.

Nora Anne called twice a week. She told Craig and me that
she would send for us when she could. She never said where
she was. "California more'n likely," said Hooter. "As far away
from cowshit as she can get."

Our conversations were always the same. I would ask her
why she had left and my mother would begin to cry. Eventu-

ally, through the tears, she would manage to tell me that I wouldn't understand until I got older. When was she coming home? I would ask. Hesitating between words, she would reply that she wasn't sure, that she had some things to work out (actually she may have used the word "resolve," although at that time the word was foreign to me). After that, at least from my point of view, there seemed to be little left to discuss. Wordlessly, I would turn and hand the phone to my brother.

Scooter was on the road all week selling bull semen. On the weekends he lived in the trailer by himself. Apparently the utility company had either fixed the problem with the gas or given the stove and its fixtures a clean bill of health. Whichever, the problem, like so many of my father's maladies, was never mentioned again. Such was the history of his varied health problems; he tended to get things—more often than not, fatal things—one time only, before ridding himself of them forever.

Scooter spent a lot of time with Craig and me on the weekends. In the afternoons we would go fishing together or on picnics or take long rides in the country—Craig and me bouncing up and down in the back of the old Chevy while my father was up front, searching for the bumps and screaming at the top of his lungs, "It's Mount Everest! Fasten your seat belts for this one, folks!" Craig found Scooter's behavior quite childish and would have preferred most times to stay home and read a book, but my father insisted that he come along, which only served to widen the already substantial gap between the two of them. As for me, I looked forward all week to these outings and only wished that I could be with my father on a full-time basis. Unfortunately, the overnight responsibilities of fatherhood were well beyond what Scooter could handle at that time, and so my brother and I remained at the big house.

We shared my father's old room. Since Scooter had moved his bed to the trailer when he and Nora Anne were married, Craig and I each had a cot to sleep on. In the trailer we had always had separate rooms, thus it was a new experience for me to lie awake at night listening to my brother wheezing and whining in his sleep. On occasion, a sharp, slapping noise, like the sound of fresh butter being thrown against a wall, would emanate from Craig's side of the room, followed shortly thereafter by a stifled moan and a quick trip to the bathroom. This, I supposed, was my brother's way of dealing with his own dancing gremlins, although Mary Jean, upon hearing of these nocturnal noises, claimed they were nothing more than Craig "choking the chicken."

The upstairs bathroom became my haven on those sleepless nights. With a *Hardy Boys* hardcover in hand, I would tiptoe silently down the hall past Looter's and Mary Jean's rooms and into the secure warmth contained within its four walls. Against my bare buttocks, the hard wooden seat bolstered me against the night. With the fan gently whirring and the door safely locked, I was isolated from the rest of the house, alone with my thoughts and consumed by someone else's mystery.

It was during one of my nightly passages to the bathroom that I ran into Uncle Hooter, or, more precisely, that he ran into me. Confronting my uncle under such circumstances was surprising on two accounts. The first was the hour, which was well past midnight. My uncle, like most farmers, was a creature of habit and a morning person by necessity. He was up at four-thirty every morning and was dressed and in the barn, shoveling silage down for morning feed, before the rest of us had washed away the previous night's cobwebs. He was in bed by nine-thirty every evening, unless it was a Friday night, when he always went into Anton and often didn't stumble home until almost sunup the next morning, whereupon he would shower, gulp down a cup of coffee, and head immediately out to the barn in his hungover state.

The second reason I was caught off guard was that in my brief lifetime I had never before seen my Uncle Hooter on the second floor of the Cooter house at any hour. There was simply no reason for him to be there. He and my grandparents shared the downstairs bathroom while the rest of us used the one upstairs. His room was located on the first floor, kitty-corner to my grandparents' bedroom and right next to the backdoor leading out to the driveway. He had insisted upon taking over that location at the time of my grandfather's accident so that he could come and go without waking the rest of the house—"I get more work done around here while the rest of ya is sleeping than the bunch of you do in a whole day's worth," he was fond of saying.

The second-floor hallway was split into two corridors that came together at a ninety-degree angle at the top of the stairs. Mary Jean's room and the bathroom were situated on one side of the stairway while my father's old room sat at the end of the opposite fork, adjacent to Looter's bedroom. I was tip-toeing quietly down the corridor leading away from Scooter's room and clinging tightly to the *Hardy Boys,* when Hooter came barreling around the corner nearest to the bathroom, running directly into me and knocking me flat onto my back.

"Ollie! What the hell! What are you doing here?" he whispered, at the same time reaching down to cover my mouth with a hand as thick as a bear paw. Anger flashed like carnival lights in his eyes. I was too terrified to respond even if it had been possible for me to do so through that massive impediment. Frozen momentarily like Greek statues around a pissing fountain, neither of us moved. Finally, glancing deliberately up and down each hallway, Uncle Hooter removed his hand from my mouth and indicated with one finger for me to keep my voice low.

"I was just going to the bathroom," I stammered, the fleshy taste of my uncle's hand still filling my mouth like the aftertaste of some vile medicine.

He stood staring down at me as if he were trying to figure out what to do next. He was dressed in an undershirt and boxer shorts that ended at his knees, his thick calves protruding like cedar posts from the bottoms of his underwear. For one terrible moment as I gazed into his flushed face, I was certain that it would simply explode; that the tight skin on the top of his head, shaved as close and flat as an airstrip, would suddenly burst into flames and fly from his scalp like an ascending rocket. He moved the plug of tobacco in his mouth to the opposite cheek and reached down to rearrange his balls, where, just inches from my face, they lay bunched in his shorts like bagged fruit.

"It's kind of late, ain't it, boy?"

"I couldn't sleep," I replied. As much as I tried to hold them back, tears filled my eyes like rush-hour pedestrians. I longed for my parents. I wanted to run into the bathroom and lock the door.

Uncle Hooter's anger subsided as quickly as it had come. He stepped back and reached his hand out to help me to my feet. "It's been tough on you, ain't it, Ollie? What with your ma leaving and all?"

He hoisted me off the floor and into his arms as easily as if I were a bale of hay. For a moment he held me, and his breath, stale and stinking of alcohol, was everywhere.

"Don't sweat it, kid. Just listen to your Uncle Hooter and everything'll be just fine. He loves ya." He squeezed me once before placing me back onto my feet in the hallway and giving me a friendly pat on the behind.

"Now run along and get some sleep."

I was ashamed for having cried in front of him, and as he passed me on his way to the stairs, I tried desperately to wipe the tears away. Even if I had thought to ask what he had been doing on the second floor, I probably wouldn't have had the courage. Around the Cooter farm, Hooted asked the questions and everyone else answered as best they could.

"Ollie?" He was at the top of the stairs now, his head turned back toward me. 'Don't wake nobody else up. We wouldn't want the rest of the house to know that you walk around in the middle of the night, now would we."

It was a statement rather than a question and Uncle Hooter didn't wait for an answer. Before I could respond he was halfway down the stairs.

My heart was still fluttering like a caged bird as I walked down the hallway toward the bathroom. Muffled noises, like nocturnal mice going about their business, came from somewhere within the hollowed walls of the house. I thought at first that it was my imagination, still overstimulated from my unexpected encounter with Uncle Hooter. But as I approached Mary Jean's room the sounds got louder.

Not mice. These were human sounds. A head face down in a pillow concealing laughter? Sobs? Perhaps Uncle Hooter and I were not the only ones who couldn't sleep. Whatever their source, the sounds were definitely coming from my aunt's room.

Mary Jean was the closest friend I had. The one person in the whole world I could cry in front of without feeling embarrassed. We had even played doctor together once up behind Hurley's Pond. Seeing each other naked, we had pinched and probed and laughed at our obvious differences, and when I had tried to put a stick someplace where I shouldn't Mary Jean didn't get mad; she simply explained why I shouldn't do it—"It hurts and besides it ain't right." We often told each other that if the whole world was drowning and we could only save one person it would be each other. Yet she had a private side to her, as if she had a full cookie jar and out of the whole thing she was hiding a couple of the best ones somewhere all for herself. I had never walked into her room in the middle of the night unannounced, and I wasn't about to without a good deal of careful consideration beforehand. Yet I couldn't just walk away. Something about the noises frightened me. Perhaps it was their simple monotony.

I stood silently outside her door hoping that the sounds would stop so that I could continue on down the hallway. They didn't. Taking a deep breath, I eased the door open less than an inch. Moonlight from the uncovered window shot through the gap and into the darkened corridor like escaping liquid. Still, it was impossible to see into the room. I pushed lightly against the door. It opened another couple of inches.

"Mary Jean?" I whispered, at the same time shoving my nose and half of my face through the opening. The noises stopped as if someone had suddenly turned off a spigot. I heard rustled movements coming from the bed.

"Who's there?" The words were strained and muffled.

"It's me. Ollie."

"What do you want?"

"I had to go to the bathroom."

"Go away." Her voice coming out of the darkness was hollow; an owl's hoot on a lonely night.

"I thought I heard somethin'," I whispered, pushing the door open another couple of inches. Her body was clearly visible in the moonlight. Sprawled face down on the bed, arms and legs loosely splayed out, she might've been a rag doll carelessly tossed aside.

"Leave me alone." The body didn't move. I hesitated in the doorway, not certain what to do next. Something was out of whack. This was not Mary Jean. I had a vision of turning the body over and of finding a stranger in my aunt's bed. My heart beat wildly, threatening to break free from my chest, to start hopping crazily about the floor under its own steam like some windup doll. Enough. I turned around and started back into the hallway, pulling the door shut behind me.

"Ollie." The voice, desperate, reached out like a hand from a starving crowd.

"Yes? I'm still here."

"He hurt me."

"Who?"

"Hoo! Hoo! Hoo! Hooter, that's who!"

"What?"

"He made me want to die. The pig-fucking bastard." The hushed whisper cracked and started to fade like a distant radio station as she spoke the words.

I pushed the door open and walked over to her bed. She was dressed in her underwear and a T-shirt, the words ANTON WARRIORS emblazoned in large capital letters across the back. Her thick auburn hair was gathered in a tangled mass at the base of her neck. The white light falling across the bed gave her skin a milky pallor, clearly setting off two black and blue blotches located at the top of each of her muscular thighs. The air was hot with a pungent order, like fresh silage mingled with sweat.

I sat down next to her on the bed. The sheets, gooey and wet, clung to the back of my naked legs.

"He done just what he wanted, like always," sobbed Mary Jean. She had her face buried in the pillow. Her entire body gently twitched as if it had been caught in the early summer breeze sneaking quietly through the open window. "He took everything, Ollie. He was so Goddamned dirty."

I didn't know how to comfort her. The roles had always been reversed. Mary Jean was the one I always counted on to have all of the answers. It was she who could make my deepest fears seem laughable. Now I sat silent and unmoving in the middle of a mess I didn't understand, my hand on my aunt's heaving backside and the pungent odor of a finished act filling my nostrils; as useless as a visitor at a deathbed. I hated myself for being so young and stupid.

Maybe Mary Jean was simply playing an elaborate joke.

Perhaps at any moment she would leap up off the bed, break into uncontrollable laughter, and say, "Ollie, you're such a melon head." But as I looked again at the dark bruises on her legs I knew it wasn't so. I felt ashamed for having even entertained such a thought. She was hurting and somehow my Uncle Hooter was responsible for her pain. It couldn't be. Nothing made sense, as if black and white had suddenly become less distinguishable in my ten-year-old mind; the two colors merging and obliterating each other to leave, in the final analysis, a mottled, nondescript gray.

Eventually—I'm not certain exactly how much time elapsed—Mary Jean rolled onto her back. Her face, swollen and red from crying, had the appearance of a bloated doll. Reaching next to the bed she found her nightshirt and pulled it on over her head. Standing up, the cloth shirt consumed her, hanging like a feedsack from her lanky frame. She plucked a tissue from a box on the nightstand and reached up under the gathered folds of the nightie with her right hand. Grimacing in pain, she wiped herself with the same short, quick motions that Mother Cooter used when scrubbing soiled laundry in the kitchen sink.

When Mary Jean removed her hand, the tissue was red with her blood. She glanced at it as if it were an interesting archeological find before tossing it into the wastebasket with a quick flick of her wrist.

"Get up," she said.

I got up off the bed and leaned against the wall. I wasn't sure what to do, but I knew that I loved Mary Jean and that I couldn't leave her there to toss and turn among those sticky sheets, crying alone in the night. I watched silently as she stripped the sheets off the bed and threw them into the laundry basket in the corner of the room. She was a blossoming beauty at the age of thirteen, with long, slender limbs that she was still growing into and the soft, yet well-defined features of a female deer.

She walked over to the bureau, moving gingerly on the outside part of her feet, and pulled fresh sheets out of the bottom drawer. She made the bed and lay down gently on the side closest to the window.

"Stay with me, Ollie."

I walked over to the bed, leaving the *Hardy Boys* somewhere behind me, and slipped beneath the covers. Mary Jean wrapped her long arms around me and shivered.

"He hurt me bad," she mumbled, and then, instantly it seemed, she was asleep. Sometime before daylight I slipped out of her bed, picked up my book, and tiptoed back to my own room.

6

Shenker Hollow is shaped like a giant horseshoe and Hurley's Pond sits at the very top of the loop. The pond was and still is, I assume, to Shenker Hollow youth what the Anton town pool was to the children who lived in the village. During the summer, unless I had to help in the hayfields or it was raining, I was there every afternoon. Despite the fact that I was a strong swimmer, Mother Cooter insisted that I had to be accompanied by an older person. "It's the buddy system, Ollie. It has nothing to do with your age, which is very young." As often as she would consent to it my buddy was Mary Jean.

Jeremiah Hurley had taken over the family farm following his father's death. Jeremiah wasn't cut out for farming. He had, according to Uncle Hooter, become too used to "city life," which meant that he lived in the village, worked nine to five at the Anton Creamery, and had his weekends free. But when old man Hurley died, his will left the place to Jeremiah for "so long as" he continued to operate it as a dairy farm.

Greed runs like a river through most men, and Jeremiah

was no exception. He wasn't about to pass up something that was free. He left his job at the creamery, loaded the family belongings into his flatbed Chevy, and made the move up the hollow along with his wife, Bonnie, and their four children.

Along with the farm, Jeremiah had inherited from his father a strong propensity for pure grain alcohol. The old man had operated a still on the premises and Jeremiah wasted little time in rounding it back into shape. He was usually too drunk to do the evening chores and too hungover to get up in time for the morning ones. Consequently, it was Bonnie and the kids who kept the farm afloat, and according to most everybody who was around to remember, they did a more than creditable job of it for a time.

Bonnie loved Jeremiah despite his shortcomings. Neither cows nor hard work bothered her, nor did living on the side of a mountain. She had only one complaint, really, about moving out of the village; during the summer months she was no longer able to swim her fifty laps a day at the Anton Town Pool. She kept after Jeremiah about constructing a pond on the premises. At long last, Jeremiah, perhaps sensing the one nonnegotiable point in his marriage and becoming more strongly convinced every day that he could never return to the drudgery of the Anton Creamery, undertook construction himself. Much to everyone's surprise, he stayed at it. He rented a bulldozer to dig with; then he hauled in several truckfuls of gravel to line the sides and bottom of his creation. The man-made crater filled naturally from a stream running through the backside of the property. Two months after he had begun work, Jeremiah announced that the pond was finished.

That night he went out on a toot. Arriving home in his customary condition, he decided to go out back and admire his handiwork. The next morning when Mrs. Hurley tiptoed down to the water's edge for her inaugural swim, she found Jeremiah floating like bloated algae face down upon its surface.

The coroner figured that Jeremiah had slipped on the crater's edge and then careered like a rollicking sea otter down its muddy banks. Being in no condition to negotiate the four-foot climb back up the slick walls to the field's edge, he had either fallen asleep or passed out, probably the latter, given that he had a blood-alcohol content in excess of .30, and had drowned then without a struggle in his self-made tomb.

The coroner's report aside, Mrs. Hurley blamed herself for Jeremiah's death. While she had been peacefully sleeping, he no doubt had been hollering for help as he wallowed in the cool waters, trapped and dying like a harpooned whale. It was Bonnie, after all, who had nagged him into building the pond in the first place. A week after his death she gathered together every piece of swimming apparel in the house and burned it all in a giant bonfire as a final tribute to her husband.

The day following this grand gesture, she loaded herself, her four children, and the remainder of the family's belongings into Jeremiah's flatbed Chevy and headed the vehicle in the general direction of Des Moines, Iowa—that particular city being selected primarily as a result of its location, which was, Bonnie had discovered through research at the local library, hundreds of miles inland and far removed from any major body of water.

The last news that anyone had regarding the family arrived approximately a year after they had moved. It was related third hand through a friend of someone's cousin who lived outside of Des Moines. The children had all been placed in foster homes, and Bonnie, following a judicial determination declaring her an unfit mother, had been institutionalized. The court's finding had been based in large part upon Bonnie's adamant refusal to bathe either herself or her children. Water, she said, was the Devil's tonic; beware to those who would frolic in it.

For ten years thereafter, the Hurley farm had remained vacant. The issue of who actually owned the property was unclear, although rumors were abundant.

There was the one concerning a fundamentalist group who planned on starting a rebirthing center at the farm. A certain amount of credence was added to this particular story after Looter reported seeing a van pull up to the front door of the house. Two long-haired men, dressed in bib overalls and T-shirts declaring that JESUS WAS A HIPPIE, got out and carried a large tank into the building. The tank, according to my Uncle Looter, looked like "a big fucking bathtub with all kinds of tubes coming out of it and a lid like on a fucking coffin." According to the rumor, members of the group were fully submerged within the tank before being mystically transported back to the womb to experience once again everything that had occurred there while they were waiting to be born. "What in hell could've happened?" asked Mary Jean. "There weren't even room to roll over."

Shenker Hollow was abuzz with the news for a while. But when weeks and then months passed and no one returned to the farm, the excitement gradually died down. No one aside from Looter had actually seen the strangers, and whenever anyone asked him about the story he would get a weird look on his face and say, "It's fucking wild, man." To my knowledge there had never been anyone in the house to verify whether or not the tank was even there.

The shrubs and grass surrounding the house had grown to a height of several feet, and vines clung to the walls and windows like unkempt facial hair. It needed a paint job and the roof was in disrepair, but beyond that the underlying structure appeared to be in pretty good shape.

The pond itself was circled by tall grass and lay in the middle of the back pasture like a liquid trap for the unwary. Unless one knew its precise location one could almost stumble over its high banks and fall into the still water before even seeing it. During the dog days of summer the stream feeding the pond was reduced to a mere trickle. The water's surface, protected from the wind by its banks and the encircling foliage, was like unbroken glass shattered only by an occasional frog shifting position or by a water bug scooting across it like a crazed cyclist.

Great clumps of frogs' eggs floated in the cloudy water as if they had been poached. One day Billy Bates, who had a crush on Mary Jean and who was constantly doing something to try to impress her, ate five large bunches of the eggs in a thirty-second span. Mary Jean, who loved the pond and all of its creatures and hated Billy Bates, told Billy that unless he went and had his stomach pumped the eggs would hatch into pollywogs and chew his insides out in their efforts to get free.

Billy, who at that time had already repeated the fourth grade twice and was not overly intelligent to begin with, took every word Mary Jean said as gospel. He complained of dizziness and said that his stomach felt a little queasy. Mary Jean explained that time was of the essence. Billy took off on a sprint. He ran all the way to his house, located some two miles distant at the bottom of the hollow, clutching his stomach and gasping for air. He dashed into the kitchen and blurted out something to his mother about losing his insides moments before throwing up jellied frogs' eggs all over her freshly mopped floor.

Mrs. Bates, never having seen vomit of such consistency and being the precursor of her son's intelligence, was convinced that Billy, who now lay green and depleted on the soiled vinyl, had just ejected his intestines along with various other internal organs. She promptly ladled the jellied contents into a plastic garbage bag and placed it carefully in the refrigerator before calling Dr. Lerner in Anton. After relating the tragic tale of events to the doctor, she concluded by proudly announcing that she had preserved the essential items in the hope that they could be reinstated into their former position within her son's body. From that day on Billy became known as Pollywog Bates.

One day that summer I sat on the shore of Hurley's Pond watching Mary Jean swim laps from shore to shore in an effortless motion, her long arms reaching out and quietly slapping the water in front of her like paddles on a steamship. With her broad shoulders and lanky limbs she had the classic swimmer's build. No one could quite figure out from whom she had derived such a body. The rest of the Cooters were short and compact and strutted about like bantam roosters, whereas Mary Jean, encompassed in her sinewy body, glided through life in the long, loping strides of an athlete.

Watching her swim was, for me, a joy. Mine was the body of a true Cooter, heavily muscled and like a rock in the water. Although I too would eventually develop into an accomplished swimmer, it was only as a result of hard work and of managing to overpower my foe. Mary Jean on the other hand, considered the water to be her ally and moved through it causing barely a ripple.

It had been over a week since our encounter in Mary Jean's bedroom, and between the two of us, it was as though the entire incident had never occurred. We hadn't spoken of it since. Similarly, any undercurrent of tension between Mary Jean and Hooter remained well concealed from the rest of the family. Their relationship seemed as always—Hooter, in his constant banter, alternating between sarcasm and tight-lipped derision and Mary Jean withdrawn and seldom replying other than under her breath. Indeed, I had almost convinced myself that the matter was a figment of my imagination, conjured up on the toilet seat between chapters of a *Hardy Boys* mystery.

What couldn't be explained away, however, was the physical evidence—those black-and-blue blotches on the backs of Mary Jean's legs, as if, fresh from her morning shower, she had sat on the comic section of the Sunday paper. It would have been impossible not to notice them as she stepped from the pond, shook the water from her hair, and started tiptoeing gingerly over the rocks like a long-necked water fowl preening for its mate. It was as if she had been branded forever with my uncle's hand prints.

"Let's go into the house." Mary Jean stood over me with a towel wrapped loosely about her shoulders.

"Whose house?"

"The Hurley house, dummy."

"What for?"

"I got somethin' to show you."

"It ain't safe in there."

"Who says?"

"Mother Cooter."

"I think you're just scared." She rolled her eyes mockingly and snapped me with her towel.

"Well, Looter says it's haunted." It was true. Uncle Looter claimed that the ghost of Jeremiah Hurley lived in the place and that it was he who had scared the rebirthers off. "Fucker probably moved into their tank," he told Craig and me.

"Looter is crazier than a shithouse rat. I've been in the house dozens of times. Now let's go, unless you're chicken." She turned and started walking through the thick underbrush, her adolescent ass bobbing up and down like a lobster buoy.

Feeling as though I had little choice in the matter, I got up and dutifully followed her through the field.

At the edge of the house nearest to the pond, Mary Jean stopped and took a look around. We were completely hidden from view by the tall grass. I was trying to figure out how we were going to get inside or, alternatively, how to talk Mary Jean out of the idea altogether, when she suddenly grabbed me by the shoulders and spun me around so that I was facing her.

"I'm gonna show you something don't nobody else know about. Do you understand?" I nodded my head up and down, not having the vaguest idea of what she was talking about.

"You gotta promise you won't tell another soul. If you ain't ready to, then leave now. Ya promise?"

"I promise."

"On your life?"

"Yes." It was easy. She was my aunt and I loved her more than anybody in the world.

She kneeled down and reached beneath the corner of the building. A second later, she stood up, holding an open jack-knife in one hand. I winced as she drew the blade lightly across her palm, causing tiny droplets of blood to appear as if by magic.

"Give me your hand," she commanded. Holding it out to her, I turned my head away and squeezed my eyes shut as tightly as I could. I felt a tiny prick and squeezed even harder.

"You can open your eyes now, Ollie. It's bleeding."

Looking down I saw the blood forming a tiny puddle in the center of my palm. Mary Jean was talking again.

"I'm gonna ask you some questions, Ollie. If you can't an-swer 'yes' honestly to all of 'em than the bond between us won't take. Do you understand?"

"Yes."

"Do you believe that there are forces more powerful than us?" Her voice had an eerie quality to it, like wind whistling through an abandoned building.

"Yes or no?" The words were sharp, insistent.

"Yes," I answered, feeling the blood from my hand seeping into the cracks between my fingers.

"Do you believe these forces can be used for good or evil? Yes or no?"

"Yes."

"Do you believe we can influence these forces with our will?"

"I guess so . . ."

"Yes or no?"

"Yes."

"Do you believe in the power of mental unity?"

"Mary Jean, I don't . . ."

"Yes or no?" My hand was beginning to throb and I was starting to get frightened by the singsong quality of her voice. Had she memorized this gibberish from somewhere?

"Yes I do," I answered, hoping the game would soon be over.

"Do you believe that you and I can form a mental unity?"

"Yes."

"Hold out your hand." When I did, I was shocked to see the amount of blood that had gathered there. Mary Jean's hand was just as ghoulish as she held it palm out toward my own.

"If the bond is good our hands will stay together and our blood will mingle and strengthen each other. If it is not they will come apart like opposite poles of a magnet."

We pressed our hands together and held them that way with our eyes closed for over a minute. Mary Jean's large hand covered my own like a red envelope, her blood flowing freely through my fingers and down the length of my forearm. I uttered a silent prayer for unity: a good bond between us. Too many people had already left me and I was beginning to believe that my blood was bad. Mary Jean was the one person I couldn't live without. I was deathly afraid that at any moment our hands would come flying apart and that I would be left bloodied and alone like some pathetic fraternity pledge in the middle of Hurley's field.

"Let this seal it. The bond is good. Our combined strength is as one. There is now a mental and physical unity between us," she chanted before relaxing her hand and letting it drop back to her side.

We wiped our hands on the grass and used Mary Jean's

towel to stop the bleeding. She looked at me and smiled without talking. I was happy that I had pleased her. I felt as though I had passed an important test, as if the final barrier between us had been lifted. I was filled with her warmth and would have followed her anywhere.

Wordlessly she moved through the grass toward the back of the house. She stopped next to a closed window in the basement and waited for me to catch up before squatting down and pushing inward against the glass. The window creaked open about a foot and a half. Mary Jean signaled for me to precede her through the opening.

"Be careful. There's a five-foot drop from the edge of the window to the floor."

"Five feet! Why can't you go first?"

"Somebody's got to shut the window and you can't reach it."

The idea of shutting the window with us in there didn't appeal to me any more than dropping into the unknown blackness below ground level. As scared as I was, however, to turn back now would be impossible. I was under Mary Jean's spell. We were one now. Acting together in physical and mental unity, whatever the hell that meant. I didn't really care so long as it was with Mary Jean.

The cellar was dark and smelled like morning breath: sour and unclean. It was filled with large, mysterious objects. Hidden in shadows, the objects seemed ready to spring to life like creatures in a Boris Karloff movie.

"This way." Mary Jean took my hand and started leading me toward the back of the basement. She moved with the confidence of familiarity. I remembered what she had said about having been in the house dozens of times in the past.

Eventually we stopped in front of a closed door. Mary Jean pushed the door open and led me into a small room. There was a dirt-stained window above ground level that left the room in dusty shadows.

"Sit here," she said, pointing to an empty spot on the floor opposite the window. She reached up and covered the opening with her towel, still stained and moist with our mixed blood. The room blinked into total darkness. I wanted to cry out but was afraid of losing Mary Jean's trust. I bit my lip instead.

From somewhere Mary Jean produced matches and a candle. She lit the candle and placed it between us. Then she sat down opposite me, shadows from the light dancing on her face like tiny ballerinas. The image sitting across from me in the flickering light could have served as the portrait of an emerging woman. Mary Jean's young nipples, brought to attention by the cool moist air, popped up beneath her bathing suit like two curious sea otters emerging from the deep. Her hair, unkempt and damp from the pond, was plastered to the sides of her head in thick layers. Her eyes were watery beads of blackness.

Her hand came out of the darkness and deposited a black box about the size of a bread loaf on the dirt floor between us.

"Where did you get that?"

"I told you, I've been here dozens of times. This house is full of secrets." She said it impatiently as if to quiet me. She held both of her hands out and placed them gently on the box while staring into my face through the light of the candle.

The imagination is an eerie phenomenon. It can take control of one's senses, particularly when one is only ten years old and is sitting in a dark cellar, bonded in blood to the only person he truly loves. Nonetheless, it seemed as we sat there that Mary Jean's pupils became suddenly immense, expanding finally to the size of small saucers. The rest of her face brightened as if a veil had been lifted from it.

"What we discuss here we discuss only here. Never outside of these walls. Do you agree?"

"Yes."

"Spit on your hand and promise."

I did so.

"There is a Power living in this house."

"What?"

"There is a Power living in this house and we can rule it."

"Mary Jean, you're scarin' me."

"There ain't nothin' to be afraid of, Ollie. It ain't gonna hurt us. It's our Power and only we can rule it."

"How?"

"With our will."

I glanced around the room, afraid that someone else, or something else, was standing in the shadows. What did a Power look like anyway? If it wasn't human I supposed it could hide anywhere. If it was ours, as Mary Jean claimed, why the hell didn't it come out and talk to us? I remembered Looter's words—"Fucker probably moved into the tank."

"The Power's too strong for one will alone. It can only be controlled by the two of us together. Through the power of mental unity."

"Whadda we want to control it for?"

"To destroy evil." Her words, spoken softly and void of emotion, frightened me more than if she had screamed them at the top of her lungs. Had it been anyone besides Mary Jean sitting across from me I would have bolted out of the place right then. If this was a game, she had won. I was ready to say uncle. If she didn't stop soon I would pee my pants to boot. I sensed, though, that this was no game; if Mary Jean wanted me to be there it was important. Her presence bolstered me like an army. Besides, as frightened as I was, my curiosity had become almost equally aroused.

"Is it the ghost of Old Man Hurley?"

"Who knows? Powers are weird things. They float around lookin' for dark, empty places to live in and if'n they find one they stay there forever. Unless," she hesitated for a moment and reached out with one of her hands, laying it firmly upon my leg, "they run into a will strong enough to rule 'em."

"How do you know our will is strong enough?"

"If it weren't, the bond woulda been broke and the Power would have run our asses out of here before we got halfway through the door."

"Whadda ya mean?"

"It don't like to be disturbed, Ollie. Either you got it or it's got you. Why do you think nobody has moved back in here? The Power has run 'em off, that's why."

I swallowed, the sound like boulders rolling down a mountainside in my ears, and glanced around the room again. I had no problem accepting the idea that there was a presence of some kind living in the Hurley place. Power, ghost, spirit, bogeyman. The label was irrelevant. I had heard the stories since I was old enough to remember and had always accepted them as true. What was harder to believe was that Mary Jean and I could somehow control this cellar-dwelling bogeyman for our own purposes. Mary Jean had never lied to me before. She was the closest thing to an unimpeachable source that I knew. Yet here she was sitting in the dirt, dressed in her bathing suit, and chanting crazy things about this Power and the influence of mental unity.

Suddenly I wanted to believe it. It was easier for me to accept her words than to believe that she would play some kind of an elaborate hoax with me as the target. And what if it were true? Jesus, it beat having a pet dog or your own horse. Would it do anything we asked? Maybe, if the thing was smart enough, it could do my homework.

"How do we control it?"

"First we gotta find a focus."

"A focus? What kinda focus?"

"We gotta focus our minds on what it is that we want the Power to do. If'n we concentrate hard enough on that purpose it will be done." She moved her right hand down to the lid of the box as she continued to talk. "The key thing is that we both got to concentrate on the same purpose. We gotta put the same thought into our heads and not think about nothing else. That is the only way that our will can be strong enough to control the Power."

She opened the box outward so that the lid was facing me and preventing me from seeing what was inside.

"What should we think about?"

"Evil. We start with the general idea, then we move on to a specific object." Reaching out with her free hand she took hold of one of my own. She closed her eyes. I did the same. "Fill your mind with all of the evil things in the world. Things you wish you could make disappear."

It wasn't hard. I thought of loneliness. A ten-year-old child abandoned by his parents, left to cry alone into his pillow at night. I thought of death. My grandfather, Nora Anne's father, when I was five years old, expired like an exhausted engine in a hospital bed somewhere. The oldest Cooter girl, second to Hooter in age. I didn't even know her name. Dead at four months before she could take her first step. Mother Cooter found her lying tiny and motionless with her hands folded across her chest like a china doll. Something called infant crib syndrome. I thought of disease. Bobby Bates, Billy's older brother. A regular guy who used to play football with the rest of us in the Bates's backyard. Strong as an ox. Like a brick wall when you ran into him. Noticed some lumps under his armpits one day and a week later he was in the hospital, frail and weak with tubes and needles sticking out of him as if he were some kind of voodoo doll. Six months later he was dead. I thought of Renee Durham, who was in my second-grade class; the mind and heart of a nine-year-old stuck inside a twisted, bent body that didn't have the strength to lift itself out of a wheelchair. The teacher called it cerebral palsy. I thought of . . .

"Think of pain, Ollie. Enough to make you cry." I remembered the time I stepped on a rusty nail out behind the barn.

As the four-inch spike entered my bare foot, all I could think of was lard sizzling in a hot frying pan. Remembering it now made me wince. . . .

"The day you stampeded the cows in the pasture."

It was two summers ago. I had seen Rowdy Yates do it on *Rawhide*. I got on Flash, our old brood mare, and started riding around the milk cows as they grazed dumb and contented in the pasture. I only wanted to round them up in a group, but one of them spooked and started to run. Then they all started in, running crazed and mindless, crashing through the fence and ending up scattered like black-and-white dominoes all over Shenker Hollow. It took hours to get them all back into the barn, and we lost an entire night's milking on account of it. Hooter whipped me so hard that my buttocks bled and became blistered. I couldn't sit down for days. . . .

"Who made you cry, Ollie?"

Hooter of course. When he found me, his face flushed and red as the setting sun, he fumbled with his belt and tore it off with one hand, yanking my shorts down with the other. His arm came down repeatedly, forever it seemed, the belt landing on my bare skin with the sound of a flat rock hitting the water. Finally I was alone in the field, my pants around my ankles, blood oozing from the fire that was my buttocks, crying into the heartless dirt of the sun-baked pasture. It was Mary Jean who came looking for me and helped me back to the house. She covered my wounds with cocoa butter and stayed with me throughout the night, holding my head when I cried and making me laugh at the thought of all those milkers strung out up and down the hollow and Hooter, red and sweaty, charging around after them like an enraged mother hen.

"He hurt me too." Mary Jean's voice was flat and toneless. How did she know what I was thinking? It was as if she had reached inside my head or else our brains were two tributaries of the same river.

"He left me the same way he left you." I thought of Mary Jean's own bruises and that night in her room. Was that what she meant? It gave me a chill to think of it and more . . . it angered me. White-hot rage that came in a wave. The kind of stuff that can melt paint. Where was it that night? I saw Mary Jean tear-streaked and ashamed, limping around like a wounded animal—"He done what he wanted, like always." And that smell. It permeated everything like a deadly toxin dropped from the sky. The stink of violation. And Hooter in the hall-way—fat and sassy—heading for the stairs in his boxer shorts.

"I hate him!" The intensity in my own voice scared me.

"He is evil."

"Yes," I agreed, not daring or wanting to open my eyes. I felt I was floating as in a dream, pent-up anger sitting there with me, ready to explode like a gas canister pushed to capacity. And he was there. Fat and evil. A red obsession filling my vision.

"Hear me! It's Hooter! Hooter is evil!" Mary Jean's hand left mine as she spoke. I opened my eyes and watched her remove from the box a short, fat cloth doll. It was a perfect replica of my Uncle Hooter, from the fatness in his cheeks to his cauliflower ears.

"Kill Hooter! Kill Hooter! Kill Hooter!" She was stabbing viciously at the doll with a long knitting needle, the words seemingly ripped from her throat in perfect synch with the blind thrusts of her arm. Tears were streaming down her cheeks. As it bounced around the basement walls, her voice was like a tomcat's screech in the middle of the night.

There was a needle in my hand. Whether Mary Jean placed it there or I plucked it from the box myself I honestly don't recall. I do remember the two of us stabbing and ripping the doll with all our strength and screaming at the blackness: "Kill Hooter! Kill Hooter! Kill Hooter!"

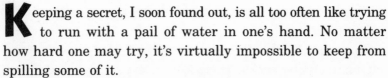

7

Keeping a secret, I soon found out, is all too often like trying to run with a pail of water in one's hand. No matter how hard one may try, it's virtually impossible to keep from spilling some of it.

One Sunday, a couple of weeks after my initial encounter with the Power, my father took Craig and me fishing. We packed a picnic lunch and drove up to a place called Sandy Pond, which was located about ten miles on the other side of Anton. It was actually a small lake that appeared to have been randomly dropped between two hills and now sat there like a giant drain siphoning off fresh water from streams to both sides of it.

Craig, as usual, had strenuously objected to the outing. "Why do you insist upon forcing me to do things that I don't wish to do?"

"The fresh air will do you good. You can't learn everything from books, you know."

"I don't want to go fishing. It's so barbaric, torturing worms like that all in the name of relaxation."

"Man is a predator. One hundred years ago if you'd refused to hunt or fish you wouldn't have survived."

"A hundred years ago," sniffed Craig, "I wouldn't have wanted to survive."

My father showed us how to bait our hooks. "You have to start the hook 'bout a quarter of an inch from the end and then just run it right down the length of the worm. Leave a small tail unhooked so's it will wiggle in the water. That way the fish can tell that the worm is alive but it won't be able to see the hook."

"Yeeeech!" said Craig. "That is disgusting! I won't sit here and mutilate innocent creatures for your amusement."

He didn't fool me. I knew my brother well enough to know that he didn't care what happened to the worms. He simply didn't want to get his hands dirty. After adamantly refusing to use the live bait, he ended up baiting his hook with a chunk of apple. Without the aid of a sinker, the hook, along with the apple, simply floated on top of the water.

"You're not going to catch anything that way," said Scooter. "Let me put some weight on your line."

"If they want it bad enough they can swim up and get it."

The lake had a reputation for having one of the most plentiful supplies of perch in the region, but you couldn't have proved it by us. We sat on shore with our lines in the water for over an hour without receiving so much as a nibble. Our frustration increased as we watched two men on the other side of the lake pull in perch after shining perch. It seemed as if the fish must have been having a contest to see which of them could get hooked first.

Craig soon gave up. Leaving his line in the water, he lay down on the grassy banks and started reading Colin Wilson's *The Outsider*.

"Maybe we're using the wrong kind of bait," I suggested.

"Nah. Worms for perch, flies for trout. That's the rule."

"Who made that rule?"

"Nobody made it, Ollie. That's just the way it is. Perch like worms and trout like flies. Just like you like chocolate ice cream and your brother likes vanilla."

"But sometimes I'm not in the mood for chocolate. I just feel like vanilla for a change. Maybe that's the way these fish are. They're just tired of worms and want flies for a change."

"Well, I don't have any flies, so they're just going to have to make do with worms."

My father really wasn't cut out for fishing any more than Craig was. He was in love with the idea of it. Somewhere in his head he had a picture of a man relaxing and fishing on a sunny afternoon with his two sons, while the three of them talked and caught enough fish for supper.

Alas, as so often was the case with my father, the reality of the day stymied him. Perhaps if we had been immediately successful—that is to say, if the fish had been biting on our side of the lake—the rest of the picture would have filled itself in as far as he was concerned. As it was, he simply had too much time on his hands and soon grew restless. It was as though he took our failure to catch any fish as a direct insult to his fatherly abilities. Had it been possible, I believe he would have swum out into the lake himself, swallowed the hook and had Craig and me haul him victoriously in to shore, so great was his need to be recognized as a successful parent.

He started fidgeting with his line, jerking on it lightly as if it were a kite string he was manipulating instead of a fishing pole. "Sometimes if you move the worm around it will attract the fish's attention," he said. So we both sat there wiggling our lines for a while until the water became choppy from our motions and it was apparent that rather than attracting their attention we had in all likelihood frightened off any fish that might have been lurking about in the first place.

Then he noticed that the men on the other side of the lake

were fishing in a shady area and decided that we should move out of the sun. He pointed to a spot beneath some poplar trees. After Craig had declined his invitation to move, my father and I gathered up our gear and relocated some fifty yards down shore.

"This is the ticket, huh, Ollie? Now we'll see who's a fisherman," he said as he brought his pole back in preparation for a mighty cast. As he whipped his arm forward there was a thrashing sound and then a splash as several twigs dislodged from an overhanging poplar and landed in the lake. The two men looked up and stared across the water toward us.

"Shit," said Scooter, gazing up into the tree, where his hook and line appeared to be hopelessly tangled amongst the foliage. "I thought I could clear those branches."

He started tugging gently on his pole. The branches swayed but the hook wouldn't come loose. He pulled harder. The line broke and this time there was a mighty splash as the pole vaulted from his hands and landed about five feet out in the lake.

The men glared in unmasked hatred in our direction. They started flapping their arms up and down like giant birds about to take flight. "They're afraid we'll scare the fish," my father whispered to me, while waving politely to the two men and preparing to wade out into the water after his fishing pole.

He had to go in up to his waist in order to retrieve it. As he climbed back onto shore he held the pole aloft toward the two men in a victorious gesture as if the three of them were fast friends.

"Let's have lunch," he said. "Maybe they'll be biting this afternoon."

We made our way back to where Craig was lying on the bank, the apple at the end of his line still bobbing up and down in the water as if it were someone's discarded garbage.

"Mother of God," said Craig, glancing up from the pages of his book. "What a spectacle that was."

"I guess it was at that," said Scooter. "But I'll bet neither of them fellas over there has ever caught a poplar tree before." He stood there with that crooked smile on his face, gazing out over the water and slowly twisting the rod back and forth in his hands. The thing about Scooter was that he could fool you with his humor. He would get a good one off—a real belly wrencher—and then act like he hadn't said anything at all out of the ordinary. So, instead of hitting you right away, it would sort of sneak up on you like Mexican chili.

The smile straightened out a little and a second later he started blowing air out from between his front teeth in powerful little bursts. Soon the shorter bursts turned into longer bursts, and these eventually turned into a full-fledged laugh. Then all three of us took it up, rolling on the bank, holding our stomachs, and guffawing as loud as we could. The men started flapping again and Scooter stood up and started flapping back. Craig and I joined in and soon the five of us were flapping back and forth at each other from across the lake as if we were exotic birds conducting some sort of strange mating ritual.

The moment was worth more than all of the perch in the lake to my mind. Rather than see it end I would have continued doing those exaggerated jumping jacks until the three of us dropped from heart failure on the grassy banks. But of course it ended long before that.

Craig's glasses fell from his head and as he stooped to retrieve them it must have occurred to him that such behavior—the flapping, that is—was completely out of character for him and didn't fit at all with the image he had of himself and wished others to have. He jammed his glasses back onto his head and, following a last glance out across the lake, stalked off in the direction of the pickup truck. Then the two men, raising all four arms above their heads with the middle finger on each hand fully extended in a parting gesture of disgust for our lack of fishing etiquette, quit their flapping and returned to their pillaging of the lake and its resources.

That left my father and me as the only remaining flappers. Our jumping gradually lost intensity as if we were part of a highlight film that was being replayed in slow motion, until pretty soon the two of us were not even leaving the ground any longer but were simply shuffling our feet and raising our arms in halfhearted motions. Finally, glancing at each other with apologetic smiles, we quit altogether and trudged off in the direction of Craig and the picnic basket.

Craig had already carried a blanket from the truck and spread it out on a grassy knoll overlooking the lake. My father and I, along with the picnic basket and a jug of lemonade, joined him on the blanket. Having been drenched with lemonade as Scooter, during the trip up, had attempted to take a well-concealed "Mount Everest" at an ungodly rate of speed, the sandwiches were soggy, but still tasted good. It was perhaps the surroundings, more than the ingredients, that added to their flavor. The sun. The fresh air; and, above all, my father. It mattered not that we hadn't caught any fish. It was the moment, however short, that I savored. These were the times that got me through the parentless abyss that so often engulfed me during those sleepless nights at the Cooter farm.

"This is the life, huh, boys?"

"You bet!" I said.

"Huh!" chortled Craig. "Some life."

"I only wish that your mother was here to share it with us."

"It's your fault she's not," said my brother.

"What makes you say that, Craig?" My father sounded genuinely puzzled.

"Because you drove her away! With all your phony diseases. If she's smart, Mother will never come back to this place."

My father gazed into his glass of lemonade as if he were hoping desperately to find a fatherly pearl of wisdom floating somewhere within its contents, something, perhaps, that he could fish out and dangle like a trophy in front of my brother.

He sighed and discarded whatever he had found with a flick of his wrist, the contents of the glass landing with a dull splat in the grass next to him.

"I am sorry that you feel that way, Craig. I only hope that you never get sick yourself. It's a terrible thing."

"Humph!" Craig shoved his wire rims deeper into the doughy folds of skin that surrounded his eyes.

"I know that I have been a disappointment to you boys at times."

Not this, I prayed, knowing all too well what was coming. Not now. Let's fish and do silly things. Let's laugh and eat our sandwiches. My stomach began twisting itself into knots.

"But I've always tried my hardest." He choked as if he had tried to swallow a piece of meat without chewing it properly. "And I love both of you."

"Do you think that's enough? To go on these corny fishing trips and tell us that you love us once in a while?"

Yes. It's enough for now, I wanted to yell out. We'll ask for more later. A hungry man doesn't turn down scraps.

"I don't know what else to do, Son. Someday, when I get the business going, I'll make it up to all of you. I promise."

"The business? Hah! That's a laugh. I suppose someday we'll all jerk off bulls together. The family that beats together, stays together. Is that it?"

"Craig, you're a very bright boy. I won't deny that. But it takes more than brains to understand the world. You don't just start a business overnight."

"How will you run a business when you can't even stand up to your own brother?"

"You mean Hooter?"

"Of course, Hooter. He makes a fool out of you in front of all of us and he does the same thing to Mother, and you let him get away with it. That Neanderthal runs your life."

That's right, I assured myself. It's Hooter. He's the cause of everything. Mary Jean was right. He's evil.

"But he's my brother. He's just trying to do what he thinks is right for all of us. . . ."

"Hah! He beat Ollie with his belt and where were you?"

"I wish he were dead."

"What did you say, Ollie?"

"Nothing."

"Well, you go ahead and start your business because I won't be here," said Craig. "I'm going to live with Mother."

"Jesus! You know where she is?" My father turned his attention back to Craig and left me to ponder alone the questions of what had caused me to say out loud what I had been thinking. It was as if something had grabbed hold of the thought and pushed it out of me.

"Don't worry. She will let me know when the time is right."

My sandwich suddenly didn't taste so good anymore. I put it back in its wrapping and threw it in the general direction of the trash can. I missed and made a mental note to discard it on the way back to the truck. I picked up my pole and started toward the lake.

"Ollie?" Oh no! Don't drag me into it. I'm only ten years old and it makes my stomach hurt.

"Yes?"

"What do you think?"

"About what?"

"Do you want to go with your mother?"

"I want her to come home. So we can all be together again." I turned back toward the water.

"Do you blame me for her leaving?"

The knots tightened, burning my gut and threatening to

twist into irreversible grannies. "No. Not really. It's some-body. Something . . . else. Evil, really."

"What?" I didn't know either. That was the scary part. The words were just coming out as if through a voice box suddenly switched on.

"It's evil that made her leave. Not you. We can kill evil, once we find it. That's what Mary Jean says. If we really be-lieve it we can kill it. Will it dead."

"Oliver?"

"Good Lord!" said Craig. "You sound crazier than Looter. You and Mary Jean have been hanging around up at the Hur-ley place too much."

"What are you doing up at the Hurley place?" asked Scooter.

"Nothing. Swimming. Playing hide and seek."

"Well, you better not go in the house. It ain't safe in there. I know that for sure. Stay away from the house, you hear me?"

"Whoa ho! Look at my apple!" squealed Craig.

Sure enough. The thing had bobbed up once, twice, and now had completely disappeared under the water's surface.

"By jove! I think you got one, Son! Reel it in, boy."

We all rushed down to the lake and started scrambling for the pole. Craig got hold of it and started pulling back on it as if he were trying to stop a team of horses, while my father and I each grabbed a handful of line. In no time the line was hopelessly tangled, and whatever had been hooked was still swimming around in the lake, probably wondering how it could possibly have been hoodwinked by anybody as stupid as the three of us.

At long last, and not until after we had all gotten drenched in the process, we managed to reel it in. It was a nice-sized yellow perch. My father got a picture of Craig and me holding on to it, one of us on each side of the fish.

Since we had only caught the one, there seemed to be no

point in bringing our trophy home. It wasn't enough to make a meal out of and we had the picture to prove our success, thus it was mutually agreed that we would return the perch to the lake, hopefully wiser after its capture and with less of a taste for apples.

Craig suddenly took hold of the fish without a word and threw it as high as he could above the water. It landed with a slapping noise—echoing off the surrounding hills with the finality of death—and then lay unmoving; a shining bauble on the water's surface.

"You killed it!" I screamed.

"What in God's name did you do that for?" asked my father.

"It would have died anyways. It had been out of the water too long," said Craig as he calmly shrugged his shoulders and turned away from the lake. "Barbaric practice, fishing, if you ask me."

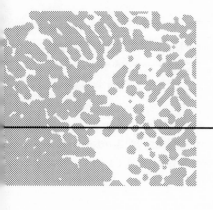

8

"Tonight is the night," said Mary Jean. "It's time for you to learn about the birds and the bees, compliments of your Uncle Hooter."

"Huh?"

"He's gonna pork her for sure and we're gonna be there."

"What're you talking about?" We were in the haymow throwing down bales for the evening feed. The mow was a haven for pigeons; their droppings covered the uppermost bales like white blobs of marshmallow. Every night Mary Jean and I tossed the bales, droppings and all, down the long chute to the main floor of the barn, where they were consumed by the undiscerning milkers. By the next morning the pigeons had done their work again. One day Looter took his shotgun and decided to rid the building of their presence once and for all. He didn't kill any pigeons but he did manage to blow several holes in the barn roof.

"Martha Wadkins. Her husband was home last weekend, which means Hooter didn't get any. He'll be horny as hell tonight. With Old Man Wadkins back on the road, big brother'll be sniffing 'round for sure."

"Sniffing 'round for what?"

"Never mind. Just meet me out behind the barn at ten o'clock." I was going to ask her how she could be so sure that Mr. Wadkins wouldn't be home, but just then Looter yelled up the chute to tell us to quit lallygagging and to get the hay down because he didn't plan on spending all Friday night in the barn waiting on us. So I never got the chance.

It had been a dry summer and the dust and chaff from the hay were thick in the mow. It danced and swirled in the shafts of light poking through the barn roof, filling our throats and sticking to our sweat-drenched skin as if Mary Jean and I had been soaked in creosote. Sometimes we would have contests to see who could get the most bales down in the least amount of time, the loser having to muck out the calf stalls all by himself, a job we usually shared. Other times we would crouch at the top of the shaft, peering down and waiting for our hired man, Earl Bailey, or Looter to appear below. When one of them did, Mary Jean and I would rain loose hay and straw down on top of whoever it was and wait for the inevitable reaction—"Fucking kids are worse than the fucking pigeons! Don't none of 'em belong in the barn, you ask me!"

That particular day we got the hay down as best we could with little extra fanfare. After telling me about the night's agenda and where I was to meet her, Mary Jean had become suddenly sullen and withdrawn.

Her silence didn't bother me as much as it normally would have. My mind was otherwise occupied. I was still thinking about our last visit to the Hurley house and how it had ended with the two of us sobbing together on the floor, our arms and legs intertwined like fighting snakes, pieces of the mutilated doll scattered about like dandelion seeds all around us. "We've reached him, Ollie! I can feel it!" Mary Jean had whispered the words into my face from a distance of less than three inches. "It's time to turn the fucker loose!"

"Turn what loose?"

"The Power, you ass! It's ours now. Can't you feel it?"

Jesus. Turn it loose? This was a new twist. I assumed the thing was already roaming somewhere within the confines of the cellar, perhaps passing judgment on our ritualistic attempts at sacrifice. Did Mary Jean have it chained up somewhere? If so, it could not be overly pleased with its present predicament. The thought of turning a pissed-off bogeyman loose, despite Mary Jean's protestations that "it was ours," was not comforting.

Mary Jean and I had returned to the cellar several times since our first visit, and on each occasion I had entered with the same mixture of emotions: fear—as intense as summer heat—and something else. Hate? Frustration? A haunting presence that I had never known was there until Mary Jean had shown me how to reach it. Whatever it was cried like a trapped animal to be set free. And after we were through, lying there depleted, our hidden wells of accumulated rage expunged for the moment, we would silently rise and, with a boost from an empty crate of preserves Mary Jean had found in the cellar, climb back through the window into the approaching darkness. And it would be gone, that other emotion. Set free somewhere within the moldy dampness of the basement.

For my part, I had come to look upon our visits to the Hurley house as a temporary reprieve from the adult world. A chance to be alone with Mary Jean in a place where we could cry together and hate out loud. That we were there for some other purpose, a mission of some sort, had become clouded and secondary in my mind. Mary Jean's comment about turning the Power loose snapped my unleashed fervor immediately back into focus.

"Come on. Let's go." She had risen to her feet and held the candle at eye level.

"How come we gotta turn it loose now? Maybe we ought to

just leave it where it is for a while longer," I suggested, hoping that the Power hadn't heard me.

"We own the son-of-a-bitch and now it's time to turn it loose to do our bidding!"

She started for the door and I scrambled after her. Outside, in the main part of the cellar, we turned right and headed for the back section of the house.

I knew what it was, lying there huge and ominous in the shadows, the moment I laid eyes on it.

It was just as Looter had described it, only its tubes were tied off at the ends and the lid was shut and locked.

"It's in there. I shut the lid on it myself. And now it's ours." Mary Jean reached under the coffinlike structure and removed a key. A part of me wanted to reach out and stop her, while something else within me silently urged her on. Wasn't this why we had come, after all? I watched her push the key into the lock, again remembering Looter's words—"Fucker probably moved into their tank."

Mary Jean turned the key and removed the lock. She looked at me, her hand gripping the lid.

"Will it, Ollie."

She threw the lid open. Dust flew and something else. A cold breeze touched my face. There was a whooshing noise like a speeding car makes as it passes a pedestrian on the highway. I felt or imagined an invisible wind rise up, circle the room and rush toward the open window. Hugging myself with both hands, I closed my eyes and heard Mary Jean scream at the darkness.

"Kill the bastard!"

9

Getting out of the house was no problem. I just had to make sure that Craig was asleep, open the window, and drop out. Mary Jean was waiting for me in the Jeep behind the barn.

"You're gonna drive to town?"

"What do you think, we're gonna walk three miles each way? Get in. I've been driving to Anton in this thing since I was nine years old, and nobody's found out yet."

Mary Jean must have had excellent night vision. She drove all the way to Anton without turning the headlights on, so that none of the neighbors would see us go by. We left the Jeep in a stand of pine trees behind the Highway Department on the edge of town and walked the additional half mile to Mrs. Wadkins's house.

When we got there, the only lights on inside the house were located in the living room. From the edge of the road we could see directly into the house, where Mrs. Wadkins was sitting on the couch watching television.

"Hooter must still be at the Moonrunner. We'll go back and wait in the bushes behind the garage," said Mary Jean.

We found an area surrounded by trees where we couldn't be seen from the road or from any of the surrounding houses and crouched down to stare at the house. Mary Jean pulled out a package of cigarettes. "You want one?" she asked.

"No."

"Why not? Ya scared?"

"I ain't never smoked one before and my mother says they give you cancer."

"Not until you're older and by then they'll have a cure. Go on, have one."

She lit the cigarette between her lips, took a puff, and handed it to me. Sucking on it, I felt the smoke fill my lungs and immediately started to cough. The cigarette fell from my mouth onto some pine needles. The pine needles began to flame. Mary Jean started in jumping up and down on the fire in some kind of crazy dance step, whipping her open hand back and forth toward her mouth while letting out whispered war whoops. I rolled onto my stomach and jammed my face into my sleeve, trying to muffle my laughter. Mary Jean got the fire out just as we heard Mrs. Wadkins's back-door open.

"Who's there?" she called. "Come on out or I'll call the police."

Grabbing hold of me, Mary Jean pushed my face into the grass, before flattening herself out next to me. We lay like that for a few minutes until Mrs. Wadkins went back inside and we heard the door slam.

"You think she'll call the police?" I asked.

"Nah. If she does Hooter won't come by and screw her."

"Why not?"

"Because it would attract too much attention. Mrs. Wadkins is married. Her husband is away all week and he'd kill her if he knew that Hooter was humpin' her."

Mary Jean took out another cigarette and lit it. This time she didn't offer it to me. It dangled there as if it were something growing from between her lips, periodically stiffening and glowing red in the darkness as she sucked on it.

"Do you like to smoke?" I asked. Nobody else in the family did, Uncle Hooter with his chaw being the only other tobacco user in the family, and it seemed odd to me that Mary Jean had developed a taste for it at such an early age. My mother had scared hell out of me with her cancer stories—which I now realize was probably her intent—and I secretly hoped that I could talk Mary Jean into giving the habit up, thereby saving her life and my best friend.

"What's it look like, nimblenuts?"

"But how come?"

" 'Cause Hooter and Mother Cooter don't like for me to."

"But . . ."

We heard footsteps not far away. I didn't get a chance to finish my question. Mary Jean put her hand over my mouth and pulled me close to her, wrapping me up in her long limbs.

I breathed in a sweet, pleasing smell, like that of freshly mown hay. My aunt's breasts were warm and soft against my chest. A confused fluttering occurred somewhere within my genitals. Whatever it was, this fluttering, it was a first, but there was no time to ponder its strange new qualities.

The footsteps belonged to Hooter. He must have left his car down the road and walked in the back way. He was no more than ten feet from where Mary Jean and I lay hidden. He stopped and turned toward the woods. It seemed as if he were looking directly at us; that he was certain to see us.

In that instant he appeared more frightening to me than ever before: a short, stocky monster who roamed the woods at night searching for kids who were out past their bedtime. The scowl on his face seemed as large as a down-turned moon. If Mary Jean hadn't had her hand over my mouth I would have screamed.

Uncle Hooter looked around once more before abruptly

turning and walking toward the rear of the house. He knocked lightly at the backdoor. A few seconds later Mrs. Wadkins opened it up and let him in.

My body continued to tremble. When I rolled over I realized that I had wet my pants. The evidence could not be concealed. Mary Jean didn't laugh. She held me close and whispered, "Don't worry none, Ollie. Everybody pees their pants once in a while."

In that moment, I loved her more than I had ever loved anyone before in my life and would have done anything that she asked.

"Weren't ya scared?" I asked.

"Of what?"

"Hooter."

"He didn't see us."

"But what if he had? What woulda happened?"

"If he'd caught us, he would have hurt us. Bad." As she talked her eyes were on some distant point at the top of the pine trees, and her body stiffened slightly like taffy exposed to the cold.

"Was he drunk?"

"Drunk as a skunk by the look of him. You could see it in his eyes."

I had seen my father drunk lots of times. He would cry and tell Nora Anne what a failure he was and pretty soon they would go into the bedroom. From the other side of the wall I would listen as Scooter sobbed and Nora Anne cooed. She would tell him that it was all right and that she was proud of him. Then I would hear funny noises: moaning and the bed creaking. After a while everything would be quiet. When I told Mary Jean she said that they were screwing. So I just figured people got drunk and then they screwed.

"Hooter gets mean when he's drunk. Dirty mean," said Mary Jean. She dropped her eyes from the pine trees and turned them on me. She reached out and touched my cheek. "I'll never let him hurt you," she said, and I believed her and felt safe.

We waited in the bushes awhile longer. We talked softly about things that seemed important and tried to stifle our voices by burying our heads under our jackets and by betting nickels against each other to see who could laugh without opening their mouth. I felt full of something, as if we were in the middle of a *Hardy Boys* adventure, on our way to recover a stolen diamond or in search of lost treasure. Mary Jean smoked another cigarette and said she wished that she had some grass. I didn't understand what she meant and didn't ask. After a while the lights went off in Mrs. Wadkins's bedroom.

Mary Jean buried the cigarette butts and smoothed over the pine needles with her hands. Then she stood up. "Let's go," she whispered.

Before I had a chance to object she was ten feet out in front of me, crouching low to the ground and moving steadily toward the house.

There was maybe a hundred feet of yard between the back of the house and the edge of the woods and about half of that was taken up by a fenced-in garden. I had once heard Mother Cooter say that Mrs. Wadkins had a naturally green thumb and that she raised the best tomatoes in Devon County. I saw them now, hanging ripe from their vines in the late-summer heat like overstuffed pinatas ready to burst. Mary Jean was halfway down the length of the garden. She was crouching outside the fence behind a large chokeberry bush. With a forefinger to her lips she signaled for me to be quiet as I knelt down beside her, panting more from nervousness than from lack of breath. From our vantage point we now had a clear view of the back of the house.

Mrs. Wadkins's bedroom was located in the rear corner of the building closest to us. There were two windows in the room; one on the backside of the house facing the garden, the other on the east side toward the driveway and the garage. The garage door was open and both it and the driveway were empty. There was a night lamp on on the front porch. Its light splashed across the front of the driveway; shadows, aided by a gentle wind in the towering maple trees on that side of the house, danced like taunting devils in the pools of light cast by the lamp. The rest of the yard was dark, illuminated only by the pale glow of the moon shining through a thin layer of rapidly dispersing clouds.

"We'll go to the back window. That way in case somebody drives into the driveway they won't see us," whispered Mary Jean.

"Do you think somebody will drive in?"

"No."

"Then why'd ya say it?"

"It's just a precaution, dummy. Just in case." She said it kindly and I felt foolish for asking. It was a question neither of the Hardy Boys would have posed.

Mary Jean started off for the back of the house on her hands and knees and I followed. Once I touched something soft that moved. When I jerked my hand back, an animal of some kind squealed and darted off through the underbrush. Something else fluttered in the branches—a bat or the wind. I gritted my teeth, thinking again of how the Hardy Boys would have reacted, and moved on.

The back of the house was covered with climbing vines wrestling for space on a wood trellis that ran to the top of the house. The bottom ledge of the window was about four feet from the ground and was partially covered on the lower portion by two huge rhododendron bushes.

When we reached the outer edge of the bushes Mary Jean signaled for me to flatten out. I did, and watched as she slithered on her stomach beneath the low-hanging branches of the rhododendrons. She disappeared for a few seconds before her head suddenly popped up on the other side, above the bushes, as if she were a giant serpent searching the night for prey.

She waved for me to come ahead. I pushed myself into the dark tunnel that ran beneath the vegetation. My elbow landed on something sharp. I gasped as pain surged from my funny bone to the tips of my fingers. Suppressing an urge to cry out, I reached over and pulled out a sliver that had lodged itself in the fleshy part of my elbow. I wished that Mary Jean, lying just a few feet away, could have seen how I had withstood the pain. She would have been proud and it might have partially made up for the earlier embarrassment of peeing my pants.

I pushed ahead until I felt Mary Jean's leg. She was sitting with her back against the house. I sat up next to her. There was only about a foot and a half of space between the bushes and the side of the building in which to stand up.

"The window is open, but the bed is against the opposite wall and the fan is on so they shouldn't ought to hear us if we keep our voices low," Mary Jean whispered into my ear. Her breath was warm, like steam rising from manure. I could feel her pulse pounding in the meat of her arm where it rested against my own.

"Have you looked yet?"

"Of course. How do you think I know the layout?"

"What are they doing?"

"They're just layin' in bed."

"Maybe they've already done it."

"Done what?"

"Screwed."

"No. Not enough time." Although it had seemed much longer it couldn't have taken us more than five minutes to move from our post in the woods to our present position.

"How long does it take?"

"It depends if Mrs. Wadkins is in the mood. Hooter has to sweet-talk her first and make her think he loves her."

"You mean foreplay?" It was a phrase that I had seen once in a magazine that my mother often read. When I asked her what it meant she said it was like a rooster preening its feathers for the chickens.

"Somethin' like that. Unless she plays too hard to get. Then Hooter will just do it anyway."

"What do you mean?"

"Never mind," she snapped. "Let's take a look."

We stood up slowly, squeezed tightly against the building and each other. Our arms were still touching and now it was difficult to tell whose pulse was whose as they beat wildly against one another like two boxers in the late rounds. Mary Jean was taller than me and had to crouch some in order to avoid being seen above the windowsill. I heard the slow, hypnotic whirring of the fan and saw clearly two figures lying side by side on the bed. Although the overhead lights were off, there was enough illumination coming through the open window to plainly see that the covers from the bed were thrown back and that both of the figures were naked.

Hooter was big and hairy. He reminded me of the bear I had seen at the circus in Durston one year with my father and Mother Cooter. A clown would pretend to shoot the bear using a long musket with a fat muzzle. Clutching its chest, the bear would fall down and roll over on its back with its arms and legs sprawled out and its stomach and barrel chest sticking up in the air, heaving like a giant locomotive.

Mrs. Wadkins lay flat on her back, her right arm out of sight somewhere beneath Uncle Hooter. She was white, almost ghostly, in contrast to Hooter's ruddy complexion. Her breasts looked to be soft and pliable and flared out on opposite sides of her chest like water-filled balloons. She had her hair down; it was long and dark and lay around her face and neck like a nest, causing the skin there to appear even whiter than the rest of her. Her legs, slightly opened, pointed outward and were crowned at the apex by a knotted mat of pubic hair.

My uncle appeared to be talking. Occasionally Mrs. Wadkins would giggle loud enough for the sound to be heard above the whirring of the fan. This was a high, nervous tinkle, like the sound of brass angels gently spinning on a candelabrum. She turned her head toward Hooter and mouthed some words into his ear. His unmistakable laugh rose above the fan's hum—"Hoo! Hoo! Hoo!"—and floated eerily out the open window. The noise startled me—as if I had been walking through the woods and a grouse suddenly had flown from cover at my feet—and I instinctively turned to run.

Mary Jean's grip tightened on my hand and pulled me back toward the window. Her face was screwed into a grimace as if it had been set in concrete. Her breathing was heavy. I followed her eyes back into the room.

Mrs. Wadkins silenced Hooter's laughter by putting her mouth on top of his. Rolling slowly toward him, she reached with her left hand someplace below his monstrous stomach. She came up with his cock, gripping it proudly in her hand as if it were a great, shining sturgeon she had just reeled in. A low growl erupted from somewhere within my uncle's chest.

Suddenly, he half picked Mrs. Wadkins up and dropped her onto her back. With another effort, he heaved his own massive body onto hers. It seemed that the weight would have to crush her. She moaned, obviously not from pain, and thrust the bottom part of her body up against his own.

Another sound, from somewhere in the front of the house. A key being inserted into a lock? Someone fumbling with a doorknob? Or was it simply my imagination? Whatever it was was quickly drowned out by the sounds now coming from the bed.

Uncle Hooter was thrusting wildly, like a man in quick-sand, and grunting with the effort. Mrs. Wadkins groaned and moved with him, her white hands clearly visible against the red background of his buttocks. A strange way, I thought, for adults to be acting. What was even stranger was that they both appeared to be enjoying themselves. Mrs. Wadkins, beneath her frail exterior, was apparently much tougher than she appeared.

More sounds. Like footsteps running through the house. Mary Jean's fingernails dug savagely into my arm. Even over the heated noises rising from the bed, I could hear her own tortured breathing.

"Whatever happens," she whispered, her eyes never straying from the intertwined figures on the bed, "shut up and stay out of sight."

As if it had been hit with a great wind, the bedroom door suddenly burst open. Light filled the room. The two figures on the bed snapped apart like brittle taffy. A man stepped through the doorway. He somehow looked ridiculous, fully dressed in a light overcoat and fedora hat, in the presence of these two naked people. A figure from a comic strip. He stood silent, arms hanging loosely by his sides as if he were waiting for someone to take his hat and coat.

"Joe!" Mrs. Wadkins gasped as she rolled away from Uncle Hooter and got shakily to her feet. She took two steps toward the intruder. Without warning, the stranger's right arm thrust straight out from his side, past the edge of the window, and was stopped only by Mrs. Wadkins's chest.

Martha Wadkins let out a sound like a punctured tire. The stranger's hand pulled back from her body, a long metallic blade now clearly visible within its grasp. The arm rose again, and this time it swung out in an arc from head level. Mrs. Wadkins's throat erupted in a geyser of red liquid, blood splattering like hot grease down her front, decorating her pale breasts and making them appear as if they had been spray-painted by an insane artist.

Mrs. Wadkins raised her arm and took a step forward as if she were about to berate the stranger for his bad manners. She opened her mouth, emitting a low bleating noise. The arm of the stranger arced and came forward again with terrific force. Mrs. Wadkins's head disappeared. It hit the floor with a thud. Her body, headless and bathed in blood, teetered for an instant before toppling forward at the feet of the stranger.

A scream of pain and rage—the noise of a bull upon feeling its genitals crushed in one lethal stroke of the veterinarian's hand—came from the opposite side of the room. I turned in time to see Uncle Hooter on his feet dancing backward, away from the stranger and what was left of Mrs. Wadkins. He was a comical figure, still naked and hopping about. His swollen scrotum, warm and pliable from excitement and the summer heat, bounced crazily halfway to his knees.

The stranger looked up as if he had just realized that there was someone else in the room. He stepped forward, directly in front of the window, and arced his right arm back over his head. He hesitated—for a moment appearing confused—his weapon poised above him. He screamed, "You piece of shit!" before the arm and the weapon came forward in a blur.

The stranger's hesitation saved Uncle Hooter. He ducked and rolled to his right a millisecond before the blade whirred over his head like a low-flying plane. There was the sound of shattering glass, the window on the east wall rupturing and exploding into the driveway from the force of the knife crashing into it.

Hooter commenced rolling across the floor; a hairy, red ball of flesh, moving with the speed and grace of a pulling lineman. He appeared headed for the bed.

Of course. That was the logical thing to do. He would roll

beneath the box spring as I myself had done on more than one occasion, with my mother, eyes blazing and thoughts of discipline in mind, in hot pursuit. At such times my first reaction was to run, in desperate search of someplace in which to wait out her rage. I soon discovered that I could slide easily into the dust-strewn haven beneath my parents' bed. Nora Anne, possessing too much womanly bulk to squeeze into such a small space, would drop flat onto her stomach at the edge of the bed, commencing then to grope blindly beneath it with her arms. We both knew it would do her no good. Lying just inches from her outstretched hands, my back pressed tightly to the rear wall, I was safely out of reach.

My uncle must have had the same thought. From his prone position, the stranger would swear and rage at Hooter, threatening to burn the bed if my uncle did not come out. Eventually, he might change his tactics, pretending then to be contrite. He would plead with Hooter. It was not his intent to hurt him, the stranger would say; he only wished to speak with him. But my uncle was too smart for that. He would wait patiently, feeling smugly safe, until the man with the fedora finally gave up. Until he took his big bloody knife and went home. Then Uncle Hooter could climb out from under the bed, put his clothes on and drive back to the farm. And Mary Jean and I would go home and pretend that the stranger and Mrs. Wadkins never existed; that they were simply characters from one of Looter's scary tales.

With a sprinkling of glass the stranger withdrew his weapon from the window. He turned toward the bed. As if he were a robot programmed to do but one thing, he raised the knife once again above his head.

I was wrong. Uncle Hooter hadn't rolled under the bed. But of course not. How could I have been so stupid? He must have realized, as I would have had I been thinking clearly, that he couldn't possibly fit; that he would have become stuck between the spring and the floor, helpless then as a beached whale while the stranger slowly hacked him to pieces.

He was on top of the bed, face down, his legs sprawled out behind him, his hairy ass sitting like a red oasis in the middle of a white sea. He was reaching for something—now clutching it in his hands. Just as the stranger's arm came down toward the back of his head, Hooter rolled over and pushed the thing in his hands outward, away from his body.

There was an explosion of goose-down feathers as the knife penetrated the pillow in Uncle Hooter's hands. A gush of red liquid burst from the center of his face, drenching the two of them in blood.

Hooter's foot came up between his attacker's legs. The stranger let out a gasp and doubled up in pain. Hooter rolled to his right, away from the other man and off the bed. The stranger regained his senses and turned, knife in hand, to renew the attack.

Uncle Hooter was on his feet now, facing the stranger, holding something in his hand. A moment's hesitation. The stranger attacked. Hooter threw the thing in his hand and screamed in a voice I had never heard before and will never forget: "Here she is, you fucker!"

Mrs. Wadkins's head hit the stranger flush in the face. He dropped like a puppet whose strings have been cut. Hooter was on him in a flash. He reached over and picked up the iron doorstop next to the wall, holding it aloft above the stranger's face. Then down it came. Again and again. The sound was like a jackhammer. . . .

10

Nora Anne arrived back at the farm some eight months after she had departed. She walked into the Cooter house in the middle of dinner, hugged Craig and me, and announced to all present that she was moving us back into the trailer.

"Does your husband know about this?" asked Mother Cooter.

"Not to my knowledge. I assume that Harold is still employed and, that being the case, is currently out of town."

"If you mean is he still peddling bull jism, then yeah, I reckon he's giving it his best shot," said Hooter.

"Shot? Did someone fire a shot?" asked Father Cooter.

"It's nothing, Dad. Nora Anne, you been gone near eight months without Scooter hearing a word. Now I ain't aiming to pry, but don't you think that you should get his feelings on all of this?"

"Scooter will do as I say."

"Well, you got that much right. He always has. Tweedledee and Tweedledum. You deserve each other, if'n you ask me."

"In case you hadn't noticed, Hooter, no one is."

"Hoo! Hoo! Hoo! Missy, if'n you was my wife I'd straighten you out right quick."

Mary Jean kicked me under the table. Pretending not to notice, I gazed dejectedly into my plate. After having burrowed a hole into a white mountain of mashed potatoes, I had just completed filling the crater with gravy when my mother walked through the door. It now appeared that the erosion of the crater walls was imminent and that the innocent side dishes that adorned the plate like clumps of unwary tourists around a volcano, were about to be drowned in the steaming brown sauce within.

"It's going to be a new arrangement. Harold and I will be living together, but not as husband and wife."

Glancing up from the table, I finally put my finger on what it was that was different about her appearance. It was her hair. It was piled like lumpy vanilla pudding on top of her head with several tiny ringlets falling out of the pile onto her neck and forehead. Or was it the rouge that was plastered like painter's putty onto her normally pale cheeks?

"Does that mean that Scooter ain't gonna be gettin' no more home cooking? Hoo! Hoo! Hoo!"

"What's that? Who's cooking?"

"Ain't no one cooking, Dad. What do you mean not as husband and wife?"

"It's really quite simple. Both Harold and I love the kids and don't feel that they should be separated or dragged through a divorce proceeding because of our own misgivings."

"Misgivings?"

"I love Harold, but he is quite obviously nuts. I can no longer function as his wife. So we will all stay together in the trailer as a sort of necessary arrangement. Harold and I will have our own lives and our own friends."

Back on my plate the walls had crumbled on all four sides.

Green beans and corn floated about in the brown mess like debris in the aftermath of a flood.

"Sakes alive," said Mother Cooter. "I hope you kids know what you're doing."

11

N ora Anne had a carpenter come out the next day. Two wooden partitions were put in place in the trailer, one on each side of the kitchen, thus dividing the trailer into thirds. In one section was my parents' old bedroom, which Nora Anne now claimed sole ownership of, the sewing room, the main bathroom, and a "roving room," so named by my mother and the function of which I will explain. Located on the other side of the kitchen was the old guest room, which was to become Scooter's new bedroom, the living room, a small bathroom containing only a toilet and stand-up shower, and another roving room.

The way Nora Anne described it, the kitchen—which served also as our dining room—was to be a neutral area; a sort of no-man's land where the four of us would get together two or three times a day for meals. In the area of food, at least, we were to continue as one big happy family. The room would remain open to everyone until ten o'clock at night, at which time each of us was to retreat to his or her respective side of the trailer.

Craig and I were each to sleep in one of the roving rooms, switching off every three months so that we could take turns living on opposite sides of what we referred to as "the wall," despite the fact that there were two of them. "I want to be completely fair about this, Harold. I think both of the boys should have an equal opportunity to benefit from our varying perspectives." We flipped a coin and I drew Scooter for the first three months.

The front door of the trailer opened into the kitchen. Each partition had a doorway heading from the kitchen in an opposite direction. When Scooter was on the road both of the partition doors remained open. The rest of the time Nora Anne's side was shut and locked from ten o'clock at night until she got up in the morning. "Don't come scratching 'round this door looking for handouts," I overheard her tell Scooter. "I'm closing up the pantry."

As might be expected, this situation didn't do much to enhance Scooter's reputation among the rest of the family. If things had been bad before, then the wall simply served to solidify his position as the chief subject of our tilted humor. He was, like the age-old fart, an easy laugh. The worst offender, of course, was Uncle Hooter. "What are you going to do when she brings home a date? Serve 'em both milk and cookies and tell Nora Anne she has to be in bed by eleven?"

But Scooter didn't seem to mind the arrangement too much. I think he was just happy to have Nora Anne back home on any terms. "Just so long as the family is back together again," he told my grandmother. "That's the important thing."

"But you ain't even sleeping together. It's not a marriage you're in for pity's sake. It's a dormitory."

"Just so long as we're all under the same roof."

"She's locked you out of your own room."

"She's just trying to make a point, Ma."

Craig and I were both pleased to have our mother back

home and to be returning to the familiar confines of the trailer. We tried to make the most of our divided lives. We painted HIS and HER in large white letters on the partition doors, and Craig, exhibiting a rare flair for the humorous, drew a picture of a female cow under the HER and a bull with its balls swollen to the size of cantaloupes and an obviously pained look upon its face beneath the HIS.

Nora Anne didn't tell us much about the period during which she had been gone from the farm. She called it a leave of absence and got all teary-eyed when she explained to my brother and me that it was because she loved us that she had stayed away for so long. "I was in no condition to be a good mother." This made me try to recall what kind of condition she had been in prior to her departure. Unfortunately, I was unsuccessful, managing only to rehash my own feelings of abandonment upon hearing the trailer door slam and seeing the blue flash from the station wagon as it passed by my window like a dying meteorite.

She wouldn't say where she had been other than to indicate that it was somewhere "away from the smell of cowshit." That much, I recalled, Uncle Hooter had already surmised. She had needed time to reevaluate her life and to decide what direction she was heading in. She claimed that the experience had been rewarding and had given her an "insight into the vast possibilities available in life." As she told us all of this Craig nodded his head as if he understood perfectly while I wagged mine up and down knowing I didn't have the vaguest idea what she was talking about.

To me she was the same Nora Anne with a different hairdo, a little more makeup, and a new taste in clothing. Whereas she had previously been partial to mid-calf dresses or slacks, she now favored earthier styles, such as long cotton dresses, full skirts, and jewelry with lots of baubles that clanked together when she walked. It was my aunt who first noticed the hair under her armpits.

"It's a protest," Mary Jean said.

"Against what?" I asked.

"The establishment, dummy, and everything it stands for."

I had no idea who the establishment was or what my mother had against it all of a sudden but it was there all right—the hair, that is—nestled beneath her arms like tiny robin's nests. I noticed it as she reached for some dishes above her head and then, having hair on the brain, I couldn't help seeing that it was on her legs as well. Good God! It must be some kind of rare disease. My mother was turning into an ape! In a state of panic, I searched her face for traces of it there as well. I was much relieved to find that there were none and was even more relieved when Mary Jean explained to me that all women naturally grow hair in such places and are required to shave if they want to get rid of it. Armed with that knowledge, I was at more of a loss than ever to understand why my mother's election not to shave was of any significance. Clearly, the protesters, if there were any, were those women who removed from their bodies that which naturally appeared there in the first place. How could Nora Anne, simply by doing nothing, be protesting something?

After dinner the four of us would break apart like diners on an overnight train before slowly drifting into our various areas of habitation. When my father was home, he and I would meet in his room to play checkers or cards. Sometimes we would just talk. Before her leave of absence Nora Anne had always insisted that Craig and I be in bed by ten o'clock, and it irked her that my father refused to enforce the same curfew on his side of the wall.

One night when the two of us—my father and I—were laughing and talking well past my mother's designated hour for silence, she opened the window in her bedroom and yelled out: "Hey! Keep it down over there! Ollie is supposed to be in bed."

"Maybe over there he is, but over here he goes to bed when I tell him to," Scooter shot back.

"You're spoiling him."

"Well, you'll have three months to unspoil him!"

"The least you can do is to keep the noise down. Craig and I are trying to sleep!"

"I paid for my room, lady. If you don't like it complain to the management!" yelled out Scooter as he fired his pillow against the wall, before we both fell on the bed together laughing so hard that it hurt.

"Mommy's going to get mad," I said after I managed to catch my breath.

"Nah. Don't let her fool you. She's over there right now trying as hard as she can not to laugh," he said as he collected his pillow from the floor and lay back down on the bed. "Now you better get to bed, Son, just like your mother said."

At times I could tell that he was sad. He would become very quiet and get a faraway look in his eyes as if his mind had taken a giant leap, leaving his body and entering some strange world of his own making. At such times he would leave the trailer and walk around by himself in the darkness. I would lie awake in bed waiting for the sound of his footsteps in the hallway, with the knots twisting and turning like sadistic earthworms in my stomach. When he returned, he would stop in my room on his way down the hallway. He would tiptoe over to my bed, kiss me on the cheek, and hug me as if he hadn't seen me in months. Sometimes he would even lie down fully clothed next to me on the bed. The two of us would stare sightlessly up at the ceiling, talking in hushed whispers.

"Do you believe in ghosts, Daddy?"

"What kind of ghosts, Son?"

"The kind that can see you but you can't see 'em back. They live in dark places and move around at night."

"Who told you about these ghosts?"

"Looter, and . . . and . . . Mary Jean."

"Well, I reckon that there are spirits around all right—ghosts if that's what you want to call 'em—but they ain't nothing more than people who used to walk and talk like the rest of us. I don't guess none of us really ever die, Son. But that's nothing for you to worry about, Ollie. In fact, life after death is probably a lot of laughs. You'll get to be with all of the folks you love the most, but you won't have to worry about 'em gettin' sick or leavin' or dyin' someday."

"Do you think some spirits listen to us?"

"Probably. If you get right down to it we're all pretty nosy. I don't imagine that changes much after we die."

"If a fella wishes hard enough for somethin' to happen do you think that maybe a spirit will make it happen?"

"Wish for what?"

"Anything. Well, not wish really, like wishing for a bike for Christmas, but asking really hard for somethin' special to happen."

"You mean willing something to happen?"

"Yeah."

"Well, Son, I believe that the human will is a pretty powerful emotion. But you better be careful with it or it can backfire on you."

"You mean there are bad spirits?"

"Just as sure as there are bad people."

So many questions and yet most of them, the ones that begged most for answers, I didn't dare ask. I longed to unburden myself, to dump the entire mess into my father's lap—after all, what were dads for?—yet I knew that was not possible. We had made a pact—my aunt and I—sealed in blood, to keep the secret of the Power. I could never break that pact now, not after I had seen what the Power was capable of. One certainty stuck out from amongst the gruesome smorgasbord of tidbits swimming through my mind—I did not want to cross it. Never again.

I had not been near the Hurley house in almost four months,

yet its secret continued to tug at me like invisible fish nibbling on a swimmer's toes. Bad spirits? The worst of the lot lived right here in Shenker Hollow, and Mary Jean and I owned it; pulled its strings as if it were a marionette hanging from a board. We had set it loose with laudable motives. Only something had gone terribly wrong. Uncle Hooter had outpowered the Power. Or perhaps he had become the Power. Whatever, Mrs. Wadkins was now dead. I could find no one to blame for her death but Mary Jean and myself.

When Scooter was on the road I slept with my bedroom door open and the kitchen light on. Nora Anne left the partition doors ajar so that the light from the kitchen would fall down the hallway and sprinkle gently into my bedroom, thus hopefully helping to keep the gremlins at bay. "If you get scared, Oliver, just yell down the hallway," she said. "I've got ears like an elephant."

My dreams were even worse than those at the big house. There I was playing by myself in one of the meadows when a man appeared in the distance, walking slowly toward me. He was a big man but his face was blurred, like an image in a kaleidoscope before it's brought into focus. He held a severed human head in his outstretched hand as if it were a church offering platter. When I turned away from the bloodied head, not wanting to see its face, the man came closer and tried to shove the thing at me. I turned to run and there he was again, or else it was someone else with a different head in his hand. He, or they, were everywhere; forming a perfect circle with me in the middle.

Suddenly, in one motion, as if on a director's cue, the heads all wheeled in their hands so that they were facing me. Someone twisted the kaleidoscope and everything snapped into focus. The blurred faces became people I knew—Scooter was there and next to him was Mary Jean—and a dozen Mrs. Wadkinses lit up like Christmas lights in their hands. In unison they cried out, "Surprise!" and started giggling in that high tinkling sound that had floated out the window past where Mary Jean and I had crouched on that bloody evening in Anton.

I woke up screaming with my mother cradling me in her arms. "It's just a nightmare, Ollie. Tell Mommy about it so that it doesn't seem so real."

But of course I couldn't tell her about it because it was real and I had seen it happen.

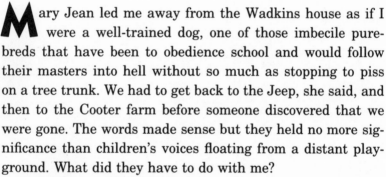

12

Mary Jean led me away from the Wadkins house as if I were a well-trained dog, one of those imbecile pure-breds that have been to obedience school and would follow their masters into hell without so much as stopping to piss on a tree trunk. We had to get back to the Jeep, she said, and then to the Cooter farm before someone discovered that we were gone. The words made sense but they held no more significance than children's voices floating from a distant playground. What did they have to do with me?

She took me through the woods and deposited me in the passenger side of the Jeep. Grabbing me by the shoulders and forcing me to look at her, she told me to stay where I was, that she had forgotten something and would have to go back to the house. I don't remember how long she was gone. It was peaceful there amongst the trees, completely silent, except for the sound of the crickets. Or were they peepers? "Crickets chirp, peepers peep. They're no more alike than English and Chinese," Scooter once explained to me. Whatever. I remember thinking I could easily fall asleep, which seemed strange given my general fear of the dark and of all the strange creatures I was certain lurked within it.

Mary Jean appeared as if she had been running. Her clothes were soaked through with dirt and perspiration. Her face glistened with sweat in the moonlight. She placed her hands momentarily on her knees, her breath coming in great gasps. She had tripped on a root and fallen in the woods, she said, as if that alone amongst the night's events was of tremendous significance.

I took little notice of the bundle that she carefully placed on the seat between us as if it were a basket of food. Whatever it was, we had not arrived with it. Perhaps my aunt had returned to raid the Wadkins refrigerator and now the two of us were about to share a midnight picnic deep within the Anton woods.

Jumping in beside me she started the engine and pulled onto the main road, heading for the Cooter farm. The motion and Mary Jean's ghastly appearance snapped me out of the reverie of the forest. I stared into the charging darkness, trying not to think, as the wind through the open cab ripped the tears from my eyes and the sound of two human heads, crashing together like midway bumper cars, pounded in my head.

About a mile down the road we turned onto the old railroad tracks. Where is she going? There's nothing this way except for the reservoir. I better tell her, I thought, but suddenly the effort seemed to be more than I could handle. Better to just sit back and be a passenger. What was that ad that always played on the radio? Leave the driving to us? Something like that. I shut my eyes.

It was a device I had employed on many a Saturday afternoon at the Durston Theater. My Uncle Looter loved monster movies—"Bela fucking Lugosi is wild, man." At least four times a year he would pile us all into the Cooter station wagon and drive us over to Durston to see the Saturday Monster Matinee.

The movies scared the hell out of me, yet I didn't dare refuse to go for fear of looking like a coward. Anything was better than opening myself up to the ridicule that was sure to follow—"We've got a chicken liver in the family do we? Hoo! Hoo! Hoo!" So I went along, pretending I was just as excited as everyone else, and as soon as the lights went off I would shut my eyes and imagine that I was back at the Cooter farm, playing cowboys and Indians with Mary Jean or trailing around behind Scooter as he puttered in the backyard. I wouldn't open my eyes until I heard voices around me indicating that the picture was over. Mary Jean was the only one who was aware of my secret, but I knew she would never tell; if anyone were to ask me what the movie was about, it was she who would immediately come to my rescue, supplying the answers I did not have.

When I opened my eyes, the Jeep was parked and Mary Jean was shaking my arm. "Stay here. I'll be back in a minute," she said before running off.

We were parked on the railroad tracks at the edge of the Antonville Reservoir. The reservoir had been created in the early 1950s at the expense of forty-two homes and fifteen hundred acres of farmland for the purpose of supplying drinking water for New York City. The taxes of all state residents were increased in order to help pay for the reservoir's construction, but none of the local taxpayers were allowed to drink the water or swim in it or even fish in it for fear of contaminating it for the city folk. "Just another example of the city sucking us dry," Uncle Hooter used to say, and the rest of the Cooters would solemnly nod their heads in agreement.

The area around the reservoir was a popular parking spot for local teenagers. Despite the prohibitions, the lake itself was well renowned for its after-hours swimming parties. Uncle Looter reportedly became famous at one of these get-togethers when he climbed to the top of a tree overhanging the reservoir, dropped his pants, and while swinging out over the water in the manner of a deformed marsupial, defecated into the crystal-clear liquid below. "Let the fuckers drink that!" he screamed as his deadly load landed like several depth charges beneath him.

I saw Mary Jean go down to the water's edge. She was carrying the same bundle she had had in her arms when she came back from the Wadkins house. I watched as she put the bundle on the ground and started to undress. Her body was white and hairless and looked especially thin in the water's reflection. She removed all of her clothes and walked into the water until it was up around her knees. She bent down and started scrubbing her hands. Then she cupped her hands together and splashed some water onto her face and began to scrub that. She looked like an egret, or perhaps a great blue heron, carefully scrubbing the grime from its feathers while gingerly wading about in the water, always on the lookout for an easy dinner. I half expected to see her head pop beneath the water's surface, only to reemerge seconds later with a glistening lake trout in her mouth.

When she was done washing she returned to the shore and picked up the bundle. She weighed the thing in her hands as if it were a letter in need of postage. It was fairly large—perhaps several things trussed together—and obviously not very heavy from the way she was holding it. Reaching down by her feet, she picked up some rocks from the shore. She added these to the bundle and then somehow tied the whole thing around her neck—rocks and all—so that it hung down her back like a knapsack. She waded back into the lake, appearing like a warped image of the perfect girl scout, the knapsack bouncing gently off her naked buttocks.

There was a slight splash as she dove into the water and started swimming out toward the middle of the lake. Her stroke, even with the additional weight, was a thing of beauty. My aunt had made the Anton Varsity Swim Team when she was in seventh grade—the first junior high student in the history of the school to do so—and had won several events that season. My grandmother bragged that she would be another in a long line of outstanding Cooter athletes. The *Anton Courier* even ran an article on her in its sports section. There was a picture of Mary Jean in her bathing suit. Underneath the picture was a caption that said, "ANTON PRETEEN MAKES BIG SPLASH." Even Uncle Hooter seemed proud of her. He started introducing her as his little sister, "the female Buster Crabbe." It was about that time that Mary Jean began to lose interest. The following season she refused to go out for the team at all, claiming that she was no longer interested in competing.

Mary Jean had swum so far out that I could barely see her. Squinting into the darkness, I could just make out her head as it bobbed above the gentle waves. Then it disappeared and reappeared again. Once. Twice. Then she was swimming back in.

A few minutes later she was back on shore, gleaming wet and slippery in the pale moonlight. She was completely naked—the bundle gone—as she ran back toward the Jeep. She reached gently for my arm. "Come on. A swim will do you good."

She led me down to the shore and helped me to remove my shirt, soaked with sweat and clinging to my body; my pants and underwear, wet and stale with urine, were next. The two of us, naked and never more alone, walked hand in hand down to the water's edge and dove in.

Everything was silent. Cool, clear silence, like swimming in an ice cube. I dove deeper—as if through an invisible curtain—into the next level of silence. Cooler and much darker; the sun's light seldom reached here. I held my breath until I was certain that my lungs would explode and wished that I could stay there forever.

What the hell had we turned loose? Even as we sat cringing and half-naked in the dirt of Hurley's cellar, chanting gibberish to some tank-dwelling bogeyman, I hadn't truly believed in the Power. Not the gut-wrenching, never-say-die, 'til-death-do-us-part, stick-a-needle-in-my-eye kind of belief. Had I? Certainly I had turned my mind against Hooter; yes, had even wished his death—all right, willed it—but I had never actually come to terms with the means. Somehow the idea of eliminating evil and the sight of Mrs. Wadkins's head rolling about on her bedroom floor seemed worlds apart. It was simply a figment of our imagination—Mary Jean's and mine; an idea that had originally been hatched in the half-deranged mind of my Uncle Looter. Not any longer. It was real and it was loose; and, if Mary Jean could be believed, it held no loyalties other than to the two of us.

Then there was Uncle Hooter, a lingering picture as real as if he were there in the water next to me; bloodstained and naked like some primitive caveman hovering over a fresh kill, and for one brief, terrifying moment, looking up and staring directly at Mary Jane and me as we watched the horror show unfolding in front of us. Had he seen us? Or was it just my own blind fear that made me think so? If we had been spotted, what now? What in God's name would happen now? I no longer had any doubt of what Hooter was capable of. He had met the Power head on, and defeated it.

Not until I was hit with that sense of panic that accompanies the instinctive need to breathe did I look upward, into the moon's light, as it dimly filtered through the water's darkness like a web of cracks in a glass prism. I lunged upward, desiring nothing more than uncluttered air, and broke into the night with a splash. I sucked it in greedily—air, life richer than gold—and began searching desperately for Mary Jean.

"Over here, Ollie."

She was behind me, her face glistening like waxed marble above the blackened water. I turned and swam toward her. She was smiling. As I came closer she splashed at me playfully before turning legs upward and disappearing beneath the surface. I followed.

Our bodies bumped together and then her hands held my own, taking us deeper. We were floating face to face, suspended like naked specimens in a solution, my ears starting to hurt from the water's pressure.

Mary Jean moved her face closer to my own. She brushed her lips against my forehead before bringing them down and gently moving them against my mouth. She mouthed some words but they were lost in a muffled garble of bubbles. I was running out of air and yet, strangely, didn't feel that sense of panic that had hit me just moments earlier. I began letting my breath out more slowly, remembering Scooter's advice in regard to swimming underwater—"Tiny bubbles, Son. That's the trick. Just think of Guy Lombardo." I had no idea who Guy Lombardo was but the tiny bubbles stuck with me.

It seemed like a game we were playing—one that I suddenly didn't want to lose. I wouldn't head for the top without Mary Jean. Finally she raised our hands above her head and we floated as one to the surface. As we broke the water she was laughing.

"Come on, Ollie. I'll race you to shore." She was off, gliding almost soundlessly through the water as I thrashed and grunted my way along behind her.

On the beach we lay on our backs, gazing up toward the stars shining like pinpricks in a black backdrop. Mrs. Wadkins and Hooter seemed as far away as the stars, a vague memory from a bad dream. Naked and wet, I shivered at the touch of the evening breeze. I heard Mary Jean giggle—a soft, friendly sound—and I turned to face her.

"It disappeared."

"What?"

"Your pecker. It disappeared."

And it had, as if it had been snipped off. I felt my face redden and my balls shrink even deeper into their protective pouch.

"I'm cold," I said and reached for my soiled shirt to dry off with. When I was finished I handed the shirt to Mary Jean. The night was warm and once I was dry the air was comfortable on my naked skin.

"It ain't through, you know?"

"Huh?"

"The Power. It ain't done yet. Hooter might have won this round, but his days are numbered. Sure as shit."

"I don't want to talk about that."

"We got to talk about it. We control it."

"No! No we don't. It ain't real!"

"Of course it's real! Didn't you see it make that fat fucker dance?"

"But Mrs. Wadkins and that stranger . . ."

"Hooter killed them!" That crazed look that I had seen at the Hurley place was in her eyes. Frothy balls of spit had accumulated at both corners of her mouth. "He's evil!"

"It ain't real, Mary Jean! It ain't! I want to go home," and I felt the tears—large and salty—fill my eyes and roll down my cheeks. I knew Mary Jean was right. It was real. We had turned it loose and now there was no going back.

"That stranger. Was he the . . ."

"The Power? Hell no! You can't see the Power, Ollie. That was Old Man Wadkins. I reckon he finally got tired of Hooter diddling his wife."

"But why did he kill her?"

"I guess he figured she was givin' away somethin' that was his. People get crazy about that sometimes."

"But why then? I mean how did he know that Hooter would be there?"

"The Power. That's how it operates. It gets other people to do things for it sometimes. I guess it just picked the wrong man for the job this time. That's all."

She sat up, pine needles and grass stuck to her naked back like carefully interwoven macramé. She gazed out toward the center of the reservoir. Several particles of sand had gathered at the top of her ass and clung there as if in the act of letting go they might disappear forever into the darkened tunnel that led to the mysteries of sprouting womanhood. I bet it's warm there. Underneath. Like the heat from a mountain of blankets on a winter's night. Safe and snug. Like a bird in its nest.

Leaning forward, Mary Jean reached back with her hand and brushed the sand from its stronghold.

"Mary Jean?"

She stood up and faced the water as if she hadn't heard me. Her nakedness was suddenly embarrassing, or perhaps it was my own. I thought of Uncle Hooter—hairy and fat— and Mrs. Wadkins—pale and lumpy like dying cauliflower— and couldn't equate the two. This nakedness standing in front of me was neither funny like my uncle nor sad like Mrs. Wadkins. It was something else—troubling and new, yet undeniably strong.

"What is it, Ollie?" Mary Jean had picked up a rock from the shore. She hurled it as she spoke and watched as it skipped crazily across the surface of the water.

"Do we have to kill him?"

"Kill who?"

"Uncle Hooter."

She turned slowly away from the water and stood over me,

her nipples pointing at me like perfectly trained rifles. "We made a pact, Ollie. Our blood merged. Hooter was the focus of evil and we willed him dead."

"Can't we call it off?"

"It's loose, damn it! Who do you think is the cause of us all—the whole family—being so fucked up? Hooter. That's who! Your old man is nuts because of him! On account of Hooter treats him like shit. He makes fun of him in front of everybody. Makes him out to be a Goddamned laughingstock. Nora Anne left 'cause she couldn't take it no more. If it weren't for him you'd be with both your parents like most kids, instead of living in the big house and seeing your father on weekends like you're a fuckin' prisoner or something!" She took a deep breath and then slowly blew it out. "Don't you get it, Ollie? It's him. Hooter. He hates everybody."

"But . . . I didn't think nothing would really happen. . . ."

She leaned down and drew me to her as if I were a soft bundle of rags. "You wanted it, kid, or it wouldn't have happened. That's the Power."

She swallowed and I felt her whole body start to quiver as if it had been hit with a cold breeze. "That ain't the only night he come into my room." Her voice was so soft that even though my ear was right up next to her mouth I could barely hear her. "He comes in whenever he feels like it—I never know when. He does whatever he wants. I close my eyes, like you do at the pictures, and pretend I'm someplace else, only I don't know noplace else. Sometimes it ain't so bad, but other times . . . ." Her voice had been slowly trailing off until finally it was nothing more than a whisper. "When he's really drunk . . . he hurts me . . . like it's fun for him . . . ."

Well-reasoned decisions, weighed carefully in one's mind, are revocable by their very nature. After all is said and done, most of us will admit an error in calculation—"So I made a mistake. I'm only human, you know?" Those emotional, gut-wrenching decisions—torn from the very soul—are a horse of a different color, however. They, it seems, are destined to follow us to the grave.

Lying on the hard-packed beach of the Antonville Reservoir, listening to Mary Jean cry helplessly into the sand, I acted from my soul—it was all I had to draw from. The bloody reality of Martha and Joe Wadkins would soon turn to restless dreams, but the sight of Mary Jean lying bruised and vulnerable in the middle of her cum-stained sheets was as close as the night.

"I'll help you, Mary Jean. Don't cry. We'll get him."

13

The Wadkins killing was the talk of Devon County for months. It was the first double murder in the county in fifteen years—since the time two woodcutters from up north were shot and killed by Lester Barlow in the Depaul Bar and Lounge after they had allegedly bilked Lester out of two hundred dollars in an after-hours card game and then, adding insult to injury, thrown him unceremoniously into the street. Lester, dazed and embarrassed—not to mention being out a month's pay—staggered to his pickup truck and got his double-barreled twelve gauge out of the back. He then returned to the game and emptied both barrels of the weapon into the unfortunate loggers. After spending most of the night searching for him, the police found Lester the next morning, sleeping off the night's excesses in the bed of his pickup truck, which he had carefully parked in his own driveway.

Of course it wasn't really a double murder at all since Joe Wadkins was alive, albeit unconscious, in the Anton Hospital. But people considered it such because whoever had clobbered Joe Wadkins with an iron doorstop had certainly intended to kill him. He had been in a coma ever since the attack, and the doctors gave him less than a twenty-five percent chance of ever coming out of it, and if he ever did happen to wake up, they wouldn't even predict what his mental or physical capabilities might be.

Theories were abundant. Several townspeople believed that it was the depraved handiwork of a cultist group. They pointed to a group of "longhairs and dropouts" who lived in a commune up Dead Creek Hollow as likely suspects. The group had moved in about two years prior to the killings and had promptly painted their life's credo in large white letters on a boulder at the entranceway to the grounds: "Mental and Physical Liberation Is the Key to World Peace." Some local teenagers had done a little editing one night and changed "Liberation" to "Copulation" and "Peace" to "Piece." The inhabitants—being apparently flexible in their politics and open to suggestions from every quarter or simply without sufficient funds for fresh paint—seemed content in adopting the new slogan and left the edited version untouched. It was unclear in what direction the path to mental liberation lay but the group's dedication to the second half of the proclamation was unassailable: "They don't wear no fucking clothes," announced Looter after he had snuck past the barriers one night in order to take a closer look.

Others labeled it a masochistic, sex-thrill killing, in which the Wadkinses had been willing participants. Why else had they been found naked together in the middle of the room? And with no sign of a struggle? The bed was neatly made and the furniture was all in place. This puzzled me as well. When I asked Mary Jean about it, she shrugged her shoulders. "Hooter," she said. "The bastard. He must have taken Joe Wadkins's clothes off and cleaned the room up."

"But why would he do that?" I asked.

"To cast suspicion away from himself," she explained. Although I was unable to follow her logic, I didn't question it further; nonetheless, I couldn't stop thinking about the bundle that Mary Jean had carried out into the middle of the Antonville Reservoir.

The Reverend Claiborne entitled one of his sermons "Sex and Violence in the Rural Community" and spent an entire Sunday morning explaining to his parishioners how R-rated movies and rock 'n' roll were the early seeds of carnage and depravity in American youth. "What I want to know is this," he thundered from the pulpit. "Did those responsible for the tragic death of Martha Wadkins ever see the movie *Easy Rider*? *The Valley of the Dolls*? *Bob and Carol and Ted and Alice*? I'm willing to wager today's offering that he or they saw at least one of those films."

The Cooter family, like every other family in Devon County, had its own varied opinions on what had occurred.

"Old Joe Wadkins was loaded," said Looter. "He had a cache of money in his fucking mattress. Sure as shit somebody cut them up to get at it."

"It weren't no local, that's for sure," said Uncle Hooter. "Nobody around these parts could keep a secret like that." I could have sworn he gazed directly across the table at Mary Jean and me as he spoke, the folds of skin in his face spreading slowly into a half-smile.

"I'll bet ya there's more than one person in town who knows what happened," said Mary Jean.

"Maybe you know something you'd like to tell the rest of us there, little girl? Like maybe you was hiding under the bed when the murder occurred? Hoo! Hoo! Hoo!"

"If'n I was," said Mary Jean, "I'd never tell."

"Well, I think it's a shame that something like this could happen in Anton," said Mother Cooter. "A person can't even feel safe in their own house no longer."

On that score my grandmother and I were in complete

agreement. I didn't feel safe anywhere for that matter. The world was filled with lurking strangers, some with fedoras and some without. I felt eyes upon me. They had all seen what I had seen. They all knew what I knew.

The person who scared me more than anyone was my Uncle Hooter. The morning after the killing he had appeared at the barn for chores same as always. I was there, at Mary Jean's insistence, despite the fact that I hadn't slept a wink the night before—the gremlins had thrown an all-night bash, with a headless Mrs. Wadkins and the fedoraed stranger as the guests of honor. Mary Jean had convinced me that it was absolutely essential that we act as if nothing out of the ordinary had occurred.

"But why?" I had asked. "What if we was to tell Sheriff Benson everything we seen?"

"If we admit that we was there, then we could be accessories."

"Be what?"

"Accessories to murder. That means we're just as guilty of a crime as Hooter is."

"But Hooter was only protectin' hisself and we was just watching. Maybe if we tell we'll only get a licking and be grounded for a while."

"Don't be an ass! It don't matter why he done what he done. It's still murder. Hooter was screwing Mrs. Wadkins and that's a crime 'cause she's married. Then she got killed and under the law that's murder. We was trespassing—that means we was where we weren't supposed to be—so we're guilty too. Just like Hooter."

I didn't follow all of it but I was certainly scared enough to believe that we were in for an awful lot of trouble if anyone ever found out that Mary Jean and I were at Mrs. Wadkins's bedroom window on the particular evening that she was killed. Aside from any legal consequences, there was a fear as real as death itself. What would Hooter do? What if he found out about everything—the Power; and Mary Jean and me turning it loose on its death-dealing mission as if it were some kind of hired assassin from the spirit world?

If my uncle had spotted us at the window he was keeping it to himself—more or less. He sauntered into the barn, bull-dog tough and barking out orders.

"You look a little down in the gills, boy." He had spotted me as I tried—on cat's feet—to tiptoe past him. "Tough night?"

"I didn't sleep much," I mumbled.

He had just sat down on a three-legged stool and was in the process of hooking a milking machine to the drooping udder of an unsuspecting victim—that being the first cow in a line that extended from one end of the barn to the other. The cow, her head through the iron bars of a stanchion, chewed contentedly on her cud and gazed down the long row of milkers as if, given her superior spot in line, she occupied a position of royalty in relation to the mere black-and-white mortals that would follow her.

"You don't say." Uncle Hooter turned the machine on and aimed the suction cups at the cow's tits, protruding like four loaded bullets from its swollen bag. "What's a trouble? You got a woman on your mind?"

The cups took hold with an awful slurping noise and the bullets disappeared. The cow groaned and swished its tail. Hooter looked up for the first time, the machine beneath his legs ejaculating in sporadic bursts as it gently sucked the cow dry.

"Wellll," he drew the word out as if he were waiting for me to interrupt. "I reckon you are still a mite young for that, ain't you?" He turned back to the cow without waiting for an answer, and I walked away with a knot the size of a cannon-ball in my stomach.

Mary Jean and I had agreed on that first night never to

talk about the night's events other than within the safe confines of the Hurley cellar. If anyone happened to ask us anything in regards to our whereabouts on that particular evening we were both home in bed when it happened.

"But what about the Power?"

"What about it?"

"Where is it?" I had this image of the damn thing hovering
around the trailer like an unwelcome relative.

"Don't worry," said Mary Jean. "I'll take care of it."

"How?"

She made it sound as if we were discussing a leaky faucet.
I had seen the Power in action and it was difficult for me to
imagine anyone "taking care of it." Anyone but Hooter perhaps.

"It'll be easy. It's got to go back to the tank and once it does
I'll close the lid on it till we need it again."

"Tonight?"

"Sure. Remember, Ollie, it does what we want. We control
it."

"You're going there tonight?" Does what we want? I certainly couldn't recall asking it to chop Mrs. Wadkins's head
off or to stove in someone's skull with a doorstop.

"Somebody's got to and you sure as hell don't look like a
likely candidate."

14

When school started back in the fall, it caught me off guard. Everyone had a Wadkins story—this was Anton, where barn fires and tractor accidents were front-page news and where double murders were seen about as often as Halley's Comet. I withdrew and felt the secret growing like a malignancy. My grades, which until that year had always been passable if not outstanding, suffered as a result. Scooter and Nora Anne were called into the school psychologist's office for a conference.

"Oliver seems preoccupied," Mr. Groover said while nodding in my direction as if I were some sort of art exhibit. "He has so much potential. I hate to see him waste it."

Fidgeting with his tie, Scooter cleared his throat, started to speak, and then apparently thought better of it.

"Mr. Cooter?"

"Uh, well, we, uh, have had some difficulties at home."

"Difficulties?"

"Yes. My wife and I, that is."

"What kind of difficulties, Mr. Cooter?" Mr. Groover was

sitting on the edge of his desk. He had his legs neatly crossed. As he spoke, his closely cropped mustache bobbed up and down like a buoy in rough water.

"Good Lord! Spit it out, would you, Harold? We were separated for eight months, Mr. Groover. We still are as far as that goes, but I don't see how that could possibly affect Oliver. You see, despite the problems between my husband and I we have managed to maintain a normally structured home environment for our children."

"Ed."

"What?"

"Call me Ed, please, Mrs. Cooter."

"Ed. All right, Ed."

"You say you still are separated?"

"In a manner of speaking, but we all live together. Oliver has two parents. That is something I have insisted upon."

"I see." He smiled at my mother, causing the ends of his mustache to shoot crazily up toward his eyebrows. Nora Anne smiled back and rearranged her hair. Scooter cleared his throat again and said nothing.

"Well," said Mr. Groover, tugging at his polyester pants, "perhaps the boy is feeling some confusion in regards to his status in the household." At first I thought he was referring to someone else until I realized that everyone was looking at me. "A parental separation of whatever nature can have a very traumatic effect upon a youngster."

"Look, Mr. Groover, why don't you ask him?"

"Ed."

"Right, Ed. Why don't you ask Ollie what's bothering him? Give him a chance to say what's on his mind. He's a bright kid."

"Oh, Oliver and I have had several discussions. Haven't we, Oliver?"

"Sure." I could recall only one, in which I had sat quietly in

Mr. Groover's office while he talked about discipline and duty before dismissing me with a curt wave of his hand and some final words of advice. "Shape up or ship out, mister."

"Sometimes I find that if I speak to one of the parents alone we can more readily pinpoint the source of the problem. Very often one feels less encumbered and is better able to ventilate his or her feelings on a one-to-one basis. Harold, I know you are on the road a good deal of the time, so perhaps Mrs. Cooter and I could get together at her convenience?" Bobbing his head toward my mother, he turned his hands palms up as if he were a stage actor taking a bow.

"Well, I suppose," said Nora Anne who once again seemed preoccupied with her hair. "If you think it will help Ollie, that is."

"Fine. Just fine," said Scooter, getting abruptly to his feet. "Pick any night. My wife always has time to ventilate." He took my hand and strode quickly out the door.

The ride back from our meeting with Mr. Groover was a quiet one. An unspoken tension hung like morning fog in the car. I studied the backs of my parents' heads while silently fidgeting in the rear seat. Whatever it was—this tension—it was charged, a live wire of current pulsing between the two of them. Scooter spoke for the first time as we turned from the highway onto Shenker Hollow Road.

"No matter what you may think, I do have my limits, Nora Anne."

"We all do, don't we, Harold?"

"I may be getting close to mine."

Instead of looking at each other while they spoke, they continued to stare straight ahead as if they were conversing with their reflections in the windshield. Did this have something to do with their concern over my grades? I wasn't sure, but somehow I thought not. In fact, I wondered if they had perhaps forgotten that I was even in the car. Then we were in the driveway and my parents exited the car without another word. The tension followed them. It seemed almost visible.

That evening Scooter and I sat in his room playing checkers.

"You know, Son, if'n you've got a problem and you want to talk about it, I'd be more than glad to listen. If you don't want to talk about it, well that's fine too. Some fellas just don't like talkin' 'bout things that are botherin' 'em. I mean the things that are really botherin' 'em instead of the things that everybody thinks is botherin' 'em. I think you may be one of those fellas. In fact you may even take after me a bit as far as that goes. And that's all right, but I suggest you find yourself an outlet."

"What's an outlet?"

"Somethin' to take your mind off of whatever it is that's bothering you. Sometimes if you concentrate hard enough on the new thing—the outlet—then the thing that's bothering you just disappears."

"What kind of outlet?"

"Well, when I was a kid I ran. I ran until I was drenched in sweat and I could hardly stand up any longer. Sometimes I wish I had never given it up."

"Why did you?"

"I got old and fat."

"Well, I dunno if I would be a good runner."

"I'll tell you what. I will if you will."

"What?"

"Run."

"You mean run together?"

"Sure. When I'm not on the road we'll go together. The rest of the time you'll have to run alone. Is it a deal?"

"Okay."

We started the next morning. Scooter was dressed in a pair of bermudas that Nora Anne had bought for him right after they were married and that he had never worn. They came down almost to his knees and were a bright red-and-yellow plaid. He had a sweatshirt on and a pair of flat running shoes that he must have kept hidden in his closet. Dressed in my cut-offs and a pair of high-top basketball sneakers, I met him on the front porch.

"You can't run in those. You'll hurt your feet," he said pointing toward my footgear.

"I don't have any others."

"Well, I guess a couple of times won't bother you none. If you stick with it, I'll get you a pair of these," he said as he held his feet out for my inspection. "That is if they still make 'em."

"Where did you get them?" This was before the running craze had begun to spread through America like a plague and I had never seen a pair of sneakers quite like the funny-looking things my father had on. They were blue and white and didn't appear to be any heavier than a pair of bedroom slippers.

"From my youth, which means they're very old now. I spent one whole summer doin' extra chores for your grandfather—I'm talking about after I had worked all day in the hay-fields—to save up enough money to buy these. The first day I got 'em I was so excited that I had Mother Cooter drop me off at the shoe store—they had to order the shoes special and it took three weeks for them to come in—and I ran all the way home from Anton."

"Are they the shoes you set the record in?"

"They sure are," he said as he bent over from the waist and tried to touch his toes. About halfway down he appeared to get stuck as if his joints had suddenly turned to cement, before he managed to bring himself slowly back into an upright position. "I reckon they only had the one record in 'em."

We planned on running to the beginning of Shenker Hollow

and back, a distance of about three and a half miles. Less than halfway down the hollow we were both exhausted. Scooter, running just in front of me, was gasping and wheezing like a steam engine, the ring of handlebar fat on his back and sides jiggling with every step; sweat stained his shirt and the bermudas where they covered the crack of his ass. I felt the autumn air fill my lungs, penetrating to the pit of my stomach before it did an about-face and was spewed back out as I exhaled. We ran by the pasture where the cows, large and slothful, grazed in dumb innocence. Despite the pain I felt quick and alive next to those plodding beasts.

For the first half mile we had exchanged a few words, but soon found the effort too exhausting. So we ran in silence except for the sounds of our labored breathing and the gurgled monotony of the brook as it kept perfect pace with us down the length of the hollow. With every step I felt certain that Scooter would stop and take a break or else totally collapse from heart failure. He did neither until we reached the end of the hollow.

Once there, he turned toward me, his face oozing perspiration, and held his hands out to stop me. "You look like you need a blow. What say we walk for a while?"

We walked without talking, catching our breath and assessing the early pains of newly used muscles. Sweat dripped from my brow and onto my lips. It tasted salty but good. I felt a vague sense of accomplishment, like a mechanic must feel when he hears the smooth purr of a re-constructed engine. I concentrated only on the taste in my mouth and the new sensations running through my body.

Soon we took up the pace again and started back up the hollow. As we moved uphill, the muscles in my legs felt as if they had been grabbed by invisible vicegrips. My lungs ached from being stretched to new limits. Overhead, birds laughed at us from the safety of the trees. Occasionally one would mock us with its winged movements, divebombing directly for us before, at the last possible second, soaring once again toward the heavens.

Twice more we slowed to a walk—but only briefly—before arriving back at the farm.

As we jogged through the yard Uncle Hooter's voice boomed out from somewhere behind the barn. "Well, well. Look at the athletes! If'n you'd only sweat like that when you worked maybe this place would turn a profit!"

Back at the trailer we lay on our backs in the front yard, staring up at the cloudless sky. I was exhausted. My legs felt as though a fire were smoldering deep within their muscles. Sweat trickled from my forehead in tiny rivers. My mind was clear at last, empty of everything but the run.

My father lay on his back with his left arm draped over his eyes, shielding them from the sun.

"Have we still got a deal?" He asked without looking at me.

"We got a deal," I said.

He flopped his right arm across his chest and held his hand out toward me. I took hold of it and shook it firmly.

15

Basketball was the game of choice for my aunt and me. At an early age we had designed a makeshift court in the dirt driveway next to the trailer. Intentionally kicking dust into an opponent's face was a foul. Approaching cars meant a timeout. Trees and buildings were out of bounds. Losing one's dribble in a pothole was a hazard of the game.

The garage was only high enough to accommodate an eight-foot rim, and the net that had once hung from it had long since fallen victim to foul weather and too many jump shots. No one had bothered to replace it, and now the rim extended netless from the garage with a forward tilt as a result of countless slam dunks by my Uncle Looter. Looter's game was totally unrefined—the dunk shot was the only weapon in his offensive arsenal, and that, of course, only effective as a consequence of the unusually low dimensions of the Cooter court. Nonetheless, my uncle played with an aggressiveness and a total abandon that were unmatched by most superstars. Rules to his way of thinking were irrelevant. He charged about the court, recklessly swatting at whoever had the ball as if it were a game of rugby that he was engaged in, and in order to execute his favorite shot, he would take off from beyond half court without the aid of a dribble.

The contests between my aunt and me more closely resembled the game of basketball. This was at a time when strategy still played a part in the game. Six foot five was still tall. Slow white men could still dream of glory. The Celtics sat atop the NBA.

Mary Jean relied on her superior height and broad shoulders to back me into the basket. Once in position, she would utilize her hook shot or turn and put up a soft jumper off the backboard. Position was everything in her strategy. The battle was won or lost in the moments leading up to her shot, as she dribbled, back to the basket, toward one of two favorite spots on either side of it. Pushing and shoving against her, I fought desperately with my body to keep her from her destination. Once she was there, I could only hope that she would miss the shot as she turned and effortlessly launched the ball over my outstretched arms.

Being of much smaller stature, I was forced to rely on my quickness and ball-handling ability in order to score. With a good enough ball fake I could generally freeze Mary Jean and drive past her for an open lay-up. During that brief moment in which my path to the basket was unimpeded and my aunt could do nothing but swipe out ineffectually at the ball with one of her long arms, I knew the single-minded savagery of success. Turning back after the ball had fallen through the rim, seeing Mary Jean, hands hanging limply by her sides, while shaking her head in disgust, I first felt the double-edged sword of victory.

The player on offense was responsible for calling all fouls. This was the source of countless arguments. The two of us were closely matched, and a blown call one way or another might mean the difference in a ballgame.

Mary Jean was a fierce competitor. She hated to lose. After coming out on the short end of a competition she would often stomp off to the big house and refuse to speak to anyone for the rest of the day. On more than one occasion I faced the dilemma of intentionally blowing a close game or of going for the win and of thus losing my aunt's companionship for the remainder of the afternoon.

A month or so after my parents' initial encounter with the school psychologist, Mary Jean and I were in the midst of one of our confrontations. I had just released a jump shot over her outstretched arms when a car pulled into the driveway.

We had been so intent on the game that we hadn't noticed its slow approach up the hill. It was a green Catalina convertible with traces of rust showing through a cheap paint job. The top was down. Music without words floated upward from its interior.

The ball bounced off the front of the rim and onto the hood of the Catalina. Ed Groover sat behind the wheel with a toothy smile on his face, waiting for me to retrieve it.

I stood bouncing the ball off the dirt-packed driveway as Groover opened up the car door and stepped out. As he slammed the door shut a piece of rusted metal dropped from the rocker panel onto the driveway.

"Hello, Mary Jean. Oliver."

He held his hands out awkwardly for the ball. I tossed it to him. He threw up a two-handed set shot that missed everything.

"A little out of practice, I guess." He chuckled. "I used to be quite a shot in my day, believe it or not." I didn't.

I picked up the ball and started bouncing it again. The sound it made as it thudded into the dirt and a dog barking somewhere filled the silence.

"Is your mother around?"

"Yup and so is my dad," I answered quickly.

"Oh really? I thought he would be working today." I bet you did. You turd.

He stood there shuffling his feet. He was dressed in a pair of plaid golfer's slacks and a button-down shirt that was only buttoned three-quarters of the way up. A gold medallion hung from a chain around his neck and was nestled among his chest hairs. The odor of aftershave emanated from his body as if he had bathed in it.

"Well, I guess . . ."

There was a sound like rushing water and Buster came barreling around the corner of the garage. Buster had been a part of the Cooter family for longer than I could remember. He was half German shepherd, half husky and half everything else, as my father used to say. Scooter had salvaged him from sure death at the hands of Hank Somes. Shortly after he had taken the job at Century Semen, my father had gone up Chipmunk Hollow for the purpose of impregnating one of Somes's heifers. When he arrived, Hank was out back by the watering trough. Four dead puppies lay side by side at his feet, and he was struggling to keep the last one under water. My father had intervened and brought the dog home with him, and Buster had been paying him back ever since. He didn't listen to anyone but Scooter. "There ain't no trick to it," claimed my father. "You just have to be able to think like a dog."

I had watched as Scooter got down on all fours and hung his tongue out the corner of his mouth, before rolling onto his back and sticking his arms and legs straight up in the air. Buster slowly ambled over and commenced to scratch my father's stomach with his massive paws. After an appropriate length of time, he stopped scratching and rolled onto his own ample back, imitating my father's earlier movements. Scooter reciprocated in kind, while moans of ecstasy emanated from an appreciative Buster. "Life is tit for tat, Son," my dad told me. "You never get something for nothing."

Groover shrank against his car in terror as the beast leaped onto his chest with its two front feet, pinning the school psychologist to the doorframe as if he were a fleeing felon. Buster began licking Mr. Groover's freshly scrubbed face with a tongue the size of a washcloth.

"Mr. Groover! Excuse me. Ed! It looks as though you've found yourself a new friend," said Scooter, walking casually out from behind the garage holding a wrench in one hand and a mangled piece of metal in the other.

"Jesus!" As he strained to keep Buster at arm's length, Groover's words came out all breathy and too fast for his tongue. "Is he dangerous?"

"Oh, sometimes. It all depends on what kind of mood he's in," said my father, making no move to disengage the two. "Sometimes he's just horny and then he'll hump anything in sight."

Having managed to push each other away from the car, Groover and the shepherd were now involved in a sort of dance in the middle of the driveway. The two of them were standing face to face, with Buster's front paws on Mr. Groover's shoulders and Mr. Groover's arms wrapped securely about the dog's neck. Thus entangled, they were slowly pirouetting about the driveway, while my father went on as if he had taken no notice of their situation.

"Are you here to talk about Oliver again, Ed? I'll be frank with you. I'm very impressed with your dedication. I understand that you've already met privately with my wife on several occasions. Well, what have the two of you figured out?"

Dropping back down onto all four feet, Buster promptly began sniffing Mr. Groover's crotch as if it were stuffed with Kennel Rations.

"Well, uh, I believe that Oliver is starting to come out of his shell. Of course these things take time."

"Of course. Have you spoken to Oliver about his shell lately?"

"Well, he . . . Oliver, that is, has been reluctant to speak with me." After his first private session with Nora Anne, Mr. Groover had called me into his office. "Oliver, I think that you and I can be good friends." He smiled and the mustache jerked up insanely from both ends of his mouth. "Is your father usually out of town all week?" I had walked out of his office and he hadn't approached me since, although my mother had been in to see him on more than one occasion.

"Well, I'll bet that you want to see Nora Anne. You two have got a lot to discuss." My father started toward the trailer and Mr. Groover took a step to follow him. Buster selected that precise moment to shove his nose into the psychologist's groin. Mr. Groover exhaled sharply and doubled up at the waist.

"Oh," said my father, putting a finger into the air as if he had just remembered something he had been trying to think of all day. Having reached the trailer door, he stopped and turned casually back toward the driveway. "One word of caution. When Buster likes the smell of something he'll take a bite out of it first and ask questions later."

Having just managed once again to reach a partially erect position, Mr. Groover reached down with both hands and clasped them firmly over his groin as if he were afraid that his testicles might suddenly sprout wings and take flight. It was in this position that Nora Anne found him when she appeared at the front door.

"Honey, Ed is here to talk with you about our son again," said Scooter. "He thinks that Oliver may be a turtle. Isn't that right, Ed?"

"Ed, I'm so sorry! Come in, please. Harold is impossible, as you can see! This is why we live separately."

Scooter turned without a word and walked back in the direction from which he had come. He whistled sharply. Buster abandoned Mr. Groover's crotch and bounded off after him.

Just before disappearing behind the garage, my father yelled back over his shoulder.

"Frankly, Ed, I think there's only one shell you care about getting into around here! And it's not Oliver's!"

Mary Jean and I resumed our game, but our thoughts were elsewhere. We sat down on the grass surrounding the driveway. We heard banging noises coming from behind the garage, where my father was working on the pickup truck. My mother and Mr. Groover disappeared into the trailer.

A door slammed. An engine started and then the pickup passed us with Scooter behind the wheel and Buster sitting up next to him, his massive head sticking out the passenger side window. The truck disappeared down the hollow. The dust rose and settled in the driveway as if someone had shaken out a dirty rug.

"I hate Mr. Groover," I said.

"How come?"

"He makes Nora Anne act different and Scooter hates him, I can tell."

"That's 'cause he thinks that Groover is screwing Nora Anne."

"That ain't true!" I said. "My mother wouldn't let him do that!"

"Maybe not, but Scooter thinks she is and that makes him mad."

We lay on our stomachs for a while without talking, searching through the grass for four-leaf clovers. Thinking about Mr. Groover in the trailer with my mother was like biting into tinfoil; it was all wrong. It was as if an intruder had entered into our lives. First the wall and now this.

"Here's one," said Mary Jean as she held up a four-leaf clover. "You take it and make a wish. It's good luck."

I gripped it in my hand and thought for a while. "I wish that the wall would disappear and Mr. Groover with it."

16

I have said that my brother was weird. At least, while we were growing up, he often seemed that way. Perhaps I should explain.

At times, it seemed that Craig did nothing but read. He would sit for hours, even on the sunniest days, reading page after page of one book or another. Usually I had never heard of the books that he became so absorbed in. He borrowed them from the library each week. Some weeks he would check out as many as ten books. These he would cart home each Friday afternoon in a satchel swung over his shoulder as if he were bringing home quantities of food to squirrel away for the winter. Indeed, there were other arboreal aspects to his behavior. The way he would hibernate in his room with these books, for example, feasting on them as if they were a pouchful of nuts he had foraged. At such times he left strict orders that he wasn't to be disturbed for any reason. "What about dinner?" my father would ask. "Or would you prefer to eat your books?"

At Parent-Teacher Day one year I overheard Craig's fourth-grade teacher tell my parents that Craig had the reading comprehension of a fourteen-year-old and a far above average

IQ. "Your problem is going to be in trying to hold him back. Intellectually he belongs with older children, but socially he is going to have problems wherever you place him."

The idea of sending him to a private school was discussed on more than one occasion. "If the Anton public school was good enough for me then it's good enough for him," said my father.

"You weren't a gifted child," said Nora Anne.

"There was a time when you thought so," said Scooter. "One particular occasion under the high school bleachers comes to mind."

"He isn't being challenged. He says the work isn't stimulating enough."

"Stimulating? Where the hell did he learn to talk like that?"

"Well, it certainly wasn't from your side of the family," said my mother.

"In case you had forgotten, N'Anne"—when Scooter became agitated with my mother he would often leave out the middle portion of her name, so as to get more quickly to the point of his agitation, I suppose—"your father was a clerk in a hardware store."

"He was a businessman," said Nora Anne. "Anyways, if you weren't so damn selfish you would be proud that we have a gifted child."

"Gifted? No one understands what he's talking about, for Christ sake. What kind of a gift is that?"

"He knows that there is more to life than cowshit! The sooner we get him into a private school the better off he is going to be."

"And who is going to pay for that? Your father the businessman?"

When he wasn't reading, my brother was composing letters or writing in his journal. He had a list of addresses for almost every newspaper and magazine published in the United States. He was constantly sending off letters to the editor, either responding to something that had been published in the editorial section or else expounding his views upon any subject that happened to catch his fancy and, of these, there were many. If one of his letters was published he would cut it out and paste it into a scrapbook, which he had entitled "The Maturing of an American—Craig K. Cooter."

One of his proudest moments had occurred upon his discovering that a letter he had written concerning the welfare system in America had been published in the *Albany Times Union*. It was entitled "The Capitalist Viewpoint" and suggested that "Man is the only species of animal that feels this inane sense of responsibility for the lazy and weak amongst its numbers. . . . The irony of the system being that it serves to undermine the very foundations of the capitalist nation by draining the resources of those who have accomplished to better the lives of those who have not." He wrote the letter when he was twelve years old.

"His view of life is so hard," complained my father. "Where is the child's compassion?"

"At this age his viewpoints aren't important," said Nora Anne. "His concern for what goes on around him is. He likes to agitate, to test people's responses. It's harmless."

"The boy is barely twelve years old and he talks like Robert McNamara. I feel foolish telling people he is my son."

"That is your problem, not his. He's a gifted child. You will just have to learn to accept it."

Following the death of Mrs. Wadkins, Craig submitted a letter—perhaps exposé would be a more accurate term—to the *Anton Courier*. It was entitled "Rural Roots of the Primitive Man." My mother persuaded him, over Craig's strong protestations, to send it in anonymously.

One should not be surprised to find such barbaric behavior among the simple folk who populate these hills. . . . We are after all essentially a backward people. . . . A throwback to the primitive man: uneducated, unrefined, and unintentioned in our behavior. Discipline has not yet reached this outback of America . . . Here we are still surviving on the most basic drives, unencumbered by any modern teachings or the need to stifle such urges . . . the most basic of all being, of course, the drive to copulate. . . .

The letter was signed "An Unsurprised Observer."

In the following weeks the *Courier* received a record number of submissions to its Opinion Section. The responses were varied, ranging from "Unsurprised Observer should be suffocated in cow [manure]" to ". . . since when does being a simple person make one a barbaric monster who cuts people's heads off?" to "Unsurprised Observer is in for a big surprise if this backward citizen ever meets him in a darkened alley."

"Jesus! If anyone ever found out that our son was the Unsurprised Observer we would all be run out of town on a rail!" said Scooter.

"I will not stifle my children's intellectual pursuits," replied Nora Anne.

"It's me and my family that he's talkin' about in all of his letters. We're the simple folk! He's ashamed of me."

"There you go with your self-pitying again, Harold. Why don't you broaden your focus? Look at all the interest that he's stimulating in the community." Ever since she had returned from her leave of absence my mother had been using terms like "broadening your focus" and "stimulation." She had amassed a large collection of books with titles such as *Crisis Non-Intervention* and *The Psychologically Embattled Adolescent*. Her bookshelf had become a quagmire of psychological jargon. At times her conversations seemed to be plagiarized bits of text.

She prided herself on being fair. In retrospect, I'm sure she would have preferred to have had Craig residing in her half of the trailer on a full-time basis. Through such an arrangement she could have more closely monitored his development and would always have been assured that my brother had someone to bounce his ideas off of without being encumbered by the banalities of farm conversation. Alas, her need for balance would not permit it. Equal access among offspring was a basic rule of good parenting. She insisted that we stick with the rotation system despite its hardships on everyone.

I don't mean to imply that my mother didn't love me. I remain convinced that she did. I simply wasn't Craig. He was a gift, her one beacon of light in a maze of cowshit. By comparison, I didn't stand a chance. His pouting spells she referred to as the "temperamental mood swings" of an intellectual, while my occasional bursts of temper were called the incomprehensible ravings of a spoiled child.

The thought that my parents may have harbored preferences between my brother and me never actually occurred to me as I was growing up. I'm sure it never consciously crossed Craig's mind either. Perhaps not even my parents would have openly acknowledged it. It certainly was never verbalized. It just was, that's all.

If Craig held a special place in my mother's heart, then I am sure that Scooter had a tiny chamber walled off somewhere in his vast reserve of emotion just for me. It was a natural leaning. Craig at times must have seemed to my father to be a stranger beamed in from another planet. Had he not been present at my brother's birth, I am certain he would have suspected that a mistake had been made at the hospital, that his real son was living in an intellectual enclave somewhere within the boundaries of a university.

Craig simply didn't respond to fatherly attentions. At least I was a child, probably much closer to Scooter's own level of mental maturity than Craig was. I was available to go fishing or to play games whenever my father wasn't too preoccupied with one of his many maladies. Unlike Craig I never questioned Scooter about his diseases or disappearances. I was simply thankful for those times when he was around.

17

I had not gone a day without running since that first morning that my father and I had pushed each other down to the end of the hollow and back. The distance was no longer a struggle. I felt my body growing hard and sinewy. "You're starting to develop a man's body," said Mary Jean. Running with the blood pounding in my temples and the wind rushing by like cars on a distant highway was the only time that I felt in control of anything.

On the days when he was home, Scooter always ran with me. He claimed that he worked out by himself when he was on the road, and from the look of him I believed it. The handlebars had shrunk and begun to tighten up like clay figurines drying in the sun. His once-swollen face was beginning to lose its puffiness. He was beginning to appear more and more like the seventeen-year-old kid who held the hundred-yard dash record for Devon County.

We had incorporated calisthenics into our workout. After we had finished our run, my father and I each did two sets of push-ups and sit-ups as well as some general cooling-down exercises. When the weather permitted, we did our exercises shirtless in the front yard of the trailer.

One warm morning, Nora Anne sat on the patio in a yard chair as we went through our routine. My father pretended not to notice, but the extra effort that he put into his push-ups and the tightness with which he held his body—as if he were a body builder posing for a panel of judges—made it obvious that he was aware of her presence. After we had finished and I had returned to the trailer, he stayed in the front yard doing handstands and one-handed push-ups. Through the window in my bedroom I saw Nora Anne smile and push some stray wisps of hair out of her eyes. Scooter finished his routine by doing a full forward flip, landing securely on his feet in front of the porch. He bowed toward my mother. Her smile grew like an expanding river. She waved and then abruptly turned and walked into the house. In my room I felt warm and happier than I had in months.

On my eleventh birthday, Scooter had two gifts for me. The first was a pair of blue-and-white Adidas running shoes. The moment I put them on I felt a new power—like liquid steel— surging through my legs.

"I could only justify getting you two presents," he said, handing me a second package, "if I got one for myself too." Inside were two gray hooded sweatshirts. On the back of the first, the letters THE had been carefully printed. On the other was the word COOTERS. "I got mediums," said Scooter, "so that you can grow into yours and I can grow down to mine." He chuckled and patted his stomach.

"Good thinking," said Nora Anne. "This way you can trade off shirts so that you won't always have to run on the same side of each other."

"And if you ever get lost, we'll only have to look for your sweatshirts," added Craig.

On the weekends my father and I would sometimes go for

long runs together. We would start early in the morning when the grass was still damp from the dew and the sun was just starting to peek over the top of the mountains as if they were mounds of bed covers. Starting out slowly—giving our muscles a chance to unfold gradually—we jogged down the Hollow Road and across the highway until we reached the old railroad bed. The rails had long since been removed from the bed and now it stretched out in a seemingly endless path in two directions. To the right was the reservoir and Anton; to the left, if one went far enough, was the village of Hartsfield and the county line. Usually we turned to the right and followed the track as it snaked alongside the river like an uncoiled rope. To one side was the water; the other was virgin woods mixed with occasional fields of corn or timothy. The only noises were the intermittent grumblings of the area's inhabitants—the screech of a crow warning of our presence, a great blue heron laboriously taking flight, a snapping turtle diving into the river for cover—and our own steady breathing.

We ran until we reached the spot where the two forks of the river came together. There was a knoll above the water where the grass lay like down pillows. My father and I would walk to the top of the knoll, sit down in the grass, and quietly watch as the two streams of water collided like a pair of rampaging bulls. The water was spun about in an angry whirlpool before being spewed out to continue its journey as one united force.

At times like these it was easy to forget about the Power and Uncle Hooter and Mrs. Wadkins. It was easy for me to believe that it was just a matter of time before Scooter would move back into my mother's room and the wall would be removed forever.

"Will we ever move out of the trailer?" I asked one day as my father and I sat gazing down at the passing river. He turned his head slowly toward me as if he were trying to work a kink out of his neck.

"Why? Do you want to?"

"Sort of. I guess."

"Well, I reckon we will someday."

"When?"

He curled his lip and placed his chin carefully into the palm of one hand before answering. "Soon as I get the business started, I reckon. Lotta things are going to start happening once the business gets going."

"Craig says you ain't never gonna start the business." The words were out before I could stop them. Scooter looked at me sharply. He took a deep breath and blew it out, his face relaxing once again.

"Well, your brother is pretty smart, but he don't know everything. I'll do whatever it takes to make your mother and you boys happy." He smiled and ruffled my hair. "Have some faith in your old man will you, kid?"

I smiled back and we both got to our feet. We started walking down the hill in preparation for the run back. "Daddy?"

"What, Ollie?"

"When we move will we all live together?"

"Of course."

"Will there be a wall in our new house?"

He stopped and turned toward me. Leaning down he put my face between his hands. They were warm and sweaty. "There won't be a wall, Ollie. I promise."

He didn't move and neither did I. Sweat glistened off his face as he held me. I was for the most part a quiet child, but now the questions wouldn't stop. "What about Mr. Groover?"

"What about him?" I felt his muscles tense.

"I don't like him."

"You don't have to."

"Does Mommy like him?"

"I guess."

"Does she love him?"

"No. No, she don't love him. She only loves you and me and Craig." He got to his feet. "It's just takin' her awhile to figure that out. When she does we'll all be together again."

The run back was the best I had felt in weeks. My feet flew over the cindered tracks. The thought of the family reunited spread like warm cider throughout my body.

18

Less then a week later, that riverside chat with my father suddenly appeared to be nothing more than a distant memory; and the feeling of exhilaration I had experienced on our last run together was expunged like the air from an exploding puffball.

It was late fall. The air was getting cooler. The days were getting shorter. By the time Craig, Mary Jean, and I had stepped from the school bus in the late afternoon and made the long trek up the hill to the farm, it would be almost pitch dark outside.

At least once or twice a week, Mr. Groover's car would be parked in the driveway when we returned from school. My mother and he would be sitting in the kitchen, drinking coffee and talking or gazing quietly out the breakfast-room window when Craig and I walked in. My father, of course, was on the road selling bull semen.

After grabbing a quick bite to eat and changing into my coveralls, I would hurry over to the barn to help with the evening chores. My brother, who adamantly refused to step foot in the barn, would slip quietly into his room to begin another session with the books.

By the time milking was over and I was ready to return to the trailer, Mr. Groover's car would be gone and my mother would be quietly humming to herself in the kitchen while she prepared our supper.

That particular evening I was already in the barn and all the way up in the haymow before I discovered that I had forgotten my work gloves. One of the first things any farmer learns about handling hay bales is never to undertake such a task without first investing in a good pair of gloves. The tightly woven twine used to secure the bales will cut through the flesh on one's hands in a matter of minutes.

After listening to a lecture from my Uncle Hooter about he necessity for arriving at work fully prepared, I returned to the house to get my gloves. Craig was sitting at the kitchen table reading by the light of the overhead lamp.

"What are you reading?" I asked.

"*Beowulf*," he replied without glancing up.

"Is it a wilderness story?"

"*Beowulf*—not *Lone Wolf*, you ass. It's eleventh-century English."

"Oh," I said, walking past him toward the partition doorway.

"You better not go in there."

"How come? I gotta get my gloves."

"It's rather a private encounter from what I gather."

"What do you mean?"

"The two of them wish to be alone."

"Who?"

"Must I always be your interpreter? Mother and Mr. Groover. Who else?"

"How do you know they want to be alone?"

"Because they went into the living room and shut the door just like they always do while you're over in the barn doing whatever it is that you do over there."

"That don't mean they want to be alone."

"That is what doors are for," he huffed. "To keep people out."

"Well, I gotta get my gloves."

"Proceed at your own risk," he said, dismissing me with a wave of his hand and turning back to his book.

My bedroom at the time was on Nora Anne's side of the trailer, which meant that I would have to walk through the living room in order to get to it. Standing outside the closed door, I heard muffled voices and hushed laughter emanating from within.

A hidden passage unlocked somewhere within my head. For a moment I was kneeling outside Mrs. Wadkins's bedroom window as the tinkling sounds of her laughter floated into the night. Panic consumed me. I didn't want to hear what came next. Fear and pain—together like some lethal drug—overtook me. I reached for the doorknob and opened the door.

"Oliver!" Nora Anne sprang up from the couch as if goosed by an electric prod. Her long country-style dress, which had been momentarily bunched up around her waist, dropped back down around her ankles, but not before I glimpsed the exposed patch between her legs, the hair there appearing even thicker than that of Mrs. Wadkins—like some overgrown garden in dire need of weeding. One hand she held over her naked breasts; in the other she gripped her underwear as if it were a handful of dust she was about to hurl my way. "You know better than to come through a closed door without knocking first!"

Ed Groover was on his hands and knees in front of the couch—naked from the waist up—the gold chain dangling like a dog's collar toward the floor. His face appeared flushed and hot as if he had just removed it from an oven. His head was twisted toward me, frozen in place like an artist's model, while his tongue traversed his lips in a reptilian manner.

"I forgot my gloves," I mumbled.

"Well, I am ashamed of you, young man! If there is one thing I have tried to instill in you it is to have consideration for the privacy of others!" Having replaced her breasts, she began to smooth the wrinkles out of her dress. She glanced at Ed Groover, who was still down on all fours.

"Get up from there, Ed."

"What? Oh, yes! Of course, Nora Anne! Oliver? Your mother lost one of her earrings here on the floor somewhere and I was just down here looking for it. I can't seem to find it, my dear." Laying his head sideways onto the carpet, he began peering beneath the couch.

"Don't be an ass, Ed! Get up from there this instant! The boy isn't stupid." She turned back toward me, the underwear still poised in her hand.

"Oliver, go to your room and get whatever it is that you need." Reaching down with both of her hands she stepped quickly into her underpants, pulling them on beneath her dress as if she were pulling on a new skin.

I walked past the two of them and hurried down the hallway to my bedroom. I grabbed the gloves from my bureau and moved rapidly out of the room. I longed to be outside, in the fresh air. I was having trouble breathing; everything in the trailer suddenly seemed very close.

Back in the living room, Mr. Groover and my mother were standing side by side in the middle of the room. Groover—now fully dressed—had his hands behind his back. Nervously working the muscles in his jaw, his mustache careened crazily from one side of his face to the other.

"Oliver?" I was halfway to the door when my mother's voice stopped me. "Haven't you forgotten something?"

"No, ma'am."

"I think you owe Mr. Groover and me an apology, young man."

We stood facing each other from a distance of less than ten feet. Her words rattled about my head. An apology? For what? For walking into the living room and catching the two of them in a grown-up game of doctor? I wanted nothing more than to have Ed Groover out of our house. It wasn't right him being there when Scooter wasn't. Yet here was my mother standing next to him, demanding that I apologize, as if it were the most normal thing in the world for Groover to have his head up her dress.

"That's all right, Nora Anne. I think Oliver has learned his lesson." It was Mr. Groover who broke the silence.

"Stay out of this, Ed. I will discipline my own children if you don't mind. Oliver?"

I thought of my father, amongst all of his fertile literature, bouncing around somewhere in the pickup truck, believing that his wife still loved him. My mother had been right; he was quite obviously nuts. I envied him his illusions. The real world was a cruel place. Suddenly I felt desperately alone, as if I were the only guest who had worn a costume to a formal party. "I'm sorry you lost your earring," I said.

"Don't get smart with me, young man! I will not tolerate impertinence from my children!"

Wasn't that what this was all about? A lost earring? Maybe it was beneath the yards of long cotton material making up my mother's dress, and Ed Groover had simply been burrowing in there after it. I felt the tears coming, embarrassing and wet. I struggled to hold them back.

"Oliver?"

"I'm sorry," I managed.

"That's better," said Nora Anne.

"Why don't you stop by my office in the morning, Ollie. The

two of us will have a little man-to-man chat. No females allowed. What do you say?" Groover winked and the mustache leaped up toward his closed eye as if suddenly he had been overcome by an uncontrollable twitch.

I turned and rushed from the room. I hurried through the partition doorway, pulling the gloves onto my hands. Craig was still reading at the table as I passed through the kitchen on my way to the front door. He glanced up, his glasses sneaking down toward the end of his nose.

"I guess you better go up on the hill," he said, "and ask your friend for some more help."

"What's that s'posed to mean?"

" 'Oh what tangled webs we weave, when first we practice to deceive,' " he said, before dropping his eyes back to his book.

As I walked down the front steps and headed toward the barn I could still hear his laughter, light and breathy like the sound of a panting dog.

19

Winter is tough on a farmer, particularly in upstate New York, where it starts in November and ends in mid-April. It is the time of year when the farmer pays for being lazy in the summer or unfortunate or just plain jinxed. There are those who would argue that anyone who has to try to make a living off the land to begin with—particularly in an area where the climate is so cold that five months of the year one can't tell the difference between rocks in the soil and frozen clumps of cowshit—is jinxed or unlucky at the start; either that or else he's just plain stupid.

In truth, brains—or a lack thereof—have little or nothing to do with a farmer's lot in life; either one is born a farmer or one is not. The farm is his birthright. As for the winter, that's simply part of his inheritance.

Of course he can buy more hay or silage if he runs low, assuming there is any available. But then everybody in the county knows that he is short and the price goes up and that cuts into profits that are meager enough during a good year. Farmers for the most part are hard-working, honest people,

138

who, when the opportunity presents itself, are just as capable of squeezing a man as the next person. It's a matter of priorities. His family or yours. "Once a man knows you're down he owns you," my Uncle Hooter was fond of saying. "You might just as well tie a string 'round your nuts and hand it to him."

My uncle was one farmer in Devon County who worked like hell in the summer to avoid being caught with his nuts in a noose come winter. But sometimes it didn't matter how hard you worked. You were just plain jinxed.

There was a drought that summer and the corn never grew the way it should have. Then the frost came early, and because Hooter had put off harvesting the corn on account of its immaturity it got hit and nearly half of it died on the plants. Stunted and lifeless—like rows of young corpses dead before their time—the plants stood in the field long after they had died.

My uncle refused to allow them to be cut until well into November, as if to do so would be to admit defeat. Or perhaps he was expecting that by some miracle they would rise from the dead and be nursed back to health by the early winter winds. When finally the order to harvest was issued, over half of the crop was useless for anything other than mulch. What was left barely filled half of the red-and-white silo that was used for its storage and that stood at the end of the barn like a moon rocket preparing for liftoff.

The hay harvest wasn't much better. What there was was all right, but because of the drought and the short growing season there was only one cutting that year instead of the usual two or three. Then too, help was short and what was available was expensive.

My uncle had become accustomed to hiring several teenagers during the summer to help with the harvest. They came from town and were usually in abundant supply. One had only to drive down Main Street to find half a dozen or more congregated like rats on the town benches. For two square meals and a dollar an hour they would work from dawn to dusk in the fields. It was a chance to get out of town, to breathe some fresh air. An experience.

That summer, teenagers just weren't around like they used to be. They were seeking new kinds of experiences. Some went to summer camps. Others took higher-paying jobs in town— "cushy gopher jobs," Hooter called them. Others simply chose not to work at all. We were, according to my uncle, entering a new era. Something was happening in the country that scared him. "These kids just want to lay around all day growing their hair and blowing dope."

"Fucking—A," said Looter. "The good life."

"Nobody wants to work anymore, Goddamnit! Some scrawny punk with hair down to his asshole asked me if I'd pay him time and a half for overtime. Time and a fucking half! And he wanted two fifty an hour!" Hooter raged.

"It's the economy," said Mother Cooter. "A dollar don't buy what it used to."

"I took hold of the slime bag and told him if he didn't get outta my sight I'd give him half a' my foot up his ass then and half after I'd shaved his fucking head!"

"These kids today are confused," said my grandmother. "Their values are different. Maybe they figure they're gonna get drafted in a year or two anyways so why spend their last summer of freedom sweating away in some hayfield."

"Overtime! Goddamn kids today talk like they're all members of some union! I told him, 'You work on a farm and there ain't no overtime and if'n you work for me it's all my time!' "

"Maybe you can't blame 'em for being a little confused, not that I'm condoning laziness, mind you. But comin' right outta high school like they is, not knowin' whether maybe they'll get sent off to some jungle in a place they ain't never heard of before, is bound to cause a child's priorities to go askew.

'Specially when they see their friends comin' home in boxes all the while."

"Well, I'm not paying it," said Hooter. "We're all just gonna have to tighten our belts and work a little harder."

So we did and we made it through the summer and the fall, and around late February we got caught short. We weren't the only ones. Most of the farmers in Devon County had been hurt by the drought and the early frost. There wasn't much feed available anywhere. Hooter had to go all the way to Drexler County to buy hay and it cost him nearly thirty dollars a ton. That's when he decided that we would have to let Earl Bailey go and that my father would have to go back to farming. Earl had been with the Cooters for five years as a milker, ever since my grandmother had retired from the barn. We all liked Earl. He was the only non-Cooter ever to work in the barn on a full-time basis and was almost like an unofficial member of the family.

"I can't afford him no longer," said my uncle. "There's too many other expenses."

"But we need Earl," said Mother Cooter. "We can't get it done with just you and Looter doin' the milkin'."

"There's another Cooter in this family." Hooter glanced across the table at my father. "There ain't no reason why he ain't over in the barn doing his share."

"Harold has a job," said Nora Anne. "He's a salesman."

We were all over at the big house for Sunday dinner. It was cold outside. Wind whistled through the windows and pelted the old house with fine bits of snow as if it were the target of some crazed giant with huge generators for lungs. Inside, my father wrestled uncomfortably with his meat, taking great interest in matters on his plate and carefully avoiding anyone's direct gaze. He had not been himself as of late. He had become increasingly withdrawn as the winter wore on, preoccupied with whatever weird gremlins danced in his head.

It had been almost three months since I had discovered Ed Groover on his hands and knees in our living room. Scooter had returned unexpectedly that same evening, complaining of fatigue and overall dizziness. The following morning he had a tingling sensation in his extremities and was unable to make our morning run. The next week at dinner he announced that he had multiple sclerosis. He produced a recent issue of the American Medical Association *Journal* and for the next half hour regaled us all with an article describing the disease. When he was finished, my mother, Craig, and I gazed silently into our plates while waiting for him to produce additional statistics and supporting literature. Instead he rose from the table without a word and left the room. When he returned, he had on his overcoat and was holding his hat in his hand.

"I just wanted you all to know why I have been acting so strangely," he said before walking out the door.

The three of us sat wordlessly, listening to the sound of the truck as it stubbornly groaned into gear and rattled off down the hollow road. After the noise had dissipated my mother stood up from the table. She told Craig and me to take care of the dishes and then she burst into tears, running into her room and slamming the door shut behind her.

"The heartless bastard," said Craig.

"Do you think he might die?" I asked.

"Hardly. He's healthy as an ox, physically at any rate. He's just looking for Mother's sympathy. He can't handle her going out with someone else."

Scooter didn't return for three days. When he did he was quiet and withdrawn. He spoke often of death.

When he wasn't on the road, the two of us continued to run together. Bundled up against the cold, with wool caps pulled over our ears and the Cooters' sweatshirts covering a layer of long underwear, we ventured out into the predawn morning, appearing, no doubt, like a pair of Arctic explorers.

Although I still enjoyed the runs with my father, we seldom spoke as we ran. At times I felt he was hardly aware of my presence next to him. The gremlins, it seemed, were relentless in their pursuit, chasing him even through the snow and cold of an upstate winter. Scooter—his latest malady aside—did his best to outdistance them. His eyes set on some distant point in front of him and his legs churning like two giant pistons, he moved straight ahead, oblivious to the changes in terrain and the unkind elements. Often I couldn't keep up with him. My legs were simply too short. I would fall in behind him and watch his breath come out in great puffs of white air, like smoke rising from a distant chimney.

After the run he would complain of fatigue. "It's the disease," he told my mother. "It's consuming me." Any day it could decide to unleash its full fury, he cautioned us, as if it were a great storm cloud that was hovering constantly above his head. When he wasn't working, he began to spend more and more time in his room, sometimes for hours, with nothing but an old tennis ball for company. Boom! Boom! Boom! The sound would echo throughout the trailer as the ball bounced off his bedroom wall and back into his waiting hand. "We're so fragile, we humans," he told me. "We must constantly prepare for our deaths."

My mother wouldn't permit him to discuss death or his diseases at the dinner table. It was one of the few places where the four of us got together, and she didn't feel it was a proper dinnertime topic. "No one wants to hear that garbage, Harold. The children and I are interested in living not dying."

"So am I. Don't you understand? Only when we are truly aware of our fragility can we appreciate what we have."

"The children would appreciate having a father as opposed to a self-obsessed lunatic."

Such discussions normally ended with my father rising from the table and mumbling, "I'm sorry. I love all of you." At which point he would walk away, leaving the rest of us to eat in pregnant silence with nothing but the occasional clink of silverware to break the tension.

Although he wasn't spending any more time on the road peddling his semen than he had in the past, it seemed to me that my father was seldom there. Or perhaps it was just that he had less and less time for me as he waged his private war against the incessant onslaught of the gremlins. There were no more weekend outings and other than on our runs—which had become more like tortured tests of endurance as opposed to morning interludes reserved for just the two of us—I seldom had an opportunity to be alone with him.

More than ever, Mary Jean was my only source of comfort. She was almost fourteen and had blossomed over the last year. Her breasts stuck out from under her T-shirt like spring buds and her hips had taken on additional weight, giving her the muscled appearance of a sculpted gymnast. At times, when we were alone together, I would be overcome with strange, sputtering sensations, as if the blood in my body was revving up like a car engine for a great race. My face would become flushed. My penis would swell and push against the fabric of my underwear like an enraged beast straining against its leash. These feelings would arrive without warning and were not subject to my control. Their origin was a mystery to me. The sensations were pleasant, yet it seemed that there was something more to be done, some further act to perform. Yet I was not certain what the act might be or of how to go about doing it.

There was a hardness about my aunt's character that may have always been there but that seemed to have intensified and become more noticeable over the past year. She disappeared, at times, within herself, exhibiting to the world a bleak mask of frozen emotions.

The mask, I somehow knew, wasn't meant for me. Like a

cheap veneer exposed to the elements, it seemed often to disappear when the two of us were alone together.

"We're the only two normal people in this whole friggin' family," she told me.

"How come?" I asked.

"Bad genes, I reckon. Soon's I'm sixteen I'm gettin' the fuck out of here."

"Where're ya gonna go?" The thought of her leaving scared me. Without Mary Jean I would have no one.

"Someplace where I ain't got to squeeze cow tits and take orders from that pig Hooter. As far away from here as I can get!"

"Can I go with you?"

"You bet, kid." Then she smiled and her face softened. "You and me against the world."

We seldom spoke of the Power, yet it was a constant presence between us. It was the bond that held us together. The thought of it lying there dormant within the bowels of the Hurley cellar was like the concept of fire to a pyromaniac: frightening, to be sure, when one dwelt upon the destructive force that he alone could bring about, yet intoxicating in its lure.

There was a reassuring quality about it as well. It was a secret that Mary Jean and I shared with no one else. It was one of a few things in my life—perhaps the only thing—that I felt I had at least partial control over. Someday, when the time was right, Mary Jean and I would turn it loose again. That alone was a sustaining thought on those occasions when the shit from the Cooter farm got so deep that it threatened to suffocate me with its odoriferous weight.

Mary Jean was sitting next to me at the dinner table on the day that Uncle Hooter suggested that my father should go back to farming. We listened along with everyone else as

Hooter berated him. We watched in silence as my father's head sank further and further into his plate as if it were being slowly lowered by invisible strings extended from the dining-room ceiling. Every word landed like a hard shot to the solar plexus.

"So he's a salesman, is he? Off selling bull jism while a certain school official is doing a little selling of his own with the salesman's wife." Tell the fat fucker to shut up! I wanted to yell but I sat silent and felt the reassuring touch of Mary Jean's hand on my trembling leg.

"What do you say, Brother? Them hands of yours get too soft for farming, what with all the hand jobs you been giving them bulls for the last eight years?"

"You'll git warts on your fingers and go blind!" exclaimed Father Cooter, who, up until that point had been silently playing with the crackers floating in his soup. All attention momentarily focused on the old man, but he didn't seem to notice. He lowered his head and returned to administering the regatta of crackers that was occurring in his soup bowl.

"Harold is retired from farming. If you have run into problems as a result of mismanagement, you will simply have to find another way to solve them," said Nora Anne. The table fell silent. The one thing that you didn't do in the Cooter family was to criticize its commander-in-chief.

"You don't know jack squat about farming, lady."

"You are so right," replied my mother without hesitation. "In fact the only thing I do know about it is that I already know all I want to know about it."

"Boy, did you ever marry into the wrong family!"

"So it seems." Brushing a stray wisp of hair from her face, she turned to face Hooter. "However, that is water over the dam. It seems that I am stuck with you. Nonetheless, I will not, unlike everyone else around here apparently, be bound by your decisions."

"Just what is it you got against farmers, lady? Maybe you think you're too good for 'em. Maybe you prefer pansy-assed school psychologists?"

"I have nothing against farmers. I simply don't wish to be married to one."

"Enough of this shit!" bellowed my uncle. "You ain't no Cooter. Let the boy speak for hisself," he said, motioning toward the end of the table, where my father's head appeared to have sunk almost to the level of his plate.

"Slowly raising his eyes, Scooter glanced around the room as if it had just occurred to him that he might be the center of debate.

"Well?" asked my uncle.

"I, uh, have to think of my family, Hooter. Nora Anne don't want me to farm and, uh, I do make pretty good money with Century." He took a deep breath as if waiting for someone to interrupt him. When no one did he cleared his throat and quickly continued. "To tell the truth, my health ain't been all that good."

"Bullshit! There ain't a thing wrong with your health. I see you out runnin' every morning all bundled up like a fucking Eskimo! And as for your wife, you ain't got one, boy. Or hadn't you noticed? She treats you like a Goddamn houseboy and plays patty pussy pully pecker every afternoon while you're out bustin' your ass to bring home the bacon!"

My stomach felt as if it were strands of spaghetti being tightly wound around a spoon. I sensed Mary Jean's grip tighten upon my leg, even as the leg began to twitch uncontrollably beneath the table.

"You are a coarse, disgusting animal," said Nora Anne. "My husband has a family to feed, unlike you, and he isn't going to do it on what you would pay him for shoveling shit."

"He's a Cooter, Goddamnit! We're family!"

"My children will not be deprived because of your perverse

ideas of family loyalty!" She stood up, knocking a glass over in her haste. "Let's go, children."

For once my father beat her to it. Having quietly risen from his chair while Hooter and my mother were in midargument, he was already standing at the door leading into the kitchen. Shuffling his feet, he hesitated momentarily before turning back toward the table. "You're wrong, Hooter," he said. "I got my own family and Nora Anne loves me."

He turned and walked out the door without looking back.

20

Bundled up and on snowshoes, Mary Jean and I made our way up to Hurley's Pond after dinner. We changed into our skates at the edge of the pond and glided silently for several minutes over its smooth, icy surface. Holding on to each other's hands, we did spinning pirouettes. Mary Jean held me extended over the ice with her long arms so that my body was less than two feet from the shining surface. She began to spin me around. Slowly at first. Then faster and faster until the world was nothing more than a twirling collage of shapes and colors. Around and around until even the shapes lost their uniqueness as if they had all been thrown together into a great blender. The speed and motion were intoxicating. I was powerless, at the complete mercy of my aunt.

The motion became slower and then stopped. Mary Jean lowered me gently onto the ice, where I lay on my back gazing silently up at the world still spinning crazily above me. None of it made sense. I shut my eyes, trying to bring it to a stop, but even the darkness spun. When I opened them Mary Jean was smiling down at me as she skated in tiny circles around my body. I smiled back. Soon the spinning stopped.

We skated over to the shore where we had left our snow-shoes sticking fat side up in a snowbank. Pulling them out of the snow, we skated back to the middle of the pond and laid them lengthwise on top of the frozen water. With running starts we began jumping over them as if we were competing in the barrel-jumping event at the Winter Olympics. Two at first. Then three. And finally all four of them lying side by side on the ice like frozen fish pulled from the water below. With a great effort Mary Jean managed to clear all four. My best attempt came up six inches short, as the runners on my skates came dangerously close to severing the tightly wound facial bindings of the snowshoes.

Mary Jean drew a line on the ice at one end of the pond. We stood side by side at the opposite end, then sprinted in a mad dash for the line, with Mary Jean announcing the event while we raced. "M. J. Cooter edges out O. Cooter at the wire for the gold medal in one of the closest races we've seen here at the Winter Olympics, folks!"

Finally we raced in circles around the pond, imagining ourselves on a banked track with the Olympic stadium bleachers filled to capacity. With the endurance and leg strength I had developed as a result of my running, I was able to beat Mary Jean in the longer race for my only victory of the day. Exhausted and gasping for lungfuls of the frozen air, we skated slowly about the perimeter of the pond.

"It's time, Ollie," Mary Jean announced.

"Time for what?" Her words caught me off guard. I thought perhaps she was referring to the start of another event and I wasn't sure whether or not I could manage it.

"To visit the Hurley house. To check out the Power."

I hadn't been in the house since before Mrs. Wadkins's death. The thought of the Power was entirely different from actually confronting it—to be sitting there in the cellar several feet from where it rested in its coffin like some mad corpse ready to spring to life. Yet I felt its pull like a mysterious odor rising from a distant oven. Mary Jean was right. It was time.

It was cold and dark in the cellar. We made our way to the back room and Mary Jean lit a small fire with some old paper and wooden pieces of a broken chair. The fire was contained in a circle of bricks that Mary Jean had discovered somewhere in the confines of the cellar. The flame flickered just enough to warm our hands and to create dancing shadows on the musty walls.

Mary Jean had obviously returned to the basement without me. It was well stocked. She produced some blankets, which we wrapped around our shoulders, and two discarded sofa cushions, which we placed beneath us on the dirt floor. She set the wooden box between us. We joined our hands over it, shutting our eyes against the maniacal shadows darting above us.

I felt as if we were embarking on a great journey. Fear pumped through my veins. But this was not the devastating kind of fear that leaves one whimpering in a pool of urine and tears. It was a bone-crunching fear of the unknown—what one must feel when he witnesses death wrap its unyielding arms around a loved one, squeezing until the last drop of life dribbles out like a bead of sweat through an open pore. The kind of fear that makes one want to strike out in the only way he knows how.

"Are we joined in mental unity?" came Mary Jean's hushed whisper.

"Yes." There was something. It flowed like molten lava between the two of us as I tightened my grip on Mary Jean's hand.

"Do we have a focus?"

"Yes." I saw my father with his head lowered toward his plate and Mr. Groover like a preacher on his knees in front of my exposed mother and Mary Jean wounded and discarded like the remains of a meal, and, above them all, fat and satiated, Uncle Hooter.

"Is it the embodiment of evil?"

"Yes."

"Cast everything else out of your mind. We must reach the Power again and control it with our will."

There was no question. It was real. I was one with Mary Jean. Our mingled fear and hate were reaching out like a great tentacle for something in the cellar. We held onto each other, chanting and crying together. Soon we were shoving needles into the cloth caricature of my uncle and screaming at the frozen walls:

"Kill Hooter! Kill Hooter! Kill Hooter!"

Some time later, well after dark, we lifted ourselves up from the barren floor. We walked back through the main part of the cellar by the light of a candle that Mary Jean had found somewhere within her cache of provisions. She stopped in front of the closed coffin, holding the candle aloft.

"It's in there, Ollie, and we've reached it. I can feel its power. Soon we'll turn it loose to do our will."

As we hiked back to the house on our snowshoes, I was filled with a strength and a sense of purpose that had been missing for months.

21

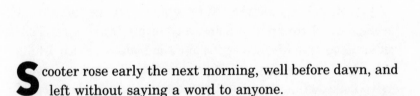

Scooter rose early the next morning, well before dawn, and left without saying a word to anyone.

Sitting in the middle of the kitchen table, leaning upright against a framed portrait of the four of us, was an envelope addressed to "My Loving Family." Inside, in my father's troubled scrawl, was his best attempt at an explanation. My mother read it aloud over breakfast to Craig and me.

> I reckon it's my turn for a leave of absence. I've been a disappointment as a farmer and a failure as a salesman. I have taken the truck and Buster in search of my true calling. Don't worry. I have a plan and need only good health and fortitude to see it through. I will send money. I love all of you.
>
> Your father,
> Scooter Cooter

Like Nora Anne before him, my father left no clue as to his whereabouts nor was it clear whether or not he was still em-

employed. One would assume from the reference in his letter to the forwarding of money that he was still with Century Semen, had found other gainful employment or, having been driven totally mad by his omnipresent gremlins, had embarked on some type of cross-country crime spree, the proceeds from which he planned to funnel back to the rest of us at the Cooter Farm. A simple phone call to Century would undoubtedly have gone a long way in ascertaining my father's present employment status, if not his whereabouts. My mother, however, would not permit it. "We must at least allow him the dignity of running away if he wishes," she said. "If he were to fail at even that I do believe it would kill him."

As for myself, I was inclined to believe that the "plan" that he mentioned referred in some way to my father's determination to operate his own artificial-insemination service. I fully expected that someday in the not-too-distant future he would arrive home behind the wheel of a cattle truck in which would be housed several prize bulls, their balls dangling like bags of golden nuggets between their well-muscled legs.

Back in my room, while preparing to change into my running shoes, I came across yet another note. It had been neatly folded prior to being stuck beneath the tongue on one of the shoes. Apparently its composer had tiptoed into my room in the middle of the night without awakening me. A cowardly gesture, no doubt, but a gesture just the same. I quickly unfolded it.

Ollie,

Don't quit on your running. It will keep you sane and healthy and will help to keep the gremlins away. I have left the COOTERS sweatshirt for you and taken THE for myself. I'll be running every morning at five-thirty. If you can do the same we won't have to miss our workouts while I'm away. Take care of your mother.

Love,
Your Father

Although I loved my father immensely, his departure did not come as a great shock, nor did it pain me as deeply as it once would have. I was somehow more prepared for his sudden absence than I had been for my mother's abrupt flight. The first scoops of rejection had already been dug from my soul; any subsequent shovelfuls would not be as painful. My defenses were more in order. Practice breeds, if not perfection, at least familiarity.

The trailer was beginning to seem like a revolving door. I had become used to one or the other of my parents disappearing without notice, leaving Craig and me behind to bounce back and forth like pinballs from one side of the trailer to the other.

The one thing that my family had demonstrated an ability to perform with aplomb was the exit scene. It seemed as if one of us was always rising suddenly from an unfinished meal, striding quickly away from a heated conversation, or scurrying off down the Hollow Road in a swirling cloud of dust and putrid exhaust. With so much practice, we were quickly honing the disappearing act into an art form. Perhaps my father would find his new calling to be something in the entertainment field—the next Houdini for example.

The adjustment process following this latest departure was minimal. My mother simply threw open both partition doorways and tied them securely in place, thus creating once more an undivided home. The ten-o'clock curfew was reinstated on both sides of the trailer, and there was immediately less confusion as to who belonged where.

"Do you s'pose they'll ever be like they used to be?" I asked Craig. "I mean stayin' together in the same room and all?"

"Doubtful. Father can't sit still long enough and Mother won't tolerate a part-time husband."

"How 'bout Ed Groover?" I asked. "He's part time."

"Hmmph," grunted my brother, peering at me over the tops of his wire rims. "Ed Groover's simply a diversion. A whimsical fancy of no more stature than one of Blanche's gentleman friends."

I inwardly castigated myself for having again made the mistake of seeking out Craig's opinion. As was so often the case, I found myself to be more confused after having heard his answer than I was before I had posed the question. I toyed with the idea of attempting to talk him into unraveling his response, but he had already dismissed me with a curt nod of his head to resume his reading. His message was clear at any rate. I sensed all too well what was meant, even if I couldn't equate it with his unique phraseology.

Mr. Groover was still stopping by about two or three times a week, usually in the late afternoon after school let out. He and my mother spent the majority of their time together cooped up in the living room like a couple of nesting pigeons. Ever since the episode involving Nora Anne's lost earring, the partition door remained shut and locked during his visits. Such precautions, as far as I was concerned, were completely unnecessary, as I had made it a point at such times to avoid the room as if it were infested with the plague.

The two of them would remain in there for hours at a time. Strange sounds often emanated from beyond the great wooden door—twittering noises much like the frenzied chatter of songbirds squabbling over scattered sunflower seeds and occasional bursts of hysterical laughter, as if my mother had sat on a whoopee cushion. When at long last the two of them would emerge from the room, they would be the picture of composure, faces set in stone, as if they had just concluded a

lengthy business conference. There appeared not a wrinkle to
be found. My mother's hair would be stacked neatly within
its swollen mounds, and Mr. Groover's mustache, wiggling just
perceptibly, bristled and shimmered above his lip like a strip
of freshly watered lawn.

Occasionally my mother would invite Mr. Groover to stay
for supper. Although his appetite was hearty, he approached
each meal as if he were more concerned not to get particles
of food lodged within his mustache than with savoring Nora
Anne's cooking. He tried on occasion to engage Craig and me
in conversation.

"How would you boys like to move into Anton?" he asked
one night.

"I wouldn't," I replied, while Craig simply let out his breath
disgustedly and resumed eating.

"You would have lots of other children to play with," he
said, "and lots of different things to do."

"I got plenty to do on the farm," I said.

"Well, then, how would you like it if I were to spend more
time out here?"

"What do you mean . . . more time?" I felt that he spent
more than enough time already. I didn't care at all for the
direction his questions were taking.

"You know . . . stay overnight." He smiled as if he were
auditioning for a toothpaste commercial. "Be like a daddy to
you boys."

"Pleeeease!" said Craig. "Don't make me vomit!"

"I have a daddy!" I exclaimed.

"Well, it was just an idea. I thought . . ."

"Who in God's name said anything about you staying overnight, Ed?" asked my mother. "Not in my house you won't!
You know my policy on overnight guests. I have all the full-
time men I can handle now. I certainly don't need another
one!"

After that Mr. Groover seldom spoke to Craig or me, and

the subject of his staying overnight was never mentioned again. Although I still resented his presence in the trailer, particularly in my father's absence, in time I begrudgingly learned to accept his visits as one learns to accept the presence of a family dog that has suddenly developed a chronic case of flatulence. Indeed, my brother and I treated Mr. Groover's appearances with the same deference that one generally accords to such an unfortunate creature as the overly gaseous pet. Realizing that we were stuck with him for at least the moment, we learned to walk around him, ignoring his very presence as if he were a part of the décor.

As for Craig, he wasn't getting any less unusual. We were still on opposite ends of life's spectrum, thrown together through common adversity and the coincidental occurrence of similar parentage. The pains he must have felt as a result of my parents' sporadic departures and misguided attempts at parenthood remained for the most part well concealed beneath his bookish appearance. He had few friends and took little interest in schoolwork, although still managing to sail by with As and a sprinkling of Bs. This was in sharp contrast to the steady diet of Cs and Ds that seemed to appear on my report card each semester with the reliability of spring buds.

My brother's passion lay in his books and in the steady stream of correspondence that left the trailer almost daily, bound for destinations throughout North America. He had not at that time expanded his editorial endeavors to encompass publications outside the continental United States, although this may have been purely a decision of economics. The cost of mailing so many submissions, even locally, surely must have been prohibitive, particularly on a budget as severely strained as that of my parents. The subject had led to more than one argument between them. Nora Anne was of the view that Craig's letter writing was a necessary part of his maturing process and labeled the money that she provided for the required postage as an educational expense. My father, on the other hand, pointed out that the IRS did not see it as such and neither did he. It was, he said, needlessly squeezing an already close-to-dry sponge.

Craig's latest contribution to the *Anton Courier* was entitled "The Rural Mentality." It was unsigned and was a general indictment of the older members of the third- and fourth-generation farm families who were sprinkled throughout the county like poppy seeds. Specifically, the letter referred to those who "are unable to see beyond their rural noses." That Craig himself was a descendant of just such a family was conveniently not mentioned but clearly seemed to be the fodder that fed the flame.

. . . And if one aspires for something more? To venture outside of this clannish environment? Perish the thought! The local cow brains will tell him that he is abandoning his family and all that is sacred in life. If one is born a backward slob he must forever remain one is their constant refrain. To that attitude this reader can only say cow plop. . . . There are no ties more tightly bound than ancestral ones. This reader is of the opinion that the sooner the roots are severed the healthier will be the offspring.

My brother cared for me as much as he cared for anyone, I suppose. It wouldn't be inaccurate to say that he was not an overly warm person. There were times, however, when he at least tolerated my presence and would regale me with his views on everything from Scooter's hypochondria to the state of the world economy. At such moments, although I seldom understood what he was talking about, I would nod my head in dumb encouragement for the sheer pleasure of hearing him go on.

When wound up there was no one else quite like Craig. His voice would rise and whine like an ascending aircraft, spittle would accumulate at the corners of his puckish mouth, and the veins in his temples would commence to throb like flashing ambulance bubbles. And the words. The words would tumble and flow like water over rocks, and even though they often made little sense they sounded pretty, or at least different. Different, that is, from the way anyone else on the farm, with the possible exception of Nora Anne, sounded when they spoke.

My Aunt Mary Jean claimed that Craig had gone directly from diapers to adulthood. "He skipped childhood. I'll bet he had fuzz on his pecker at the age of five."

That, at least, I knew not to be true. My brother had a pale, doughy body that was completely devoid of hair anyplace other than his head. He gave the appearance of being underdone, as if he were a loaf of bread that had not been allowed to remain in the oven long enough. "Might as well throw that one back," Uncle Hooter is reported to have said when first laying eyes upon the firstborn child of his younger brother. "He ain't never gonna make a farmer."

Craig was self-conscious about his appearance. He wore long pants even on the hottest days of summer. On those rare occasions when he went for a swim he dressed in shorts that came almost to his knees and a T-shirt that he refused to remove even upon entering the water. His skin, being pale, was sensitive to the sunlight and prone to rashes. As a result, he seemed to be constantly scratching one part of his body or another.

One thing that my brother and I did have in common was our dislike for Uncle Hooter, although undoubtedly for different reasons. Uncle Hooter seldom spoke directly to Craig. Even when they were in the same room together, my uncle referred to Craig as if he weren't present or, even worse, talked about him as if he were a deaf mute. In conversations, he would indicate Craig's presence with a nod, while referring to him in the third person as the "doughboy" or that "bug-eyed twerp," in reference to the bottle-thick glasses that my brother had been required to wear since the age of six on account of his nearsightedness. For reasons of his own—probably solely as a result of Craig's underdone appearance and unique manner of speech—Hooter assumed that Craig was a homosexual. "First fairy the Cooter family ever had. He even tiptoes through the barn for Christ sakes."

All of those things certainly irked Craig, but what upset him more than anything else was the way Uncle Hooter treated my mother. Craig was one of those individuals who seem capable of loving but one person. For my brother, that person was Nora Anne. She was to him a torchbearer, a rose amongst the thorns. He could not abide the slightest criticism of her. It was not, I believe, a Freudian hangup. Craig simply viewed my mother as a cultured lady, dignified and out of place like himself amid the squalor of the Cooter farm.

He could tolerate Ed Groover, although he certainly didn't warm up to him. Groover at least was a gentleman as far as my mother was concerned. He treated her with the respect that Craig felt she so richly deserved. Hooter on the other hand made no secret of his feelings in regard to my mother. He disliked her and felt that she put on airs. She wasn't what he felt a farmer's wife should be. He openly belittled her and often made her the laughingstock at family gatherings. On one occasion Craig became so upset at some remark that Uncle Hooter had made to my mother that his little body commenced to quiver uncontrollably. His glasses steamed over. Trembling with rage he shook his fist in Hooter's face. "You barbaric redneck! If you talk like that to my mother again I'll kill you!"

"Hoo! Hoo! Hoo!" laughed Hooter, barely acknowledging my brother's threat. "The twerp can chirp can he?"

It was impossible to ascertain what was on Craig's mind. He seemed always to have a secret, like a hearts player who always holds back a trump card. Since the night of the lost-earring incident he had not again made reference to "my friend on the hill." At times, however, I would find him staring at me over the top of one of his periodicals as if I were a rare type of fauna that he had unaccountably stumbled upon. If he caught me returning his gaze, a rare smile would flicker across his face. The sides of his mouth would turn slowly up in the shape of a half-moon. After a few moments his mouth would rearrange itself and his eyes would drop gradually back to the hidden pages of his book. I feared that he knew much more than he was letting on and I wondered for what purpose he was saving whatever secret it was that he possessed.

22

It had only been in the preceding five years that the Cooter farm had begun to utilize milking machines. Prior to that time all of the milking had been done by hand, and chores would often take three or four hours to complete. The machines were a great timesaver. Once hooked up they operated themselves, thus freeing up a pair of hands to help in other areas. They were, however, both bulky and expensive. It took an experienced, adult hand to ensure not only that the machine was properly attached to the cow, but also to disengage and empty it once it was full.

With the firing of Earl Bailey in early March, my uncles were the only two experienced milkers remaining in the barn. There were three machines and only two people available to operate them. Neither Mary Jean nor I had developed enough muscle or expertise to operate the machines effectively. Besides, we had our own duties to perform in the barn. There just wasn't enough manpower left to handle sixty milk cows.

Much to everyone's dismay, Mother Cooter was forced out of retirement. She volunteered to return to the barn just until the immediate crisis was over and we could afford to hire Earl back.

Of course it was beginning to look as though the crisis might be a bit longer in duration than had at first been expected. This was at a time when things were beginning to get rough for small farmers everywhere. The creameries were charging the farmer more and more for the expense of transporting his milk to their facilities. The government refused to provide any price breaks. The cost of machinery and interest rates had gone up. The big dairy coops with creameries at their backdoors and having the advantage of tax breaks not available to the individual farmer were slowly making all but the most well-rooted of the family farms a relic of the past.

None of that, I'm sure, had registered with my grandmother as a threat to our way of life. Not because she was an unintelligent woman, but simply because she was a farmer, and farmers, everyone knew, periodically had rough times. We were, then, in the midst of rough times. She had seen them before and she, as well as the farm, had always survived them. We would survive them this time, she assured us, so long as we all stuck together and worked hard.

My grandmother was a proud, no-nonsense woman who put loyalty and the welfare of her family above all else. She was the daughter of a third-generation Devon County farmer. She and my grandfather had met at the Devon County Fair, the two of them being pitted against one another as contestants in the horseshoe-throwing contest. Father Cooter took the championship with a leaner on his last toss, and promptly asked his opponent to join him for a stroll through the midway. They were married six months later, the day after my grandmother's seventeenth birthday.

Mother Cooter's father operated one of the most prosperous farms in Devon County at the time. It was all flatland, and the hay and corn grew like weeds with the help of the natural irrigation provided by the river. He had offered to bring my grandfather in as a partner, but Father Cooter—knowing that his new wife's younger brother would someday undoubtedly take over his father's farm—declined the offer and elected instead to go in with his own father up Shenker Hollow. "That," said my grandmother, "is how I ended up on this pile of rocks."

Pile of rocks or not, she had given herself to her new life with the fervor of the pioneer spirit. She had worked seven days a week in the barn until the age of fifty-seven—"she can handle cow teats better than any two men," my grandfather reportedly used to brag. In addition to her other duties she managed to bear and raise four children. If it was a difficult life it was the only life she knew, and I never once heard her complain about her draw of the cards. When it appeared that we had no choice but to let Earl go, she shrugged her strong but sagging shoulders and said: "I might just as well get back to doin' somethin' useful. All of this free time is turning me soft."

But even the return of my grandmother couldn't turn things around. The snow stayed on the ground until well into April. There was no grass for the cattle to graze on, so we had to continue to buy hay and feed until the ground thawed. Hooter was forced to sell five heifers in order to pay the feed bill. They were two-year-olds that he had planned on adding to the herd of milkers once they had freshened the following fall. "We're going backwards Goddamnit. How's a man suppose' to get ahead when he's got to sell his herd off to pay for feed?"

"We've had bad winters before," said Mother Cooter, "and we've always seen them through."

But Hooter trusted neither fate nor nature. He misperceived the problem. To his mind, where there was a shortcoming there had to be a solution. To believe otherwise, to simply leave things in the hands of Mother Nature, was to give up. He was convinced that there was but one reason for the recent downturn of events.

"It's the Goddamn attitude 'round here. That's why we're

losin' money hand over fist. Everybody should be in the barn helpin' out. That's how it was when I was growin' up. A farm ain't no place for slackers, Guddamnit!"

He was enraged by the fact that his mother had to return to the role of a milker. He considered it a personal slap in the face. It was disgraceful that Scooter could sit by and let it happen. He officially disowned my father and swore that if he ever showed up at the farm again Hooter would run him off with a load of buckshot.

He went so far as to suggest that Craig should begin taking an active role in the operation of the farm. "Maybe we can still make a man out of the twerp," he said. "He don't do nothin' now but sit around all day chokin' the chicken and writing his crazy damn letters to the newspapers. I s'pose his old lady thinks he's too lily white to get smeared with a little cowshit!"

"And you," he said, pointing at Mary Jean, "why don't you quit school and help out full time? You're flunking everything anyhow."

"I can't quit until I'm sixteen. It's the law."

"The law! What's the law know 'bout farming? I'm the God-damned law round here and what I say goes!"

He was grasping at straws. No one, it seemed, was immune to his wrath. He wanted Looter to give up his weekly salary— "You get room and board. That's more than plenty for all the help you are." When Looter threatened to quit entirely and take a job at the Anton Creamery, Hooter flew into a rage. He threw Uncle Looter onto the barn floor and pummeled him with his fists, bloodying Looter's nose and knocking out two of his teeth. Beaten and bloodied, my youngest uncle got slowly to his feet, carefully placing the extracted teeth in his shirt pocket. Five minutes later, he was back with a shotgun in his hands. He aimed both barrels at Hooter and told him that if he ever laid a hand on him or anybody else in the family again, Looter would blow his head off.

"Don't nobody panic!" bellowed Hooter to the rest of us. "Jis' give the sum bitch your Fritos!"

He jumped up from his stool, holding a fresh pail of milk in his hand, and pushed by Looter on his way to the bulk tank as if he weren't even there.

"This is no fucking-A joke!" raged Looter. His voice was starting to crack, though, and the gun sagged pathetically in his hands. As he reeled crazily about the barn, his eyes looked like they might well up with tears. "You ain't the only one what—what . . ."

A second later he turned and made his way shakily out the barn door, mumbling to no one in particular, "Somebody oughta deep-six the mother fucker."

Mary Jean and I had been working on doing just that up at the Hurley house. Ever since that cold day in February when we had returned to the original site of our baptism into the world of the unknown, my aunt and I had been meeting on a regular basis in the old abandoned cellar.

Sometimes we just talked. Bundled up against the cold and snuggled together for warmth, we talked about places we would like to go. Mary Jean liked Australia because it was so far away. I, on the other hand, was partial to Africa on account of its miles of untamed jungle and the myriad of strange creatures that lived within it. I was a great fan of the television program *Wild Kingdom* and hoped someday to replace Jim as Marlin Perkins's chief assistant. Perhaps one day, I thought, Jim would get wrapped up by a boa constrictor and Marlin wouldn't arrive in time to save him. Then my big chance would arrive.

We talked about school. Mary Jean maintained that it was a waste of time. What you need to learn, she said, they don't teach you. "It don't matter how much you know if you ain't got smarts," she told me. I couldn't see how school could possibly aid me in the pursuit of white rhinos through the damp heat of the African jungle.

Mary Jean told me about guys. They were jerks, she said. They acted tough but really weren't. She knew how to make them squirm and beg like a hungry dog for scraps. Sometimes, she told me, she did things for them just to see them get all flustered and become like pools of melted butter at her touch. It was as if she owned them for a few moments; but when she finally gave them what they wanted they would leave her and pretend that the whole thing had never happened. She didn't tell me just what it was that she did to make them act so strangely. "Don't worry," she said. "You're not like them. You're just a kid."

But sometimes I didn't feel like a kid around her. Those strange sensations that I had first noticed that steamy evening out behind Martha Wadkins's house had begun to arrive more often of late. Appearing to follow no consistent pattern, they would hit me without warning. My balls—no bigger than ripe acorns at that age—swelled and felt like large grapefruits in my pants. Sensations akin to growling hunger arose from my stomach and spread to the outermost portions of my fingers and toes, like tiny messages being conveyed by coded pinpricks. I was too embarrassed to tell Mary Jean about these feelings, but at times I felt certain that she knew.

At other times we chanted at the walls and reached out for the caged-up soul of the Power. Pent-up hatred spewed forth like a viscous liquid and spread throughout the cellar. Mary Jean and I were one, a combined power of our own that had a chance in a sometimes cruel and disappointing world. The cellar was our place; and the Power was our secret.

"When will we turn it loose again?" I asked Mary Jean.

"When we're sure that it's time," she answered.

"How will we know that?"

"We'll know."

23

The death of a farm does not arrive with merciful quickness. The path to finality is, instead, a tortuous process of decay, involving much pain and suffering. Sandwiched between all of this heartache and despair are brief interludes of optimistic respite, in which, for the moment at least, it seems likely that alternatives are at hand; that perhaps there is a back door out of death's chamber.

Winter eventually became spring throughout Devon County, and the Cooter Farm, although not prospering, was still in business. We had survived another winter, one which, like the long-forgotten relative who suddenly appears without warning, had shown indications of staying forever. With the melting of the snow and the sudden appearance of buds and early vegetation on the trees came a fresh hope, a second wind, akin to what the marathon runner must feel halfway through a race.

It was sixty-five degrees and sunny on a day in early May when Mother Cooter decided that it was time for a Shenker Hollow barbecue. "We made it through the winter in one piece," she said. "That's reason enough to celebrate."

The Cooter Farm

The event was scheduled for the following weekend. Notice was circulated throughout the hollow. Neighbors from up and down the road were invited to attend and to bring a dish to pass.

Uncle Hooter dug a large pit in the backyard and filled it with seasoned wood and charcoal. On the evening before the planned celebration he lit the fire. By the time the next day arrived the pit was a glowing bed of embers. Having earlier butchered a young steer, he then skewered it on a large spike and left it to cook all morning over the hot coals. The smoke from the simmering meat lingered tantalizingly in the morning air. After chores Mary Jean and I sat around the pit, our hunger slowly building as we listened to the steer pop and sizzle in the fire.

Most of the guests arrived early, anxious for any excuse to celebrate after such a long winter. Every farm family in the hollow was in attendance. Most folks were dressed in their best casuals—pressed and sparkling clean—as if to illustrate that the winter had not defeated them. Family pickup trucks had been washed and waxed for the occasion.

My father was the only member of the immediate family not in attendance. He had been sending money and letters home on a regular basis, but had still given no indication of when he would return to the farm. Questions as to his whereabouts were dissuaded by my mother's glacial silence.

Looter brought a girlfriend. It was the first that any of us learned he had one. Her name was Lila and she lived in the commune up Dead Creek Hollow. She was delicate and pretty, with a face as white as porcelain china. She wore a loose-fitting cotton dress and a plaid bandana for the occasion. Her blond hair stuck out from the bottom of the bandana and was decorated throughout with long-stemmed daisies. She brought a guitar, and several of the children from the hollow sat around her singing songs while she played. Looter was on his best behavior, scrubbed and dressed in summer leisures. I hardly recognized him and heard him use his favorite word on but one occasion. Standing proudly by while Lila strummed her guitar, he suddenly blurted out, "Isn't she the fucking best?" to no one in particular.

Mary Jean was beautiful, dressed in a long, sleeveless dress, her finely muscled shoulders bare and already bronzed by the spring sun. Her smooth hair was tied in a ponytail that bounced off her naked back like the tail on a wild mare. She had just turned fourteen, and the boys from the hollow flocked around her like disciples to the Messiah, but she brushed them all off to eat dinner with me.

After dinner my uncles organized a softball game. The rear pasture was used as a diamond. Discarded shirts became bases. The plowed portion of the field was foul ground. Each team was composed equally of men and women.

Even Craig played. He came up to bat adorned in his full-length Bermudas and a long-sleeved sweatshirt and promptly slapped a single to right field. He tore off down the base path, his glasses bobbing crazily up and down on the end of his nose, his pudgy legs squeaking together like hinges in need of oil. Everyone cheered when he arrived safely at the first base bag. Turning toward where I stood in the first-base coach's box, he broke into a smile that beamed from ear to ear across his face. "It's actually quite an elementary game," he said, but was unable to conceal the excitement in his voice.

After the game Mary Jean and I struck up a conversation with Lila. She was from Long Island and had left home when she was fifteen. "I couldn't dig the scene no more," she explained. "My parents had their own establishment thing and were always trying to impose it on me. At least out here I can breathe."

"Don't you miss your folks?" I asked.

"Sometimes, I suppose, but we were outta tune, man. I could never go back to that scene."

"How come?"

"My family is here. At the commune I mean. We're all brothers and sisters. We all take care of each other."

"I'd like to go to New York City," said Mary Jean.

"It's big and dirty and really lonely," said Lila.

"It couldn't be no lonelier than it is here," answered my aunt.

"Hey there, Blondie! Is it true you people out there don't wear no clothes?" Uncle Hooter had suddenly appeared from nowhere to drop in on our conversation. He had a mug of beer in his hand. From his staggering appearance, it was obviously not his first.

"We believe in free expression, Mr. Cooter," answered Lila. "Nobody has to wear clothes but then nobody has to go without if it isn't their scene."

"How 'bout you?" He smiled lewdly and sloshed his beer. "What's your scene?"

"What do you mean?"

"Well, I was just wonderin' if you was takin' your clothes off for my little brother."

"What's it matter, Hooter?" asked Mary Jean, flicking nervously at her ponytail.

" 'Cause if she'll take 'em off for a piss ant like Looter I figure maybe she'll take 'em off for just about anybody. Hoo! Hoo! Hoo!" His big barrel chest, naked and hairy, heaved from the effort of his laughter.

"Your brother has a lot of qualities you probably don't know a thing about, Mr. Cooter."

"Oh, is that right?" He raised the beer mug to his lips and took a long draw. "Well, I know he can't farm for shit, he's lazier than a whupped dog, and he's a Goddamn thief!" Glancing at his almost empty mug, he threw aside the remaining contents with a flip of his wrist. "Did I leave anything out there, Blondie?"

"Why all the hostility, Mr. Cooter?" She seemed unperturbed, as if she had had similar conversations in the past. "I don't think you're being fair to Bradford."

"Hoo! Hoo! Hoo! Bradford, is it? Well, you're right. I did forget about one of his better qualities," he said, taking a step closer to Lila. "That boy can spot a piece of ass even if it is dressed up like a hippy."

"Bradford is a very warm person."

"Well, if it's warmth you're after then you're chasin' the wrong brother." He reached his arm out and slung it heavily about Lila's shoulders, pulling her to him as if she were a bundle of straw.

"Let her go, Hooter!" said Mary Jean.

My uncle's head snapped quickly around. His nostrils flared. He looked directly into Mary Jean's eyes. A smile slowly appeared upon his face.

"Sure 'nough, baby sister, I'll let her go." The smile grew. "Now you ain't gettin' jealous, are ya? You know there ain't nobody prettier than you in my eyes."

Releasing Lila, he took a step closer to my aunt. Reaching out with his right hand he placed it firmly upon Mary Jean's bottom. Mary Jean didn't move as Hooter began slowly massaging her tightly muscled mounds through the cotton fabric of her dress. His hand tightened momentarily at the top of her legs. The fabric bunched noticeably into a ball between his fingers.

"You know you're my favorite blossom," he whispered as he leaned over and kissed her quickly on the cheek. He let out a breathy chuckle and removed his hand. A second later, he sauntered off in the direction of the beer keg.

"I guess your brother's drunk, huh?" said Lila.

But Mary Jean had already turned and walked hurriedly

away without saying a word. Sometime later I saw her talking to Billy Bates and another boy who lived at the bottom of the hollow. They were all laughing about something and then the three of them disappeared behind the barn.

I didn't see my aunt again until it was almost dark and most of the guests had already gone home. Her dress was stained and wrinkled. Her hair was out of its ponytail and lounged in tangled disarray about her face and neck. She pushed by me on her way to the big house.

"Where you been, Mary Jean?"

"What's it matter?"

"I was just wonderin'."

"Well, quit your wonderin' and go on home." She turned and quickly walked into the house. "The party's over," she said, without glancing back.

I walked back out to the yard and found that everyone with the exception of Uncle Hooter and four or five other farmers from the hollow had returned to their own homes. Hooter and the others were sitting around the smoldering remains of the barbecue pit. They were drinking what was left of the beer, smoking cigars, and talking in hushed, conspiratorial tones.

The day that had begun with so much promise had suddenly turned black. The guests were gone, Mary Jean wouldn't talk to me, and my father was God knows where. I sat down by myself on the side of the hill, several yards above the huddled farmers and out of sight behind a large weeping willow tree. I listened to the garbled voices as they blended together, reaching me like the drone from a nest of bees. The words were indecipherable. On occasion my uncle's all-too-familiar laugh would rise into the night like a distant owl's hoot before being swept away by the early summer breeze. The orange glow from the dying fire danced across the farmers' faces and gave them an eerie pallor. My eyelids grew heavy. Sleep seemed like a pleasant alternative.

When I awoke the moon was directly above me in an otherwise empty sky. The lights were out in the Cooter house. There were only two men left by the barbecue pit, my uncle and Andy Yoemanns, who had the last farm up the right fork of the hollow. The two men were standing up, facing the pit and pissing on what was left of the fire. The sound of rising steam was clearly audible in the still night. It was this sound, I realized, that had woken me.

When the two men were through urinating they zipped up their flies and started walking in opposite directions, both of them weaving and making unsteady progress toward their respective destinations. Mr. Yoemanns took off down the hill toward where his pickup truck was parked. In the other direction, Uncle Hooter began weaving erratically toward the big house and the willow tree behind which I lay hidden.

I made an effort to push myself deeper into the heavy grass and hoped that Hooter wouldn't have to stop and relieve himself again before he reached the house. Feeling wet and clammy from the evening dew that had settled over my body as I slept, I tried not to exhale. He was so close I could hear his labored breathing and smell the mixture of smoke and alcohol that clung to him like cheap cologne. Stopping directly in front of the willow tree, he turned slowly back toward the barbecue pit. Putting his hands to his mouth, he called down the hill.

"Hey, Andy! Fuck the old lady once for me, will ya?"

Mr. Yoemanns yelled something back up the hill that I couldn't make out, but I heard clearly my uncle's delayed response. "Oh, I reckon I can take care of that all right," he mumbled more to himself than to anyone else. "Yes sirree, that ain't going to be no problem at all."

Mr. Yeomanns obviously hadn't waited for Hooter's answer. His truck started up and moved slowly off down the hill, its headlights weaving back and forth like searchlights across the meadow. Uncle Hooter turned and walked the rest of the way to the house. The kitchen door squeaked open and then quietly shut again, Hooter apparently having the presence of mind to prevent it from slamming on its loose hinges.

The air escaped from my lungs in a great gasp. I lay on my back, breathing deeply and staring up at the sky. I searched for inspiration and found none. How I despised being a child, a person without answers. A person without power. How was it that my uncle could be the driving force behind the entire Cooter family and yet the focus of so much hate? Mother Cooter said he was our strength; that without him we would be nothing more than a directionless family of misfits sprouting off like ragweed in every direction. Mary Jean said he was evil, the cause of the pain and loneliness that seemed to have become as much a part of our young world as the quantities of cowshit that we shoveled from the barn each evening.

Did I really want him dead? I'd seen dead animals before. Lots of them. When I was six years old, one of my favorite milk cows got sick, some kind of intestinal disease, according to my uncle. For days it lay in a stall emitting low moans of agony and spitting up frothy blood. The veterinarian was called. He said that it would have to be put to sleep, that it had a sickness that could spread to the other cows. I cried and begged my grandmother to find some way to save the animal. She told me that it couldn't be saved, that everything dies eventually, and that by being put to death now my cow could save a lot of others from going through the same misery it was going through. Uncle Hooter made me watch as the veterinarian took a long needle from his bag and gave the cow a lethal shot. "It's for the good of the herd, Ollie," he told me. "Death is just a part of life for a farmer." The cow mooed softly and then stopped breathing, its big eyes staring glassily up at me. It looked peaceful. I was thankful that the rest of the herd would not have to suffer as it had.

I rolled onto my stomach in the wet grass and turned my

attention back to the Cooter house. As I did, the kitchen light blinked off, leaving the entire building in darkness. I sighed and started to get to my feet, mentally preparing myself for the lecture that would surely be forthcoming from Nora Anne upon my arrival back at the trailer.

Another light suddenly blinked on in the house: upstairs, the second window on the right. Mary Jean's room. An unseen hand grabbed hold of my testicles. The truth unfolded itself like the pages of a book.

A figure, short and stocky, filled the window. In the light I could tell that the figure was naked. I could see its swollen genitals hanging down like Christmas ornaments between its legs. The figure quickly pulled down the window shade and a moment later the light blinked off. The hand on my genitals squeezed viciously, sending a searing pain through my bowels and making me feel as if I would throw up.

24

Sheriff Robert "Bobo" Benson was one of those rare exceptions that prove the rule in the area of rural law enforcement. Being neither a stumbling ex-jock who flunked the written portion of the State Police entrance exam, nor a closet Nazi whose sustaining pleasures in life appear to be derived from squealing the tires on the black-and-white and/or crushing the heads of unfortunate villains and innocent bystanders alike, he was an anomaly amongst his peers. It was agreed by almost everyone, other than the occasional villain holding a grudge, that the people of Devon County were lucky to have him.

Bobo was slow competent. He liked to size a situation up from every conceivable angle before finally commencing to chew on it as if it were an overdone roast; and he would keep right on chewing until he got the thing gnawed down to a consistency he could handle. Law work, as he saw it, was a matter of persistence. If one kept shoving different-size pieces into a puzzle, sooner or later one was bound to find a piece that fit.

Sheriff Benson was in the habit of stopping by the farm on occasion to make certain that Looter was staying out of trouble or just to get the latest news from the hollow. Being a lawman, he liked to stay informed. Keeping his hand on the pulse of the county, he called it. In order to do so he made regular stops, much like a local politician, at various farms thoughout the county. He would customarily drop in after evening chores so that he could sit awhile. My grandmother would offer him a cup of coffee and a piece of whatever was to be eaten for dessert. I had never seen him arrive in anything other than his Ford pickup truck.

I watched from the front porch of the trailer one day that spring as Bobo approached the Cooter house in one of only two police cars that the county owned. The car moved unhurriedly, much like the man himself, up the winding hill toward the farm. Swirling clouds of dust rose from the car's wheels like fleeing spirits. Its red bubble, although unlit, rode in swollen splendor atop the car's roof, the first indication that this was not just the occasional neighborly visit.

The day was overcast—the clouds appearing as if they might, at any moment, elect to lighten their load. It was less than a week after the hollow barbecue and already the festive mood created by that occasion was a thing of the past. Having just returned from an early-evening run, I was cooling down on the porch with a few light calisthenics. Snatches of *Mystery Theatre*, as narrated by E. G. Marshall, floated through the open window in the kitchen where my mother was preparing dinner.

The Sheriff was a tall, lean man with charcoal-gray hair combed straight back from the temples—"ramrod straight and tough as nails like a lawman ought to be," Mother Cooter was fond of saying. He was a member of the First Presbyterian Church, same as the Cooters, and was the last one into the church every Sunday morning. He cut quite a figure as he strolled down the aisle in his Sunday suit, Stetson hat in hand and a look of tempered steel lining his face.

Acknowledging all of the ladies, including my grandmother,

with a nod of his head and a courteous "Morning, ma'am" or "Pleased to see you, Mrs. Cooter," he would head directly for the left front pew, where he always sat. No matter how full the church was, his spot was always empty. It was as if he had a deal with the rest of the congregation or perhaps, as my grandmother often suggested, it went even higher than that. The Reverend Claiborne would never commence the service until the Sheriff was seated in his pew. "If'n he's ever sick we'll be there till Doomsday, for Christ sake," complained Uncle Hooter.

The police car came to a stop in front of the big house. The Sheriff stepped out of the cruiser, hitched up his belt, and shoved the long-barrelled pistol that he always wore into its holster. Glancing casually toward the trailer, he pointed his finger and shouted out, "Hey, Ollie." I waved and watched as he carefully placed the Stetson on his head before slowly walking toward the house. When he knocked on the front door, the sound pierced the morning air like successive gunshots.

Mother Cooter answered the door. The Sheriff, in a characteristic gesture, bowed his head and tipped his hat to my grandmother. I imagined him saying, "Evening, ma'am." The door opened and shut behind him. E. G. Marshall's voice drifted through the open window at my back. The smell of baking lasagne filled my nostrils.

I leaned against the porch railing, sweating from my workout, and gazed in the direction of the big house. The first drops of rain started to fall. They landed in the dust of the driveway, each one a miniature explosion.

Craig appeared without warning in the kitchen doorway. He pulled up a chair next to me on the porch and sat down without a word. He opened the book he had brought with him, lowering his eyes to the print. From the kitchen my mother yelled out, "Dinner in ten minutes."

The front door of the big house opened again. The Sheriff

came out, preceded by Uncle Hooter. Short and tightly packed, my uncle appeared in sharp contrast to Sheriff Benson as the two of them walked down the front steps. With his low center of gravity, and being propelled by such short legs, Uncle Hooter always appeared to be in a great hurry as he walked.

He began moving across the lawn in the quick, choppy strides of a bull terrier as the Sheriff, in his unhurried gait, fell in a step behind. Halfway across the lawn, Hooter glanced toward the trailer. In a voice loud enough for Craig and me to hear plainly, he yelled back over his shoulder, "This hadn't better take long, Bobo. I gotta be back in time to finish up the chores. Sure as hell ain't nobody 'round here gonna pick up the slack."

At the car, the Sheriff took a pair of handcuffs off his belt. Placing Hooter's hands behind his back, he snapped the cuffs around my uncle's wrists. Facing the porch, with his hands momentarily out of sight, it appeared as if my uncle's arms had been cut off at the elbows.

Why would Sheriff Benson put handcuffs on Uncle Hooter? I wondered. They appeared to be engaged in a child's game, something akin to Pin the Tail on the Donkey. I half expected the Sheriff to place a blindfold on Hooter before spinning him about in circles, at which point my uncle presumably would have to maneuver himself without help into the police cruiser.

Instead Sheriff Benson opened up the back door of the car and Hooter climbed in behind the caged partition. The door slammed shut with a solid thud. The Sheriff got in behind the wheel and started up the ignition. As I watched them drive off down the hill it suddenly occurred to me that it was the first time that I had even seen Uncle Hooter riding in the rear seat of anything.

I watched until the cruiser turned onto the Hollow Road and disappeared from sight. The rain had increased in intensity. The drops pounded off the porch roof in a frenzied staccato of wet bullets. As I turned to walk into the kitchen my brother looked casually up from his reading. His lips curled upward, into a hideous half-moon. His pale face beamed with pleasure.

"First the cheese," he said, "then the trap."

25

Despite Uncle Hooter's prediction to the contrary, the rest of us did pick up the slack that evening, and part of the next day as well. Like subservient house pets, pissing repeatedly into the same corner, we knew no different. Hovering constantly above us, as foreboding and close as a wadded-up newspaper, was my uncle's image.

I felt his presence in the barn as I carelessly sloshed the contents from a pail of milk onto the barn floor, and glanced nervously about for the eruption of words that never came. Looter, arriving characteristically late for chores, surely knew no different as he mumbled to no one in particular that his alarm had not gone off. My uncle not being present, no one seemed to care.

The morning after his departure, following chores, I stayed on for breakfast at the big house. Everyone was there, with the exception of Nora Anne, Craig, and, of course, Hooter. His absence was not mentioned. It was a great hole that sat in the midst of us, a hole we gingerly avoided without comment.

There was much throat clearing, and not a small amount

of clanging silverware. There was, however, very little conversation. No one even saw fit to comment when the Sheriff's car appeared unexpectedly at the bottom of the drive. Nor did the conversation increase as the car turned off the Hollow Road and began to make its way slowly up the long driveway. We watched in silence as it approached like a great black-and-white beetle through the early-morning sunshine. It passed the dining-room window with galling slowness before coming to a stop, momentarily out of sight, in the backyard. A door opened and shut before the car appeared once again, descending down the hill in its same unhurried pace.

Uncle Hooter appeared suddenly in the dining room. He pulled up a chair and sat down to eat without saying a word. He wolfed down a plate of pancakes and reached for a second cup of coffee. The rest of the family, eyes averted, waited without comment as he slurped it down.

At long last, wiping his mouth with the palm of one hand, he leaned casually back in his chair. Belching deeply—the sound shattering the silence like the unannounced arrival of schoolchildren—he surveyed the table in a measured glance, his face erupting slowly into a great smile.

"The fucker can't prove a thing and Bobo knows it."

"What're you talking about, Son?"

"He thinks I'm the one carved up old Martha Wadkins and her husband."

Probably all of us, with the possible exception of Father Cooter, had at least a sneaking suspicion as to why Sheriff Benson had deemed it necessary to cart Uncle Hooter off to town in the back of the police cruiser. Nonetheless, my uncle's sudden verbalization of those suspicions came as quite a shock.

"Well, sakes alive! If that ain't the most ridiculous thing I ever heard! Isn't it?" Mother Cooter looked quickly around the table. "Why, of course it is! Bobo must have lost his marbles!"

"Yeah, it sure 'nough's ridiculous," said Hooter. "And don't none of you forget it neither." He cast his eyes in a semicircle, taking in each one of us with his gaze. I stared down at my eggs, desperately wishing that I was somewhere else. Anywhere else would have suited me at that moment.

"Well, what did he want from you?"

"He wanted to know where I was the night she got killed." Hooter folded his huge arms across his chest and leaned forward in his chair. "And he wanted to take some of my blood and get me to give him some of my spit. A saliva sample, he called it."

Mary Jean exhaled slowly, the sound like a slow leak. Her hand found my own under the table and squeezed.

"Why in blue blazes would he want that?"

"Seems they found a plug of tobacco under Martha's bed and old Joe never could tolerate the stuff. Then there was the blood on the sheets. Some of it was Martha's. Some of it was Joe's . . . and then some of it was somebody else's."

"And Bobo thinks it was yours?"

"Maybe."

It seems that Sheriff Benson hadn't had many leads at all, except for the plug of tobacco and the bloodstains and they weren't much good without somebody to match them up with; until about a month before he decided to pick up Hooter for questioning, that is. That's when Harley Sambo got caught serving minors over at the Moonrunner and was just a hairbreadth away from losing his liquor license. As if propelled by a lightning bolt from Providence Himself, an idea suddenly popped into Harley's usually vacuous head.

It was one of those "I'll rub your back if you'll rub mine" kind of propositions, and Sambo knew just who amongst Devon County's citizenry was in most need of his type of massage. He just happened to mention to Sheriff Benson about how Hooter Cooter had been in the Moonrunner the night that Martha and Joe Wadkins had got their heads caved in.

"Yeah? So what?" said the Sheriff.

That's when Sambo volunteered the information that Hooter had left the bar around nine-thirty with a full package on.

"You still ain't given me nothing worth spit," said the Sheriff, but by then he was sitting up a little straighter in his chair. Feeling nauseated and starting to break into a cold sweat over the possibility of having to work for a living were he to suddenly lose his liquor license, Sambo mentioned as how he had asked Hooter where he was going at the time.

"Well, what in hell did he say?" asked the Sheriff, who was starting at this point to get a little impatient with the bartender's drawn-out rendition of the night's events.

"Well, sir, he winked at me like this." Sambo scrunched up his right eye, seeming to revel in his role as a narrator and appearing to feel that perhaps his true calling lay somewhere in the acting profession. "And then he says to me with a big smile on his face, 'I reckon I'll just go over and sample some of them tomatoes that Martha Wadkins is always bragging on.'"

Had anybody else heard what was said? wondered the Sheriff. That's when Harley threw his ace.

"Sure," he said. "Sonny Woodrow was sitting directly across from me like he is most every Friday night."

Sonny generally spent more time at the Moonrunner than he did either at home or at his part-time job as a sweeper on the Anton Town Highway crew. When he got drunk, which was almost every night, he would do one of two things—pass out on the bar or, if the mood so compelled him, drop his pants and display to the remaining patrons of the bar a penis that, despite Sonny's smallish physical stature, was, even in its most flaccid state, of reportedly legendary dimensions. On more than one occasion he had been seen unfolding the thing onto Sambo's pool table as if it were a flexible pool cue before taking a swipe at the eight ball, much to the delight of the evening's patrons.

Sonny allowed as how he had been somewhat drunk that night and had in fact spent a good portion of the evening in his customary position face down on the bar, but he did clearly recall Hooter's little aside in regards to Mrs. Wadkins's tomatoes. He had thought the remark real clever at the time, particularly since Hooter had bragged to Sonny on several prior occasions about how he had spent more than one evening tending to Martha's garden while old Joe Wadkins was out of town.

That set the Sheriff to thinking about the lab samples that he had sitting back on his desk and about how, come to think of it, he couldn't remember the last time that he had seen Hooter without a chaw of tobacco in his cheek. He also recollected seeing my uncle in church one or two Sundays a little over a year before with a big white bandage over his nose. In fact, he recalled that he had even inquired as to how the injury had occurred and Hooter had said that he had been kicked by a heifer as he bent over behind the animal to pick up a pail of milk. All things considered, it seemed like a good idea to bring my uncle down to the station house for questioning.

"There ain't nothing to worry about then," said Mother Cooter, breathing a visible sigh of relief. "That's good."

"What's good?" asked Hooter.

"It's good that the Sheriff is testing your blood and all. That way he'll find that they don't match the samples he took from the Wadkins place and the whole durn mess'll be cleared up."

"It's not good."

"Why not?" asked my grandmother.

"Supposin' they do match? I mean it's possible, ain't it? Lots of folks got the same blood type and what can anybody tell from spit that's over a year old for Christ sake?"

"What are you saying?" My grandmother's head was cocked to one side, giving her an owlish appearance. She peered at Hooter through squinted eyes as if she were having trouble making him out.

"I'm saying don't none of it make a difference if I weren't there and I can prove it. I got old Maynard Heathcote to represent me. The bastard'll probably charge me half of the farm in fees but at least I know I got me the best in the county. Anyhow, Maynard tells me that them kind of tests ain't conclusive. A good alibi'll knock 'em out, he says."

He stopped and looked slowly around the room, his eyes halting momentarily on each one of us as if they were taking a photograph. He took a deep breath, scratched the stubble on his chin thoughtfully, and then quickly expelled the air as if it tasted bad.

"So. I got me an airtight alibi."

I noticed for the first time my uncle's adam's apple. It was as prominent as a stone statue, like one of those faces carved into the side of a mountain, and jerked ludicrously in his throat as he talked. It seemed odd that I had never noticed it before.

"How so, Son?"

"I was right here . . . playing cards with you all."

"But it was Friday night. You was at the Moonrunner like always."

"Maybe so. But I left there 'round 'bout nine-thirty just like that bastard Sambo told the Sheriff." It looked painful—the adam's apple—moving around in his throat like that. Watching it reminded me of something I had seen on *Wild Kingdom*. A giant python was filmed swallowing a rabbit. It had taken the snake three days to digest its meal, while the poor rabbit sat in its throat like a boulder.

"I was home here by ten o'clock." He smiled softly and held his hands out, the gregarious host prepared to field questions.

"Ollie?" He turned and calmly faced me, the smile covering his entire face.

"You was here that evenin'. Do you recall what time I got home?"

"No. I . . ." Jesus, why was he asking me? "I guess I was in bed."

"Wrong!" His hand came down with such force that the dishes jumped right off the table, half of them landing on the floor in a hideous mess of china and leftover breakfast food.

"Hit the dirt!" screamed Father Cooter. "The bastards are hittin' us with everythin' they got!"

"Shut that old man up or I'll do it myself!"

"It's all right, Dad. It's only Hooter," cooed my grandmother as she reached for the trembling old man.

"You are fucking-A wrong, boy!" He was standing over me now, the Adam's apple pointing at me like a jagged piece of stone. I had seen the same crazed look in his eyes the night Joe Wadkins came at him with a kitchen knife.

"I don't want to have to show you how wrong you are!"

I felt Mary Jean's hand fall limply away. I was vaguely aware of my grandfather's whimpering. He cried onto my grandmother's shoulder, while mumbling through the tears, "I peed my pants. I peed my pants."

"You seen me come into the house at a quarter to ten and then we all played cards together until everybody went to bed around eleven o'clock!" Again his fist came down on the table-top. Again the dishes jumped. "You got that?"

"Yes sir," I managed.

"That's good. I'm glad you remember now." He leaned back in his chair, the tension draining visibly from his face. "What time was it that I got home, Ollie?"

"Quarter to ten."

"Why do you s'pose ya remember that so well?"

" 'Cause we played cards together until eleven o'clock," I answered without hesitation.

More of the tension left his face, draining away like ice melting from a windowpane. The smile reappeared as he turned to face Mary Jean.

"Blossom? Do you remember what time I got in?"

"Yes sir. It was a quarter to ten." I reached for her hand but couldn't find it beneath the table.

"I knew you would remember, Blossom," Hooter said as he leaned forward and lightly pinched her cheek. He turned in the direction of Looter.

"Brother? I ain't going to have no problems from you, am I?"

"Nine-thirty. Quarter to ten. Why not twelve fucking noon? I don't give a damn!"

"Good! Just see that you don't forget it! Now, that's what's so nice about having a family. Everybody pulls together." He looked directly at my grandmother, who was still cooing and holding on to Father Cooter. Bits of Cheerios and fried egg dribbled from the old man's mouth and stained the back of his wife's shirt.

"Ain't that right, Ma?"

"Yes, Stewart. I reckon you're right." She dabbed without success at the food on my grandfather's chin. "Just don't scare your father no more. It ain't good for his heart."

Uncle Hooter pushed his chair away from the table and scratched at his armpits.

"Do you believe that son of a bitch Bobo kept me there all night? Wouldn't let me go till my lawyer showed up."

He reached over and placed his hand on my grandfather's shoulder. "You'd stand up for me if'n you weren't scrambled eggs, wouldn't you, Dad?"

Without waiting for an answer he walked out of the dining room, leaving the rest of us searching for somewhere to look besides at each other. My grandmother bent over and started picking up pieces of broken china from the dining-room floor while Father Cooter stared at her and blew tiny spit bubbles through his teeth. The kitchen door opened and shut and Hooter passed by the window on his way to the barn.

"What are we going to do, Ma?" It was Looter who broke the silence.

My grandmother, crouching there on her knees and holding

on to broken pieces of the family breakfast set, suddenly appeared very old. The wrinkles that had been there forever were now as deep as plowed furrows in her face. Her ponderous breasts hung toward the floor like two exhausted beasts. She cocked her head in that odd way again and looked up at her son.

"We're going to do what's right."

"What is fucking-A right!" It was unclear whether Looter's response was intended as a question or a statement.

"I'll tell you what is right," said Mary Jean. "What is right is to tell the Sheriff the truth and to get that shit-for-brains lunatic locked up for good!"

"What is the truth, Mary Jean?"

"The truth is I don't know what time he got home! But I know he's plenty scared and more'n likely with good reason."

"Wouldn't you be?"

Mother Cooter stood up, placed the china in a pile on the table, and smoothed the wrinkles out of her dress. She ran a hand through her bristly hair and sat back down.

"Now listen to me, all of you, and I will tell you what is right. What is right is for us to keep this farm and to keep living the life we're living, to keep food on the table and clothes on our backs. We're farmers. All of us. Ain't none of us trained to do nothing else. I'm too old to pay rent to somebody and to collect a welfare check each month." She took a deep breath and held it in as if it were some type of drug she had inhaled.

"And the truth? You want to know what the truth is? The truth is that without that man out there in the barn we'd all be on welfare, beholden to some sleazy landlord and beggin' for scraps." Women, I suddenly realized while watching my grandmother, have no adam's apples. They talk and nothing below their mouths moves. Words tumble smoothly forth without impediment. What, I wondered, did God have in mind?

"If he goes to jail who's going to run this place? You, Looter?

That's a fine thought. Half the time chores wouldn't get started till noontime and the fields wouldn't ever get harvested. Scooter maybe? Whenever he gets back from his latest escapade? 'Tween his diseases and his dreams it would be a miracle if anything ever got done. I'm too old and, Ollie, you're too young and that leaves Hooter. Say what you want 'bout the man but can't nobody deny he's a farmer and without him we're through."

"Well, what if he is guilty?" said Looter. "I mean s'posin' he did deep-six Old Lady Wadkins. Don't that mean a fucking thing?"

"He didn't! No son of mine would do such a thing."

"You don't know the half of what your Goddamn son'd do!" blurted out Mary Jean. "And you don't want to know!"

"I'll tell you this," my grandmother replied. "Hooter didn't kill them people, but even if he did I wouldn't sacrifice the rest of my family to put him in jail for it."

She got up from the table and started dabbing at my grandfather's mouth with a napkin. The old man's eyes had gotten all rheumy and glazed over, like a television set gone out of focus. All the excitement had caused him to drool more than usual. His mouth was working and he was mumbling something about his boys and the farm.

"We're a family and by God we'll stick together," said Mother Cooter. "The discussion is closed."

"You'll see!" screamed Mary Jean as she ran from the room with tears streaming from her eyes. "You'll see what your precious son is really like!"

26

We saw the storm coming minutes before it hit. We stood watching its relentless approach from the bottom of the hill where the school bus had dropped us off. The clouds, dark and heavy as milk-filled udders, moved with deceptive speed across the horizon. They had, since our departure from Anton, sat above the right shoulder of the bus, an ominous, laughing combination of overstuffed devils preparing to pounce on those unfortunate stragglers forced to leave the steel confines of the yellow enclosure. "It's gonna be a mean one," the bus driver had warned us. "You kids skedaddle on up the hill soon as your dogs hit the pavement."

Despite his admonition, we stood for a moment looking into it much as the condemned man is said to stare into the eyes of his executioner seconds before the switch is thrown. It seemed to have a face, this storm, a mouth wide open, drooling in brazen anticipation, eyes without pupils, staring with blind ferocity, and a great lumpy forehead composed of piles of cumulus gray poison. The effect was hypnotizing. The lure of evil.

Overhead, the sun still shone as if the two—the cumulus devil and the godly sun—were charging knights preparing to collide and do deathly battle in the sky above us. Faster and closer it came, and yet Mary Jean and I could not turn away.

Craig had already waddled off in haste toward the trailer. "You two can get struck by lightning if you wish," he had hissed. "I'll watch the fireworks from a warm, safe place."

"Let's wait till it's right on top of us, Ollie, and then try to outrun it," said Mary Jean.

A car was advancing up the hollow ahead of the storm. We heard it before we saw it, the muted, muffled roar of a decaying muffler shattering the heavy afternoon air. It turned the corner and came toward us at a dangerous rate of speed for the bumpy dirt road. The rusted, puke-green Catalina that I was all too familiar with rambled toward the turnoff, disgorging flatulent clouds of bluish smoke and emitting sounds of dire distress.

With a sudden popping noise, not unlike that made by a bursting egg, the car swerved and came to a halt, its two outside wheels in the ditch, just feet from where Mary Jean and I stood. The driver-side door opened and out slid Mr. Groover, dressed in his golfer's plaids and Hawaiian print shirt. His mustache twitched in agitation.

"Shit!" he exclaimed, barely acknowledging our presence. "This is one hell of a time to get a flat."

He looked at us and at the damaged wheel. "How about you two trying to change it while I make a dash for the house?" The hair on his lip moved upward in a half smile. "As you can see I'm not really dressed for it."

The wind stirred in quiet circles, bending and whipping the tall grass and causing Mary Jean to gather her hair in a tail behind her head. She secured it with a rubber band and glanced at the advancing storm.

"There ain't time," she said.

"Maybe you're right," said Mr. Groover. "I'll wait here and you two come back and pick me up in the Jeep."

"Can't do that," replied Mary Jean.

The sun had lost its brilliance, its light mottled by a thin layer of cirrus clouds preceding the main storm like advance scouts from a platoon of soldiers. The grass and surrounding fields took on the color of orange soda pop. Rolls of thunder rumbled in a cacophony of hollow sounds as angry clouds jostled each other in their elbowed rush to explode.

"Why not?"

"Ollie and I ain't goin' up to the house," answered my aunt. "We're headin' up to the Hurley place."

"The Hurley place? Why, don't be ridiculous. You'll never make it before the storm hits."

"We got a better chance of gettin' up there dry than we do makin' it to the farm." She nodded in the direction of the storm and then straight up the long hill to the big house.

"The storm's comin' straight for us. It ain't gonna hit us no sooner than it hits the house." Turning away from the clouds, she pointed up the hollow toward the Hurley farm.

"Thataway, we at least got us a chance to outrun it."

Up the hill, Craig was a smudged dot in the distance as he entered the yard to the trailer. The orange sky had become darker, as if an unseen hand had thrown a pail of blood-red paint over the sun. The temperature had dropped. The cool wind whipped the dust from the road into frenetic circles and dispersed the blue smoke coming from the sputtering Catalina immediately into the fray.

"Do what you want, children," sniffed Mr. Groover. "I'm afraid, however, that you'll only be causing your parents needless worry when you fail to show up."

"They'll figure it out soon enough. And as for worry there ain't gonna be none of that on my account unless I ain't back in time for chores . . . which I will be."

"Well, I think you're being childish. It's just a little water, after all," he said, pulling open the door to the Catalina and preparing to step inside. "You're welcome, however, to wait it out inside the warmth of the car if you wish."

"No thanks," said Mary Jean. "We'd rather make a dash for it."

And make a dash for it we did, leaving Mr. Groover in the process of rolling up the windows of the old Catalina. I looked back once as Mary Jean and I trotted off ahead of the storm. The psychologist sat in apparent composure behind the steering wheel as clouds of billowy exhaust were discharged from the tailpipe of the car and quickly blown asunder by the rising wind.

The vehicle, being in such unkempt disarray, stood as an exception to the usual orderliness of Mr. Groover's life. Once I had overheard my mother castigating him for his aversion to parting with his money. He lived, she pointed out, with his mother and had few if any day-to-day expenses. For what purpose, Nora Anne had asked, was he hoarding nearly every penny he made? For a rainy day? I couldn't help but recall the conversation as I took note of him sitting in his bucket of rust and choking on the car's exhaust in the face of what promised to be a very rainy day indeed.

Regardless of the weather conditions, Mary Jean and I had planned on meeting up at the Hurley house ever since Hooter's triumphant arrival home that morning. There had been no need for either of us to mention the place or its incorporeal inhabitant; the nearness of both had summoned us like hypnotic notes from a Pied Piper's instrument. Fleeing the breakfast table, fear bubbling up from my stomach in a thinly veiled disguise of poorly digested eggs, I had longed for nothing but a friend, a very powerful friend who could erase once and for all what quickly I was coming to perceive as the source of my constant and varied nightmares. Thus, when Mary Jean had whispered hurriedly into my ear—"Tonight. After school"—I had nodded my anxious and silent assent.

We ran ahead of the storm as it chased behind us, thunder rumbling like satanic laughter in our ears. Occasional bolts of lightning lit up the sky like tracers fired from a heavenly bastion. We covered the mile and a half to the Hurley farm without speaking, using our energy instead to fill our lungs and to hold down the gnawing fear that one inevitably feels as the enemy breathes down his neck.

I could feel it tearing behind us through the grass, a crazed killer reaching a frenzy as he smells the first scent of blood. The sky became darker, until finally it was black as night, the sun completely obliterated.

We scampered across the last bit of meadow and struggled through the cellar window as the first drops began to pelt our backs. We sat down in the cellar moments before the sky exploded.

The thing was on top of us. Rain slashed and tore at the old house, as claps of thunder boomed in evil applause at the attack. Then another sound, much too loud for rain and too steady for thunder. It crashed against the walls and roof of the house with such volume that attempts at conversation were useless. There was a shattering of glass and then some more as the cellar windows were blown into the basement. A flash of lightning illuminated the cellar for an instant and I saw Mary Jean's face as stark and white as Mrs. Wadkins's once had been. She screamed something at me but it was caught in the fury and torn from her mouth before I could make it out. "Hell" is what it sounded like and it wouldn't have taken much to convince me. Then she pulled my ear up next to her mouth and tried again. Hail. "Hail," she said. We were in the middle of a hailstorm.

It was as if two great doors had opened in Heaven and dumped its debris down upon us. Mary Jean and I huddled in silence in our secret room. Once I knew what it was, I was no longer afraid. This after all was nature, a well-documented phenomenon and not some unseen evil that lurked in darkness.

Soon the hail stopped, its fury spent. We walked into the main portion of the cellar. There was broken glass on the floor and there were several round pieces of ice that had come through the holes in the building. Some of the pieces were bigger than golf balls. The rain continued in sheets. Mary Jean led me back to our room.

We sat down cross-legged on the dirt floor. Mary Jean lit a candle. A wasp appeared from somewhere within the walls. It buzzed around my head like a low-flying crop duster before settling onto my arm. I waited until it had brought its wings together and arched its back before swatting it with my opposite hand.

The wasp dropped from my arm and began spinning crazily in the dirt, both of its wings broken and useless. I watched, hypnotized by its helpless attempts to take flight—as if it were unable to comprehend why it suddenly could no longer go wherever it wished. I wondered vaguely if it was aware that its death was imminent. I wondered if it even knew what it meant to die. Feeling a sudden pang of guilt, I brought my heel down upon the insect in crunching finality.

The cloth doll sat between us: the effigy of evil. Mary Jean held one of the long needles in her hand. I took the other. The bond came quickly and was stronger than ever. There was no choice after all and that made it easier. The blood and saliva tests were not conclusive yet but soon they would be. Soon we would all be questioned and without exception we would state whatever Hooter wanted us to. Such was his power over us all.

There was no holding back as we chanted and tore at the cloth doll, ripping it apart piece by piece, throwing the pieces about the cellar as if they were buds from an exploding milk-weed. Obliteration was our goal. It had to be. There was Hooter and there was evil; and they were the same thing.

My mind swayed but once. For a moment only it was filled with the image of Mr. Groover on his hands and knees at my mother's feet and of Scooter as he walked from the Cooter house with his head hanging to the level of his chest. Then it was gone and there was nothing left but Hooter. We willed him dead.

"Now, Ollie," said Mary Jean, "we turn it loose!"

We walked together to the tank. Mary Jean stuck the key in the lock and removed it. We threw back the lid and ran to the nearest wall. This time there could be no doubt. Above the sound of the pounding rain there was a whooshing noise like steam escaping from a pressure cooker.

The Power—what else could it have been?—rose up from the coffin. Less than a shadow, it was more than a wind. And colder. I imagined it whipping madly about the room, rising from the floor to the ceiling, touching everything in be-tween—including my aunt and me where we huddled to-gether at the base of the wall—before disappearing finally through a square of shattered glass. Mary Jean grabbed hold of me. I shivered in her arms. Our voices followed the thing through the window and into the rainy afternoon air.

"Kill Hooter! Kill Hooter! Kill Hooter!"

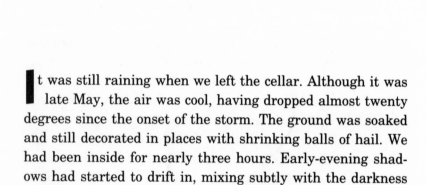

27

It was still raining when we left the cellar. Although it was late May, the air was cool, having dropped almost twenty degrees since the onset of the storm. The ground was soaked and still decorated in places with shrinking balls of hail. We had been inside for nearly three hours. Early-evening shadows had started to drift in, mixing subtly with the darkness brought on by the storm.

"We'll be late for chores," I said. "Hooter'll be madder'n a wet hen."

"Soon it won't matter."

"Mary Jean?" I waited for her to look at me before continuing. "How come Mother Cooter says that without Hooter we'd lose the farm and everythin'?"

" 'Cause she's scared just like everybody else. I seen Hooter hit her before on account of Ma standing up for Looter."

"No! Hit Grandma?"

"Sure as shit. It was after the second time Looter got hisself arrested. Hooter was beating on him real bad, right in the living room. Hooter said he wouldn't tolerate no punks in the family. Ma stepped in on account of she was afraid Looter might get hurt and Hooter backhanded her up against the wall. And that weren't the only time neither."

We walked in silence, the rain penetrating our clothing and getting up next to our skin. Mary Jean's hair was wet and slick as an otter's back. She walked with her head down. Drops of rain rolled from her forehead and down the length of her nose before dropping into the deepening puddles at our feet. Our shoes had filled with water and they sloshed as they landed on the muddy surface of the road.

"Mary Jean?"

"Yeah?"

"How come you never told Grandma 'bout them things that Hooter done to you?"

She didn't look up. I thought at first she hadn't heard me. When she finally answered, the words were muffled and slow as if she were suffering from the lingering effects of novocaine.

"I tried . . . one time anyways."

No place looks beautiful in the rain. Everything around us drooped and bowed like hackled prisoners, beaten into submission by the relentless onslaught of the storm. Overhead the branches on the trees hung within inches of our heads, seeming almost apologetic in their weakness.

"I was only jist eleven then. He all of the sudden showed up in the middle of the night one time. Woke me up out of a sound sleep. I thought it was time to get up 'cept I could see through the window that the moon was still high."

She looked at her feet, seemingly hypnotized by the constant squirt of water forced from between the holes in her sneakers.

"Then I seen he was drunk . . . and naked. I never seen a cock so big. Up till then I thought everybody had little ones . . . you know, like yours." She giggled, the sound like a twittering bird.

"I didn't know they got hard nor nothing, but when I seen

him standing in front of me like that, I swear it looked like a Goddamn baseball bat, 'cept it was all purply-veined and pointing right up toward his chin. A real Goddamn diamond cutter. And I guess I musta opened my mouth, like 'Wow,' you know, 'cause I never seen nothin' like that before. But when I done that he smiled and said, 'You like that don't ya, little sister?' Then I got all the sudden real scared, like I never been scared before, 'cause I just knew he was gonna try and stick that great big fuckin' thing inside a' me and there weren't a Goddamn thing I could do about it."

In the road in front of us there was a tree down. It was a big oak, probably four arms' lengths around. Lightning had struck it and split the trunk right down the middle. Its branches, still green with life, lay scattered along the road like debris blown from the back of a truck.

"He fumbled around on top—hammering away like a son-of-a-bitch—but it wouldn't work right. He was too big or I was too small. He couldn't git it in. Then he got all pissed off and rolled me over on my stomach and tried it thataway. When he finally forced hisself in I thought my legs 'd split apart at my asshole. I kept on bleeding for days.

"I told Ma. Even showed her the blood on my sheets." She stepped carefully over the fallen trunk without looking up and continued walking as if she hadn't noticed the obstruction. "She called me a liar and said that I was an evil child, that I was tryin' to tear the family apart. She said the blood was on account of my havin' my first period."

Off to the side of the road an animal of some kind lay unmoving in a pool of mud. It was a bird, a flicker. Its neck and head lay at a contorted angle against the side of its body. A dark trail of blood oozed from its skull and stained its black-and-yellow feathers. Mary Jean leaned over it. She reached out to touch it with her hand and the flicker's head flopped forward like a door on its hinges.

"Its neck is broke. Must of been hit by the hail."

Of all the birds in the world why this one? I wondered. Had it done something bad? Was God punishing it? Maybe it had abandoned its young, left them without food in the nest. Or maybe it had just been unlucky enough to be sitting in the wrong place at a time when the earth was being bombarded by chunks of ice. It seemed senseless and unfair. Mary Jean picked the bird up and placed it carefully under some brush off the driving portion of the road.

"At least it didn't suffer none," she said.

Somewhere in the darkness above us a flock of crows flew noisily by, cawing in sardonic pleasure at being alive. How had they managed to escape being pounded to death? Where had they hidden? Mary Jean and I took up the pace once again, resigned now to the damp chill that had pervaded every portion of our bodies.

"That's when I quit the swim team," she said. Her words caught me off guard. I wasn't certain what she was talking about.

"How come?" I asked.

"It was the only thing I was any good at. They all bragged about me." She looked directly at me for the first time. "I wanted them to hurt like I hurt. So I quit."

"I wish you hadn't quit, Mary Jean," I said mostly because I could think of nothing else to say. I hated myself for being so young and stupid. "You woulda set some county records for sure."

"It didn't matter none anyhow. He started comin' more after that. I guess he figured no one would ever believe me. He made me do things. Dirty things. And pretty soon I stopped fighting. It never hurt so bad as that first time and I never told nobody ever again . . . 'cept for you."

"I love you, Mary Jean." She looked up and smiled. Touching my arm, she laughed lightly and started to run.

"Come on, Ollie. The exercise will warm us up."

I sloshed after her, feeling twenty pounds heavier than my actual weight. The road was awash with living things: night crawlers and frogs at home in the muck; buds broken from trees, floating and desperately hoping to catch onto a piece of solid ground; thousands of insects driven from hiding, now wet and seeking shelter much as we were. Our feet landed rudely amongst this sea of life, coming down with impudent disregard for their individual plights. We came around the last big curve before the turnoff leading up to the Cooter farm. Ahead was the driveway, and still sitting off to one side, at the bottom of the hill, was Ed Groover's rusted-out Catalina.

We slowed to a walk, taking large gulps of the cool, wet air as we approached the car. It was as we had left it over three hours before—two tires in the ditch, the flat untouched. Coming out of the back, visible through the rain as we drew nearer, was a sputtering stream of exhaust.

"Damn fool never turned the engine off," said Mary Jean. "He's probably been sittin' there with the heater on since we left."

Approaching closer we heard the unsteady thumping of the sick engine as it coughed defiantly into the night air. Each turn of the motor sounded as if it would be its last and yet, like the dying man waiting to receive his final rites, the car hung desperately on, driven by some inner strength.

We walked up to the driver-side window and peered in. Mr. Groover was sitting behind the wheel in a reclining position. The seat had been pushed back as far as its rollers would permit. Mr. Groover's legs were sprawled out in haphazard fashion beneath the dash.

A closer look through the fog-covered glass revealed that his pants had been lowered to the level of his ankles. Appearing like unearthed turnips, they lay in bunched mounds of fabric about his feet.

In his right hand he held his flaccid member as if it were a microphone attached to a wire. The psychologist's head was slumped against the headrest. His eyes were shut. His lips were set in a pleasant smile, the mustache angled up in perfect form.

"Son of a bitch!" exclaimed Mary Jean. "He fell asleep chokin' the chicken!"

She tapped lightly on the window. Mr. Groover did not stir. Tapping harder, she called out his name. Still the psychologist didn't answer. Reaching down with her hand, Mary Jean unlatched the door and pulled it open. She reached through the open doorway and tapped Mr. Groover on the shoulder.

He leaned to the right and sprawled lengthwise onto the seat, his right hand pulling away from his genitals as he did so. His other hand sprang up from where it lay hidden beneath the seat and flopped onto his chest. In this hand he gripped a piece of paper. It was a photograph of my mother. She was naked, smiling with her eyes at the camera, her mouth being otherwise occupied with Mr. Groover's swollen prick.

28

" It was this little hole that damn near killed him," said Sheriff Benson, pointing beneath the rusted Catalina at an opening in the floorboard. "It must've broke through when he slid into the ditch. 'Course only a damn fool would sit in a tub of rust like this with the engine on and all of the windows rolled up."

"Well, I reckon you 'bout summed it up with that last part," grunted Uncle Hooter. Leaning back against one of the huge tires on the John Deere, he spat tobacco juice onto the driveway. "Damn fool is just what he is."

"Probably never smelled it," said Looter. "Rolled the windows up and figured he was safer than a bug in a fuckin' rug."

"How could you not smell it for Christ sake?" this from Claude Bates, Pollywog's father. "Whole Guddum car was churnin' out exhaust like a friggin' factory smokestack."

"Only thing he could smell was pussy and that was settin' a half mile away. Hoo! Hoo! Hoo!"

"Say again?"

"Forget it, Claude. A man has to start spellin' things out

and they lose their meanin'. Besides"—Hooter glanced over at Mary Jean and me before smiling—"what's family business ought to stay family business."

"Hell, everybody in the hollow knowed he was putting the pork to Scooter's old lady every time he got the chance," said Billy Bates. I lunged for him, meaning to tear his beady little eyes from their sockets, but managed only to connect with a quick shot to the stomach before Mary Jean pulled me away.

"Billy, you're dumber than three layers of paint," she snorted. "Maybe the folks would like to hear 'bout the time you got caught pullin' your doinker in the back of the school bus?"

"That ain't true!"

"Is so!"

"All right, everybody settle down," said the Sheriff. "The excitement's over. I want whoever ain't got business here to get on home."

That meant Billy, his father, and a couple of other hollow families who, having heard the ambulance siren, had flocked to the source of the excitement like street juicers to a bottle of wine. The Sheriff had been the first to arrive, just minutes after Mary Jean and I had discovered Mr. Groover and before we had fully realized what had occurred. "What the hell is this?" he had asked upon spying Anton's school psychologist lying supine across the front seat of the sedan, his pants in a tangled knot about his ankles and his penis lying limp as an overcooked vegetable atop his abdomen. "Is he dead?"

It was a thought, in truth, that had not occurred to Mary Jean or me, so diverted had we been with the physical scenario. The photograph, for example. I could not stop staring at it. It was such a strange picture: Mr. Groover standing there with his inflated appendage and Nora Anne attempting to swallow the thing as if it were a submarine sandwich. But who had taken the picture? Perhaps it didn't matter. I felt nauseated without knowing exactly why.

No. He wasn't dead. Sheriff Benson reached into the car

and switched off the engine. He placed a hand on Mr. Groover's neck and found a pulse. "Let's get him out of the car," he said. "And for God's sake pull his pants up before someone happens by." Someone already has, I felt like saying, but knew that the Sheriff meant someone in addition to the three of us.

We managed to pull him from the car. As the Sheriff held him upright Mary Jean and I worked his polyester pants up the length of his legs. The legs were flabby and covered with red dots, the kind of limbs meant to be adorned with clothing. His underpants, too, were strange, unlike any I had ever seen before. They were blue and small, like the bottom to a woman's bathing suit, and were decorated with what looked to be mermaids doing flips. Packed like sardines into this cloth harness, Mr. Groover's genitals appeared pinched. Devoid of trousers, he seemed somehow transformed, as if he had evolved from the swaggering school psychologist into nothing more than a little white man with pimples.

Once we had him back in his trousers, Mary Jean and I were left holding Mr. Groover upright against the car while Sheriff Benson went to radio for an ambulance. Groover's weight swayed against us, threatening to tumble us all into the muddy driveway. He was lifeless, limp. Amenable to physical prodding. I thought of a bag of oats.

The Sheriff returned and suggested that we walk the unfortunate victim about in order to get some oxygen flowing into his blood. As he reached to relieve me of my half of Mr. Groover's bulk, he noticed the photograph in my hand.

"What you got there?" he asked.

I wasn't inclined to show him, but as he leaned down for a closer look I saw in his eyes kindness and trust. I thrust my hand out toward him. Taking the photograph, he looked at it for several seconds without speaking. I searched his face for a barely perceptible trace of humor or disgust. There was neither. He swallowed deeply, the sound like a plunger being forced into a clogged drain.

The Sheriff carefully placed the photograph in his shirt pocket before turning his attention back to Mary Jean and me. His face appeared slightly flushed. His smile, when it came, was all that I could have hoped for. "I don't reckon nobody else need know about this," he said. "Or about how we found him. It'll be our secret. I'll give the picture back to your mother, Ollie. That's where it belongs. No one else will know about it unless one of you two tells 'em."

He got down on his knees so that he was facing me. The smile slowly faded from his face. "It's tough to understand a lot of things on account of your being a kid, Ollie. I ain't so old I don't remember that. I reckon everything seems personal to you. As if folks you love are out and out trying to hurt you. When you get older you find out that ain't always true. Folks can love you and try their darnedest not to hurt you and end up doing it just the same." He mussed my hair with his hand. "I don't rightly know what's going through your head or even how much you understand, but I do know your mother loves you. Very much." He stood up. I looked at Mary Jean. She was looking away, toward the farm. Her mouth was rigid, a straight line of unbroken steel.

The Sheriff and Mary Jean led Mr. Groover around in circles through the mud until the ambulance arrived. Two men in white suits got out and pulled open the large red-and-white doors. The opened ambulance looked like a great, hygienic mouth, white and filled with sparkling instruments. There was a cot in the middle. One of the men was Mr. Tweedie who worked at the feed mill in Anton. It seemed strange to see him in the clean attendant's uniform. At the mill he always wore dirty coveralls and smelled like grain. He tweaked my cheek and said, "Hey, Ollie," as he moved past me into the open mouth. He removed a mask from the wall of the ambulance and placed it over Mr. Groover's face. The men laid the psychologist onto the cot. Mr. Tweedie got in with him, and the other man shut the big doors. "He'll be all right," he said. "We'll take him to Durston." He turned and climbed in behind the wheel of the ambulance. "Damn fool," he mumbled out the window just before he drove off.

By that time, of course, the crowd had arrived. One couldn't expect to drive up Shenker Hollow, siren blaring and lights flashing, without managing to attract the majority of the populace. My uncles drove down in the Jeep. After sizing up the situation, Hooter went back up to the barn and got the John Deere 10-40 to haul the Catalina out of the ditch. He backed the hulking green monster up to the front of Mr. Groover's car and hooked a chain around the front bumper. "Damn thing's so rusted," he said, "it'll more'n likely break off like a Goddamn pretzel."

Everybody moved around the car then, gawking and offering opinions on how best to proceed. "Might better fix the flat first, so's you don't ruin the rim."

"And how in hell you going to get at her? Maybe you'd like to crawl in there in three foot a' mud to stick a jack under her?"

"It ain't my car and I'm damn glad of it. Thing's as rusty as an old tin can."

"You're right. It ain't your car so why in hell you so all-fired worried about the rim for?"

"Who says I'm worried? Just telling ya. Rims ain't cheap."

"As if I didn't know. Well, we'll have to take a chance on her, that's all."

"Well, if that's all you ruin you'll be lucky."

"Whatdaya mean by that?"

"Way she's hooked up now, you won't no sooner get the tractor in gear than the bumper and the whole front end'll come off."

"What's your suggestion, genius?"

"Hook her up to the ass end. Ain't so rusted there."

So the chain was hooked to the back bumper. Hooter got

onto the tractor and slipped it into gear. He gave it a little gas. Diesel fuel spewed forth in a powerful burst of black smoke from the pipe over the engine. The huge wheels dug into the muddy turf. The John Deere moved forward, followed by the Catalina, all of its rusted parts hanging miraculously together. The onlookers cheered. Hooter gunned the engine in a victory salute.

The rain had stopped. Clouds of moisture hung suspended in the night air as if rejected by the oversaturated earth. Water ran in a confused web of tiny rivers down the dirt driveway, taking soil and rocks with it. The air was clear and still and felt good to breathe. The people of the hollow dispersed. It was a night they would remember—the night that the school psychologist damn near killed himself in his own car. Thanks to Sheriff Benson only a few of us would remember the intricacies behind the big event.

Our neighbors walked off in small groups of twos and threes, talking amongst themselves.

"Reminds me of the time Chester Barlow rolled his pickup and got hisself trapped in the cab. Stayed there all night, hanging upside down on account of the door was smashed shut and he couldn't get his feet out from under the dash."

"Only difference is this fool psychologist went and trapped his own self."

"Deke Spaulding happened to be driving by next morning and seen Chester just hanging there. Said his head was redder than a boiled lobster on account of every ounce a blood in his body was a-settin' in it."

"Well, that musta been an improvement. Old Chester sure didn't have much else up there."

Their voices slowly faded. The Sheriff and my uncles were standing by the tractor talking, their voices muffled by the sputtering sounds of the idling engine. Mary Jean and I stood a few feet away, leaning wearily against the rusted Catalina.

The dampness had permeated our clothing and lay against our skin in moist, intimate layers. Our teeth chattered against the cold.

I gazed listlessly into the interior of the car. Against the rear passenger-side door a suit lay wadded up in a plastic bag. Above it, an empty hanger hung uselessly from its hook. Several books lay in disarray on the back seat. Amongst them, a Polaroid camera sat untouched, its open lens smiling blindly into the darkness.

"We'll leave her there till morning," said Looter. "I'll come down and change the tire after chores."

"Why don't you kids get in the cruiser," said the Sheriff, "before you catch pneumonia. I'll give you a ride up to the house soon's we're through talking."

"No need for you to drive up, Bobo," interjected Hooter. "They can ride up on the tractor."

"Well, somebody has to tell Nora Anne what happened. I reckon that's my job."

"Suit yourself," grunted my uncle, grabbing onto one of the roll bars at the tractor's front in preparation for hoisting himself onto the seat.

"Besides, I was on my way up to the house anyhow." Sheriff Benson ran two fingers around the brim of his Stetson before tilting it forward on his head. Droplets of water fell from the hat onto the driveway. "I drove out here on other business."

"Other business?"

"It was just plain luck I showed up when I did."

"What other business?" Hooter had stopped with one foot up on the tractor. His body turned halfway around, he peered at the Sheriff over his left shoulder.

Sheriff Benson hitched up his trousers and readjusted his gun in its holster. "Go on now, kids," he barked at us. "Get in the car 'fore you freeze to death."

Mary Jean and I sloshed obediently through the mud to where the cruiser was parked. We got into the backseat and shut the door. The engine was running. The heat washed over us in luxuriant waves. We sat behind the wire partition, feeling like prisoners.

"Mary Jean?"

"Yeah?"

"How come Mr. Groover had that picture of my mother?"

"It's hard to explain, Ollie." She reached behind her and retrieved Sheriff Benson's wool jacket from where it lay beneath the rear window. She wrapped the jacket around my shoulders. I was lost in it. "That's just the way men are."

"But why would my mother want to do that?"

"Folks do a lot a things they don't really want to do."

"But she was smilin' sorta."

"That don't mean nothin'."

Behind us Looter had gotten into the Jeep. We watched as he drove up the hill toward the farm. My uncle and Sheriff Benson stood by the tractor, still talking. The Sheriff was unmoving, his hands on his hips, the lights from the tractor glistening off his rain-soaked slicker. Hooter was waving his arms wildly, water flying from his jacket as he did so.

"Mary Jean?"

"Yeah?"

"I'm the one almost killed Mr. Groover."

"Whatcha talkin' about?"

"I willed him dead. Up at the Hurley house. Leastwise for a minute."

"How come?"

"I figured if he was dead then my dad would come home, and when I seen that picture I wished he was dead."

A squelched voice came from the front seat, causing us both to jump. It was the two-way radio. The voice turned into unintelligible static before fading away completely. Mary Jean reached over and put her long arm around my shoulders, drawing me to her.

"It weren't you," she said. "Only way we can control the

Power is together. I told you that. Besides, Groover ain't the problem. He's nothing but a horse's ass. He ain't evil. He ain't the Devil."

She turned and nodded up the hill toward where Hooter and the Sheriff were still talking. "That there's the Devil. When he's gone your dad'll come back home for sure."

"Promise?"

"Sure. We'll be like a family again."

Hooter was climbing up onto the tractor, still talking to Sheriff Benson. He got behind the wheel and put the big John Deere in gear. The engine roared, black exhaust shot into the night, and the tractor took off up the hill. The Sheriff stood, hands on hips, gazing after it. Finally he turned and started walking back toward the car.

"Mary Jean?"

"Yeah?"

"Who took the picture?"

"Groover did. They was lookin' into a mirror when he snapped it." She smiled and hugged me. "It ain't really them, Ollie. It's just their image."

29

I aimed the stream of warm water directly between my shoulder blades, at the base of my neck, and let it roll down my back and chest. Upon arriving back at the trailer, I had passed by Nora Anne without a word, heading directly into the bathroom and a hot shower. The water turned my back red and filled the bathroom with thick steam. Still my insides were cold, as if I had swallowed ice.

Sheriff Benson was in the kitchen talking to my mother, filling her in on the night's events no doubt. Perhaps he had already handed her the photograph in which she was making a meal of Mr. Groover's prick. I tried to imagine what her reaction might be. Maybe she would share a laugh with the Sheriff: the two of them pointing with derision at the image of the psychologist, as he stood there, hands on hips and a slightly bemused look upon his face, as if he couldn't quite comprehend my mother's cavernous capabilities. Or perhaps she would frame the act of coupling and place it on her bedside table, next to the picture of Scooter in his track suit. "And here I am blowing Ed Groover," she would tell her discerning guests.

I turned the shower off and stood there dripping water into the bathtub. Despite having remained beneath the hot water for close to half an hour, I still felt a chill. Hosts of images, swimming in serpentine lines before my eyes, refused to disappear. They grappled and fought, becoming hopelessly intertwined like a ball of earthworms.

There was the still-vivid memory of the only other time that Mary Jean and I had turned the Power loose and the nightmare that had ensued: the picture of Hooter and Mrs. Wadkins, rolling naked and laughing on the bed; the sudden entrance of the fedoraed stranger, and then Martha Wadkins's head bouncing across the floor like someone's lost earring.

"That was Old Man Wadkins," Mary Jean had said. "I reckon he finally got tired of Hooter diddling his wife." Her words kept repeating themselves. "The Power. That's how it operates. It gets other people to do things for it sometimes." I saw Nora Anne and Mr. Groover. I heard their high-pitched laughter coming from the living room, so much like that of Martha Wadkins. And I remembered my father's words: "I have my limits, Nora Anne."

I stood in front of the mirror, shivering and staring at my own image, but the face I kept seeing was that of my father. He was dressed in an overcoat and a fedora. He held a long-bladed kitchen knife in his hand.

Of such images were my dreams composed. It was not a restful night.

The next morning when I awoke, my mother was in the bathroom and Uncle Hooter was in jail. The Sheriff had waited for him to finish supper—so abruptly interrupted by Mr. Groover's near fatal hand job—before arresting him for the murder of Martha Wadkins. While I had slept in fitful turmoil, Uncle Hooter had rested on a cot in the local hoosegow, tormented no doubt by dancing demons of his own.

The blood and saliva tests had been completed the previous

afternoon. Both were as close to a match as the legal doctrines of scientific similitude would permit; i.e., someone with a blood type matching that of my uncle's had been amongst Mrs. Wadkins's sheets and whoever he was he chewed the same type of tobacco as Hooter did and exhibited a similar bite mark when he did so. That, in conjunction with the sworn statements of Harley Sambo and Sonny Woodrow, as well as the Sheriff's own observations of Hooter's injured nose shortly following the murder, constituted legal grounds for an arrest in the eyes of Sheriff Benson.

Such, at least, was the information I gathered from Craig as the two of us sat at the kitchen table waiting for my mother to evacuate the bathroom. She had been inside for an inordinate amount of time. The door was locked. A strange sound emanated from within. It was a buzzing noise, not unlike that made by a distant chainsaw or a blender running at high speed.

I had not seen my mother since the Sheriff had left the previous evening. After my shower I had gone directly to bed and thus missed not only Uncle Hooter's arrest but Nora Anne's reaction at being handed photographic evidence of her oral impaling of Ed Groover. Was there to be an explanation? I wondered. Perhaps my mother had swallowed one of her earrings and Mr. Groover, out of courtesy, had taken it upon himself to blindly probe for it?

Each member of a household in time comes to understand the bathroom habits of each of the other members. It is a necessity of communal life. Certain patterns arise. Based upon such patterns an organized household develops. When one member strays from his or her norm anything from chaos to panic may set in.

Unlike some women, Nora Anne was not a person who enjoyed the bathroom. She rarely remained within it any longer than was necessary to conduct her business. Often she was in such a hurry to escape from its confines that she would emerge from the room still in the process of adjusting her clothing. With a look of consternation upon her face she would gaze about as if in fear of someone entering too quickly behind her and thereby catching wind of some offending odor. Rarely if ever did such odors exist. Even had they been present, their detection would have been nearly impossible, given the copious amounts of air freshener that were sprayed about the place.

Had it been Scooter who had locked himself in the bathroom for the better part of a half hour neither Craig nor I would have taken notice. The bathroom to my father was a second home. At times one would almost become convinced that he sat anxiously awaiting the early signs of an approaching bowel movement so that he could retrieve the latest copy of *Sports Illustrated,* saunter casually into the bathroom, and take his seat, to read in contented bliss while nature took its course. Air freshener to him, who most required it, was superfluous.

The buzzing from the bathroom continued. Craig and I chewed on our toast, while staring in silence across the table at one another. It wasn't just the length of my mother's stay that was of concern. It was her timing. Every weekday morning I had first dibs on the bathroom. Everyone was aware of this. It was so because I was the only one amongst us who went to the barn before breakfast to help with the chores. Now, when I was most needed in the barn as a result of Hooter's absence, my mother had totally disregarded this well-established pattern of behavior.

Craig swallowed the last of his orange juice and placed his glass on the table. An orange mustache had formed above his lip. He rose from the table and shuffled off toward his room, leaving me to contemplate alone what course of action to follow. Just as I had determined to head for the barn without first urinating and brushing my teeth, the buzzing stopped.

The bathroom door opened and my mother appeared. She had a large towel wrapped about her. Her hair was flatter; or perhaps it was just wet. But there was something else lacking about her appearance. Her legs. They were as smooth and polished as the surface of an apple. The thin forest of hair was gone. I gazed up toward her armpits, to just above where the towel stopped. The pits too were bare. She had shaved it all.

"Ollie," she smiled pleasantly. "I'm sorry if I held you up. It's just that I didn't have a chance to bathe last night and I woke up feeling unbearably dirty."

I said nothing, but stood staring at her naked legs. I wasn't yet ready to look her in the face, afraid perhaps of what I might find there.

"I wanted to get started early," she said. "I'm going to Langston. To the Century Semen office. I want to see if your father is still employed there."

Her skin actually shone. I could make out part of my face in the taut skin covering her shinbone. Tears—salty and wet—filled my eyes. The image of my face glistened in her leg.

"Ollie . . . please don't cry. I made a mistake. Lots of them." She swallowed and I heard it down in her stomach. "I thought I could do it—raise you children—all by myself. I won't tell you that you will understand when you get older. You deserve better. I got so lonely. . . . I let you down."

She swallowed again and cleared her throat. I felt a warm drop of moisture hit me on the head. I looked up. My mother was crying. I hugged her bald legs.

"I love you, Ollie. I love you with all my heart."

30

When one repeats something enough times the truth is no longer relevant. What is relevant is what is said and what is said becomes the truth.

Uncle Hooter was at the big house on the night that Martha Wadkins was killed and her husband was brutally beaten. He was home at nine-thirty. He played cards from nine-forty-five until eleven o'clock, at which time he went to bed as did the rest of the household.

That is what my grandmother, Uncle Looter, Mary Jean, and I told Sheriff Benson. We told him individually at the station house and we told him again over milk and cookies while sitting at the table in my grandparents' kitchen.

"Well, sir," said the Sheriff as he stood up from the table and reached for his hat, "I don't believe it. Not for one minute do I believe that Hooter was home like you all say he was."

He glanced at our assembled faces. His steady gaze lay upon us like a great shroud. I couldn't look into his eyes. They would be filled with disappointment. I felt them reaching out and boring into the top of my lowered head. There is no reason for you not to trust me, they said. On a cold and rainy night I showed you my worth. I kept the wolves at bay. If not for me they would have ripped into your parents with their angry teeth, tearing them apart with meticulous care, piece by piece. I smiled and buried our secret in my pocket. And this is how you repay me?

"You leave me no choice but to go down to the jail and let him out." He placed his hat squarely onto his head and reached into his pocket for a stick of gum. "It's on your heads," he said as he shoved the gum into his mouth, turned, and walked slowly from the room.

I was filled with shame. It washed over me in waves of self-disgust. What the eyes had said was true. Sheriff Benson had talked to me as an equal that night, giving weight to my feelings as few adults before him. I had been afraid that he would laugh at my mother's predicament or make fun of my father and call him weak as so many others had. Instead he had smiled warmly, sent the group of gawking onlookers home, and hidden the offending evidence deep within his pocket. I felt that I had found a new friend. But now I had let him down. Because he knew the truth, or at least part of it; and I knew the rest, but I had held it from him.

But what choice did I have? There was so much that the Sheriff did not know, not the least of which was my uncle's strange and brutal power over our family. What good would my voice be in the face of silence from the rest of the Cooters? And if I were to tell the truth? What then? According to Mary Jean, the two of us were something called accessories. If Hooter was guilty of a crime, she said, then so were we.

But was my uncle a murderer? I had seen the stranger hack off Mrs. Wadkins's head and then chase Hooter around the bedroom with his bloody knife as if my uncle were a chicken fleeing from the chopping block. Under such circumstances who wouldn't have acted as Hooter had? Perhaps if I told the

Sheriff what Mary Jean and I had seen, nothing would happen to Hooter. Perhaps he would be free to return to the farm, more determined than ever to wreak havoc upon the rest of the family. We couldn't take that chance, said Mary Jean. The law would let Hooter go. The Power would not.

The Power, of course, was the thing actually responsible for the beheading of Martha Wadkins. The stranger was simply its tool, a warm body with which to implement its mission of destruction. Through such tortuous logic, I surmised that ultimate guilt could rest with none other than Mary Jean and me. The two of us, after all, had sent the thing on its ghastly mission in the first place. We had abandoned Sheriff Benson and his ways over a year before, the first time we had unleashed the lethal wind that was the Power. Whatever it was that lived within the Hurley cellar, I was certain that it was not legal. If anyone was guilty of murder, perhaps it was my aunt and me.

Thus we all sat in silence, each for our own reasons, as the Sheriff strode casually from the room. He drove off down the hill, the retreating sound of the cruiser's engine lingering about the breakfast table.

Hooter would arrive home a free man. The lab reports alone were not enough. They were, according to the District Attorney, purely circumstantial evidence. The results of the entire investigation could be explained away as one big coincidence. With no way of placing my uncle at the scene, and an airtight alibi, the prosecutor would not even seek an indictment.

There were other matters of which the Sheriff had no knowledge. Matters that made me even more determined to maintain my silence and to let the Power go about its mission unimpeded by the law.

My father was coming home. We were to be together again. Or so he had said. Nora Anne, with her bald appendages and another new hairdo, had set off for the offices of Century Semen, seeking information about his whereabouts.

"Yes," she was told, "your husband still works for the company."

He was stationed in the southern part of the state and rarely came into the local office. Peddling to customers along a regular route, he was on the road constantly. Doing a damn good job too, according to the office manager. I'm sorry about the problems at home, he told my mother. But with no offense intended, Mrs. Cooter, your husband has been a tremendous asset to this company since the two of you split up. Why, he's even in the running for our biannual Big Shot award. It's given out twice a year to the salesman who has managed to impregnate the most heifers during the preceding six months. As we say in the business, "your husband is really fillin' 'em up."

"Yes," said the manager. "You can leave a message. He generally calls in three or four times a week."

Her message, my mother informed Craig and me, had been brief. She had had, she wrote, an opportunity to do a lot of thinking since he had been gone, to digest certain things. Although she still felt as strongly about the perspectives that she had been exposed to during her own leave of absence, she now realized the need for compromise. People must, she emphasized, take time to understand each other. A good marriage requires work. A certain incident had taken place that made her realize the importance of a strong bond to her offspring. There was no need to go into the details of the incident. It was a message from whatever God one chose to believe in. The point is that how we handle our responsibilities is the true measure of our worth. One must bear them—these responsibilities—with whatever pain is necessary. Perhaps we can get together and talk? I'm willing to negotiate. P.S. I'm no longer seeing Ed Groover, if it matters.

The phone call came a few days later. Craig picked up the receiver on the second ring. He listened for several seconds, his face screwed into a prunish scowl, before wordlessly extending the instrument toward me with two fingers as if it were in some way diseased.

"I just got in from my run, Ollie," my father said. "I could feel you out there next to me."

"I was there, Daddy." In fact I was still in my sweats, dripping perspiration onto the living-room rug as I talked. My mother and Craig stared at me from the sofa.

"Do you want to talk to Mommy?"

"No. Not yet. I got good news, though."

"Are you comin' home?"

"Soon, I hope. I got somethin' in the works. There's just one little detail I've got to take care of and when that's done I'm comin' home."

I held my hand over the mouthpiece and whispered excitedly to Craig and Nora Anne.

"He's coming home soon. He's got somethin' in the works." Craig scoffed openly, spitting laughter into his chubby hand.

"If only I had a dollar for every time I have heard that before," he whined. "Ask him what he's got in the works."

"Craig wants to know what you've got in the works," I said into the receiver.

"Well, I'd rather not say just now. . . ."

"Please."

"But . . . I guess I can give you a hint."

"What?"

"We're moving."

"Movin'? You mean all of us?"

Craig, his eyes peering slyly over the top of his hand, appeared like a large tortoise rising slowly to the water's surface. My mother lifted her hand suddenly to her hair and began poking at it with her fingers.

"Of course all of us."

"But where to?" I asked. "Away from the farm?"

"I can't say yet. That's one of the things I've got in the works.

Don't worry, I'll tell you more soon." He hesitated for a moment. "What's the news there?"

"Nothin'," I replied. I suppose I could have told him that his brother had been arrested for the murder of Mrs. Wadkins, before being subsequently released when everybody else in the family lied to cover up for him; that Mary Jean and I had released some evil spirit, for the second time, with orders to kill; or that Ed Groover had been caught with his pants down while viewing a photograph of Nora Anne in the midst of undertaking an oral gyration that would have been the pride of any circus performer. I could have said all or any one of those things, but I loved my father dearly and knew he had enough on his mind already, so I said "Nothin' " instead.

"Tell your mother that I have her message," he said. "I will talk to her soon . . . soon's I got somethin' more to offer her."

"Okay."

"My love to everybody."

"I love you, Daddy."

"I love you too, Son. Keep running."

Perhaps, I thought, we really would be reunited. As much as I loved the farm, I would have gladly moved if it meant that the whole family could be back together again. I would miss Mary Jean, but maybe she could come with us. Everything else, including the gruesome nightmares that so often merged with reality, I would happily leave behind.

With such thoughts in mind, I faced the return of Uncle Hooter. He had remained in prison for two days. When he returned, it was as if he had never been gone. Within minutes he climbed into his coveralls, put on his manure-crusted barn boots, and pulled his John Deere cap tightly onto his razored head.

"Vacation's over," he said on his way out to the barn. "Let's see how bad y'all fucked up while I was gone."

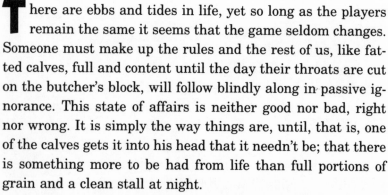

31

There are ebbs and tides in life, yet so long as the players remain the same it seems that the game seldom changes. Someone must make up the rules and the rest of us, like fatted calves, full and content until the day their throats are cut on the butcher's block, will follow blindly along in passive ignorance. This state of affairs is neither good nor bad, right nor wrong. It is simply the way things are, until, that is, one of the calves gets it into his head that it needn't be; that there is something more to be had from life than full portions of grain and a clean stall at night.

The idea may form slowly, beginning as little more than a bothersome itch, but soon it's growing in malignant leaps and bounds until it's pressing against one's vocal cords. The thing is cumbersome, like a boulder in the throat. It can no longer be quelled. One must get it out or die choking upon it. With a final effort, this formless mass is spit up. Suddenly, in front of one's eyes it takes on magnificent proportions, brilliant in its clarity, and it is something called justice.

Several weeks after Uncle Hooter's return, in the Thursday edition of the *Anton Courier* appeared the disgruntled rumblings of one of the fatted calves. It was amongst the letters to the editor, lodged between an article propounding the fertile qualities of liquid cow manure over those of the solid variety and a piece detailing the meteoric rise of the Anton Heifers to the final round of the playoffs in the Devon County Women's Softball League. It was an untitled cry for justice.

> There is an animal roaming loose amongst us and Sheriff Robert Benson knows who it is. It lives in plain sight, scoffing at the laws of our quaint community. Vicious, primal instincts rule this beast, it having long ago shoved aside the reasoned discipline ingrained in the majority of us since birth. This reader has reliable information, from sources which I am not now at liberty to disclose, suggesting that our esteemed District Attorney has more than enough evidence to prosecute the person responsible for the gruesome butchering of two of this town's citizens. Yet he has failed to act and this farmer gone berserk is still amongst us. He is short and fat with a laugh that conceals evil, and he is biding his time until the urge to kill overcomes him once again. This community must not wait for that eventuality. If our law-enforcement agency won't act to protect us, then let us act to protect ourselves. Don't we as citizens have a right, in fact a duty, to recognize evil and to eliminate it as one would destroy a rabid dog? Let the message go out that when one plays with a sword, or in this case a long-bladed kitchen knife, he takes the risk of becoming impaled upon it.
>
> A Beholder of Justice

There could have been little doubt amongst the Cooter clan as to who the Beholder of Justice was. His cryptic style was all too revealing, his savage thrusts all too familiar. More damaging perhaps, leastwise in my uncle's eyes, was the revelation that had been squarely planted in the collective mind of the citizens of Anton. It was as if my brother's pen had been an exploding flare. Having finished with their morning papers, any local need only cast his eyes up Shenker Hollow in order to ascertain the true identity of "the farmer gone berserk."

No one had even bothered to consult Craig about the big coverup. After all, what could he have said? As always he had been in bed by nine on the evening that Martha Wadkins was killed, reading no doubt, about some faraway place and wishing that he was there. When the time had come for the family to present its united front, Hooter had ignored my brother as usual, and the rest of us had taken for granted that he would tell the Sheriff the truth. And he had. He was in bed, he said.

I recalled the wheezing lump of humanity that lay fidgeting on the bed next to mine as I dropped quietly from the bedroom window that evening. He was asleep, wasn't he? With Craig it was often difficult to tell; once under the covers he seemed never to be still, as if his body were finally releasing the physical energy it had retained from passing the daylight hours in a largely inert state. And when I arrived home early that morning? I hadn't thought to check, my mind functioning as it was at the level of soggy shredded wheat. But he must have been there. Where else would he have been? Yet he obviously knew something about what had occurred. Or thought that he did. Or perhaps his hate for Hooter had simply overflowed. Then again, perhaps he was hurt at not being asked to take part with the rest of the family in the great lie.

Whatever his motives, he was now a Beholder of Justice. Whatever that meant. Perhaps it is one who not only has the ability to recognize justice in one of its varied forms, but is also quick enough to reach out and latch onto the concept long enough to hold it aloft like a great trophy for the rest of the world to gawk at. I am certain that my brother had justice in mind when he sat down to compose his letter to the *Courier*. One thing was obvious—thoughts concerning his personal health and well-being were not uppermost in his mind.

Door-to-door delivery of the *Courier* did not extend beyond the village limits. For those subscribers who lived out of town and chose not to drive into the village to pick up their paper hot off the presses, the Thursday edition was delivered along with their Friday mail. Given the lack of urgent content contained within the pages of the *Courier,* this slight delay in delivery was of small consequence to most readers. Thus it was not until Friday afternoon that the family first learned of my brother's latest composition.

After school I returned to the trailer to find my mother and Craig standing above the kitchen table with the front section of the *Courier* spread open beneath them. Nora Anne was studying the fine print as if it were a road map. Her index finger scooted back and forth beneath the lines while she read. Craig stood next to her, his disheveled body straight as a mast, barely able to suppress an expanding smile. He appeared ready to burst into a chorus of "God Bless America."

Neither of them took apparent notice of my entrance into the room. After standing by the door for several seconds, I began walking past them toward my bedroom. My mother's head suddenly snapped up. She removed her finger from the page and pointed it at me. "Ollie," she said, "lock the door."

"What?"

"Lock the outside door. Quickly." She turned toward Craig and lowered her voice. "Go to your room, Craig, and stay there."

I did as she asked. Craig cleared his throat and looked up at Nora Anne. "That won't be necessary, Mother."

What in the *Anton Courier,* I wondered, could cause such

strange vibrations between a mother and her son? As I con-
templated the possibilities, there commenced a terrible
pounding upon the kitchen door. My uncle's voice boomed
through the locked partition.

"Where is he? So he thinks he's the fucking judge and jury,
does he?" The door shook as he beat on it with his fists..

"Craig! Go to your room now!" Nora Anne's voice was insistent.

The three of them appeared to be in the midst of some type
of drama, leaving me, or so it seemed, as the only member of
the cast without benefit of a script. My brother glanced once
at the vibrating door, adjusted his wire rims and slithered
quietly from the room.

"Open the door!" screamed my uncie.

"Go away!" My mother yelled back. "You're shaking my
trailer!"

"I'll huff and I'll puff and I'll blow the fucking thing down!"

"You're a Goddamn Neanderthal, Hooter Cooter!" Nora Anne
shoved a chair in front of the door. She propped it up on two
feet and lodged its back up under the door handle. "Get away
from my house!"

"Not till I get what I come for!"

"Never!" She got on her tiptoes and reached above the
kitchen sink. When she turned back to face the door she
gripped a rolling pin firmly between the fingers of her right
hand.

"Fee fee fi fi fo fo fum! I smell the blood of a fairy faggot
Englushmun!" There was a splattering of glass and Hooter's
hand, tightly wrapped inside a piece of cloth, came crashing
through the window portion of the front door.

The hand groped blindly for the handle, latched onto it and
turned. Nora Anne brought the rolling pin down upon my uncle's wadded-up appendage. From the other side of the door
Hooter screamed in pain. In the next instant he came crash-

ing into the kitchen, pushing the kitchen table, the chair, and my mother into the opposite wall.

He got up, shaking his injured hand. His face was the color of the setting sun. His nostrils, flared in anger, were dark tunnels in its center. He was the Devil come a-calling.

"Now!" he spit out the word as if it were phlegm. "Where is the fucking faggot?"

My mother was pinned behind the table. She heaved against it and tried to free herself. "If you touch a hair on my son's head I will kill you!"

"Hoo! Hoo! Hoo! You best get off your ass first!"

Summoning up all of her strength, Nora Anne pushed the table from her chest. She straightened up and in one motion lunged at my uncle. His left hand shot out, catching my mother in the throat. She tried to scream but the sound that came out was high-pitched and ludicrous, like the voice from a wind-up doll. Uncle Hooter held her upright and slapped her in the face with the back of his opposite hand. Blood erupted from her nose and flew against the wall. He slapped her again and then threw her aside as if she were someone's discarded teddy bear.

From somewhere I had grabbed a baseball bat. I swung blindly and caught Hooter just below the right knee. He howled and reached for his injured leg before turning toward me and lashing out with his fist. I ducked and yelled out: "Run for it, Craig! He wants to kill you!"

Hooter swung again and this time his fist caught me in the mouth. I landed in a heap next to my mother. For a moment he stood over us, sucking in air and grunting like a great scavenging beast. Then he turned and lumbered into the back portion of the trailer. In an instant he returned with Craig slung over his shoulder like a rolled-up carpet.

As Hooter rushed out of the trailer, I caught a final glimpse of Craig's face as it bobbed up and down on my uncle's back.

His glasses were half off and his normally groomed hair hung like overdone spaghetti across his forehead. Contained within his features was a bemused, almost calm look, as if he had just finished reading one of his books and was now contemplating the strange and varied paths one must sometimes travel in the pursuit of justice.

32

Years later, after I had left the Cooter farm forever, I became somewhat of a philosopher. Of the dime-store variety to be sure; that is, I had no formal education. I came to enjoy a good phrase and to attribute to it all kinds of significant meaning that the speaker no doubt never intended. Perhaps philosopher is not the right term. Symbolist may be more accurate. At any rate, at some point in those later years, someone—and I don't recall who—explained to me the difference between a friend and a mother. A friend, he said, will do ninety-nine percent of the time, but when you're hip deep in the shit, only your mother will suffice.

She was crying, my mother, and bleeding from her lip and mouth. The front of her dress was a collage of red puddles. She was, in short, a wreck. Nonetheless, I wanted nothing more than to cling to her polished legs. They were warm stanchions of flesh. I latched onto them with both arms and burrowed my head up under the folds of her skirt.

It was dark there, the air musty and forboding. Not a place, it seemed, for the faint of heart. The insides of her freshly shaven legs were smooth as waxed marble. I slid along them with careless ease until I could go no further, until I reached the source of the heat. The furnace. I turned my head face down in this patch of warmth and let everything go. I cried—bellowed really, as if in pain. My body shook with the effort. Embarrassing, crocodile tears streamed from my eyes. They ran in frantic rivers down my mother's legs. It was, I realized, where I had longed to be for over a year, ever since I had first encountered Uncle Hooter in the upstairs hallway of the big house, and the secrets had started piling up in my mind like toys in the attic.

My mother sputtered and cooed. She patted my back and told me not to cry. No one can see me up here, I thought to myself. It's safe to cry at last. No secrets will be divulged in this warm room and my tears will fall and disappear like rainwater into a musty patch of jungle. My mother is here, patting my back.

The telephone's ring was barely audible. It was a distant sound, insignificant, like that of a flock of migrating geese. My mother stirred. Her legs tightened, coming together like closing doors. She sat up. My head slid rudely to the floor.

"Oh my God!" she said. "The bastard stole Craig!"

She was attempting to stand up. I knew that soon my head would pop out from under her dress and emerge once again into the cruel light. I struggled to swallow my sobs and to wipe my tears on her legs as they slid out from under me. The telephone blared on, louder, somehow more urgent this time.

Then I was free and the light was everywhere, embarrassing in its brilliance. My mother, once free from the kitchen table, sprang quickly to her feet. As the phone rang again, her head snapped to attention. Tiny drops of blood flew from her nose to the kitchen wall. She looked down to where I lay, now abandoned amongst the debris on the floor. Smiling through her bloody teeth, she reached her hand out to help me up. Brushing the hair from my eyes, she smiled once again and kissed me on the forehead. I reached out to hug her, but she held me firmly by the shoulders.

"All right, Oliver, pull yourself together," she said. "It's time to be a man. We've got to get your brother back."

The phone rang again. My mother took a deep breath and pushed the hair back from her forehead with both hands. She wiped her nose on the sleeve of her dress and turned toward the telephone.

"Who on earth do you suppose that is?" she asked me. "They certainly are calling at a most inopportune time."

She made her way through the debris of the trailer, stuffing a large wad of Kleenex into her damaged nose as she went. She reached the phone and picked it up.

"This is the Cooter residence," she said. "Would you call back later please. We are in the midst of a crisis at the moment."

The receiver was halfway back in its cradle when a voice came from the other end. "Nora Anne! Don't hang up! It's your husband . . . Scooter."

My mother hesitated. Holding the phone away from her body, she stared at the receiver as if it had just emitted an obscene noise. Shrugging her shoulders, she frowned and lifted it quickly back to her ear. "Harold, I'm afraid that I don't have time to talk right now. Your son has been kidnapped and I'm going after him."

There was a brief interruption, a flurry of garbled words, from the other end of the line. It was soon silenced by my mother's own insistent barrage.

"No. Not Oliver. Oliver is standing right here, recovering from the blows that you should have warded off. He is holding up well, however. It was your other son, Craig, who was carted off like pirates' booty from his own bedroom. He too, I might add, proved to be a good deal stronger than his father in dealing with shit and adversity. The adversity being this godforsaken farm and everyone on it and the shit being your brother Hooter." There was another hesitation, scarcely the length of a heartbeat. "That's what I said. Hooter, who, if I have my way, may very well be dead by the time you arrive home."

She pulled a red piece of Kleenex from her nose and flung it in the general direction of the wastebasket. With her free hand she began rolling up a fresh piece between her thumb and forefinger. Scooter's voice gushed forth like rainwater from the receiver, the words hurried and indecipherable. Nora Anne shoved the fresh wad of tissue into her damaged nostril and broke in on my father's torrential outpouring.

"I must go, Harold. Your views on our marital failures, although intriguing, will have to wait for another time. I've already talked too long." She paused before continuing. "Whatever is necessary I will do." Another pause. "Yes. He's right here." She started to hand the phone to me and then quickly pulled it back in response to something my father had said.

"I'm glad that you love me, Harold," she said hurriedly into the phone, "but what earthly difference does it make if you are not here?" She handed me the receiver and walked without hesitation from the room.

I brought the receiver up to my ear and winced in pain. The right side of my face was swollen and painful to touch. I moved the phone to my other ear and waited for my father's voice.

"Ollie?"

"Yes sir?"

"I want you to take care of your mother till I get home."

"When are you comin', Daddy?"

"Tonight. Everything's gonna be just fine. It'll take me a while to get there though."

"But what about Craig? Uncle Hooter stole him! He threw

him over his shoulder and took him. I'm afraid, Daddy. I think Hooter might kill him and it's all my fault!"

"What? Hold on there, boy!"

"He does bad things. I seen him. I think he's crazy."

"Ollie! Get hold of yourself. Hooter ain't gonna hurt your brother. He's not that crazy."

Not that crazy? Why don't you ask Mary Jean or Joe Wadkins how crazy he is? Or my mother with her bloody nose and lower lip split open like an overripe melon? With a sudden chill I realized that my father knew nothing of these things. That he knew nothing really about anything that went on at the Cooter farm. Even while he was at home he hadn't seen. He lived in his own world, oblivious of the lives around him. I remembered what Mary Jean had told me long ago and knew now that she was right. It really was her and me against the world.

"Ollie?"

"Yes sir?"

"There's one other thing I want you to promise me. It's the reason I called in the first place." He hesitated. I heard his breathing through the phone. "Are you listening?"

"Yes sir."

"I want you to stay away from the Hurley house. Do you understand?"

A painful obstruction appeared suddenly in the midst of my throat. My words became trapped, impeded in their progress by this great lump.

"Ollie? Are you there?

"Did you hear me? Stay away from the Hurley house and make sure that everyone else does as well."

"But . . . why?" I managed. "What for? I mean how come you said that, Daddy?"

"Never mind why. I'll explain later." The pause was shorter this time. The breathing more troubled. "I know that you and

Mary Jean used to like to play there . . . when you were younger. Well, it isn't safe anymore . . . and I just want to make sure that you stay away for a while. Okay?"

I had been foolish to believe that it was just Mary Jean and me. Others too had apparently discovered their own secrets up at the Hurley place. Looter, Craig, and now my father. "Yes sir . . . I guess so. I mean okay."

"You sure?"

"Yeah."

"Good. Now don't worry, Son. Stay with your mother and don't worry none about Craig. Hooter ain't gonna hurt him. I'm counting on you to take care of things. You're the man of the house till I get back." The phone clicked dead. The monotonous sound of the dial tone buzzed in my ear. I replaced the receiver in its cradle.

Suddenly, in the space of five minutes, both of my parents had informed me that I was the man of the house. It seemed terribly unfair. I was not yet ready to assume such responsibilities. Especially not when the world was taking shots at the Cooter farm as if it were a piñata at a free-for-all. Not just a man: "the man" according to my father. Where the hell was he? The thought came quickly and I choked it off like rising bile.

"Oliver." My mother had suddenly reappeared in the doorway. "I want you to get cleaned up. Your face is a mess."

She had changed her clothes and done the best she could with her wounds. Her lower lip, swollen to twice its normal size, had been coated with some type of shiny ointment, giving it the appearance of a glazed doughnut. Her nose, wrapped in a large white bandage, dominated the center of her face. The long dress was gone. In its place were blue jeans and a turtleneck. She held my father's twelve-gauge shotgun in her hands.

"Where are you going?"

"To get your brother back." She shrugged. "Where else?"

"But we don't even know where Hooter took him."

"That is what I am attempting to find out, Oliver."

"Hadn't we oughta call the Sheriff?" I said, trying to sound as I imagined the man of the house should.

My mother shifted the shotgun to her right hand and let it dangle loosely by her side. She reached out with her free hand and placed it firmly upon my shoulder. "To the law this is nothing more than a family squabble, Ollie. The Sheriff wouldn't even bother to drive out here."

"But he beat you up and he stole Craig."

"Those things happen in families and to the law—leastwise in Anton—it's no big deal." She shrugged. "Besides, if the Sheriff can't keep a man in jail for murdering two people I don't imagine he's going to get too excited about someone beating up on women and children."

The realization that one lives in an inequitable world does not leap suddenly into one's field of vision. It does not come as a slap in the face. Rather it is a realization that occurs over time, that grows like a pile of manure as each new injustice is thrown onto the heap. Nonetheless, there are certain times or events that serve to highlight the reality, that underline it so that, for a moment at least, one sees it as clearly as the black marble in a jar of impostors. Such was the vision of Nora Anne. Beaten, bruised, and armed to the teeth, she stood ready to face insurmountable odds. In the pursuit of justice. And she would lose just as Craig had. Just as Mary Jean and I had. It was an unjust world. We were all howling at the moon.

My mother bent over and kissed me on the forehead. "Get some ice on your cheek and keep the door locked," she said. "I won't be gone long."

She slung her weapon over her shoulder and walked through the kitchen. At the doorway she turned and blew me a kiss. I remembered a movie I had seen on television with Scooter. Battle of something or other, it was called. The hero had gone off to war in a train. His girlfriend had stood on the platform waving and dabbing at her eyes with a handkerchief while the train pulled out of the station. "How come she's crying?" I asked my father.

"Because her boyfriend is going away to fight the Germans," he said, "and she's afraid he won't come back."

"Will he?"

"Yes, Son. He'll come back."

"But how do you know, Daddy?"

" 'Cause it's a movie and the hero always comes back."

She pushed open the door. A summer breeze whipped through the doorway, rustling the pages of the *Anton Courier,* where it sat unfolded atop the kitchen table. Nora Anne stepped onto the porch. I waved goodbye. The door slammed shut, causing several pages of the paper to fall from the table. They landed in confused disarray amongst the dust on the kitchen floor.

I cleaned up the kitchen and then went into the bathroom to tend to my face. It was swollen and discolored on the right side. Yet my image, reflected in the mirror, did not totally displease me. I stripped off my shirt and stood in front of the full-length mirror. Tensing my muscles, I tried to look nonchalant. I held my mouth in a tight-lipped frown and snarled into the mirror, "You got my brotha' and now I'm gonna get you." I imagined I looked tough. I smiled inwardly at how I had taken a swing at Uncle Hooter as if he were a hanging curveball out over the plate.

Back in the living room I sat down on the couch. The late-afternoon sun shone through the wooden slats that covered the windows. One of Craig's books sat face down on the end table. I picked it up and started to leaf through it. It was called *The Painted Bird*. It seemed to have little to do with birds. Reading was slow and tortuous for me. Words with more than one syllable blurred together like rocks in a stream. Why would anyone sit down to read in the middle of the day? Page after page of someone else's thoughts. Endless strings of words and with no pictures to break the monotony. Why? It could never replace the feeling of the sun on one's back or the cool waters of Hurley's Pond after a day in the hayfields.

I put the book back and replaced it with one of my mother's magazines. One called *Ladies' Home Journal*. At least it had pictures. There was a big one in the middle, covering two whole pages. It was a portrait of a family: two smiling parents and three children—a boy and two girls. They all had perfect teeth. Underneath the picture was a caption: "An American Family Portrait." Where, I wondered, were the uncles and grandparents?

On the next page was a picture of two women beaming at each other in their underwear. More perfect teeth. Everyone seemed so happy. "Three full days of protection," the print beneath the picture said. Protection from what? I hated to read. It made me realize how ignorant I was.

Flipping the magazine onto the end table I got up and switched on the television set. Grown people dressed as fruits and automobiles were leaping up and down and trying to get someone else to give them money. The show was called *Let's Make a Deal*. I had watched it before. I could never understand why so many people were willing to trade what they had for some unknown item behind a curtain. I turned off the set and leaned back on the couch, trying to think of anything but the events in my own life. I looked up at the clock over the mantel. Almost four-thirty. It seemed to take forever for the minute hand to go around once. I closed my eyes and listened to the ticking of the clock.

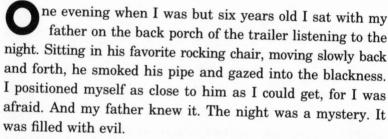

33

One evening when I was but six years old I sat with my
father on the back porch of the trailer listening to the
night. Sitting in his favorite rocking chair, moving slowly back
and forth, he smoked his pipe and gazed into the blackness.
I positioned myself as close to him as I could get, for I was
afraid. And my father knew it. The night was a mystery. It
was filled with evil.

One had only to listen. The night was alive with sounds.
The Devil's symphony. Or so I believed. Which is why my
father made me sit and listen that night.

"There's a whole different world comes alive at night," he
told me. "But them that are a part of it ain't no worse than
what you find in the daylight."

"But everything sounds so scary, Daddy."

"That's just on account of you can't see nothin'. If you could
only see what was making them sounds, Ollie, why you'd laugh
at yourself for bein' afraid."

I sat on the floor next to his chair, gripping tightly to his
leg while he rocked. We listened in silence. They were every-

where, these sounds—screeches, hoots, chirps, howls, and peeps. The trailer was surrounded. I could only imagine by what. How long would they stay away? I tightened my grip on my father's leg.

"Tell you what, Son," he said at last. "You let me know which ones you can't figure and I'll let you see what they are."

Without warning he pulled his legs up into the chair. He dropped his arms down and pulled them in tight to his body. Scrunching his head down into his shoulders so that it appeared as if he had no neck, he peered out at me. I forgot for the moment my fears and laughed out loud at the sight of him.

"This here's an owl, Ollie," he said. "It's what's doin' all that hootin' you hear." He smiled. "Real scary-looking, ain't he?"

Suddenly he leapt up from his chair and got down next to me on the floor. Squatting there on his haunches, he squeezed his shoulder blades together and commenced rolling them back and forth as if he had an unreachable itch in the center of his back.

"This here evil-looking creature's a cricket," he said. "All he's doin' is rubbing his wings together like this." He sped up the motion of his shoulders, appearing like a mechanical toy gone berserk. "He's the cause of all that chirpin' goin' on. I reckon maybe his wings need oilin', is all."

Soon we were both on our hands and knees, hopping about on the porch floor and laughing as we attempted to outdo each other with our impersonations. "All's you got to do is draw a picture of what's scaring you, Ollie, and pretty soon it don't seem so bad. It's the not knowing that gets ya."

But what if the pictures one draws cause one to grope for one's shrinking genitals as if they are a lifeline? And what if these etchings of horror are not just figments of one's imagination? What if they are real? And he has seen them all before? My father did not prepare me for such an eventuality. As was so often the case, his detailed analysis skirted unkind reality.

I woke up surrounded by darkness. The night was silent except for the ticking of the clock. The room was filled with figures; large, unmoving figures that sat about the room in evil nonchalance. Waiting for what? For me to wake up perhaps? If I moved they would surely see me. My mouth tasted sour. My heart beat frantically. How did these creatures get here? What did they want with me? I have to get out! I won't wait for them to tear me apart limb by limb. Dropping from the couch, I rolled sideways across the floor. I jumped up and started to run. Ow! It was too late! One of the creatures had me. He hit me and rolled back on his haunches. I fell on the floor and screamed. He came toward me once more. Then rolled back again. And forward again.

I opened my eyes and looked up at the ceiling. Above me the rocking chair moved steadily back and forth. The clock ticked monotonously. My breath came in painful gasps. I got to my feet and groped for the light switch. The darkness became a living room, the creatures, tables and chairs. The clock above the mantel said ten minutes to eight.

I had slept through evening chores. Why had no one woken me? And dinner. Where were my mother and Craig? I went to the living room window and looked down the drive. The road was dark. Off in the distance a couple of lights flickered in the scattered houses along the Hollow Road. Panic arrived in a nauseating wave. Was I all alone on this hill?

I hurried blindly through the unlit hallway, toward the end of the trailer, where it faced the Cooter house. Entering my mother's bedroom I reached for the light switch, momentarily frightened of what might be hidden in the darkness. I flicked on the light.

My mother's bed was neatly made, its surface like that of an untouched lake. A framed picture of Scooter, younger and thin as a willow in his track suit, and a book entitled *The Language of the Body* sat atop the bedside table. Going over to the large picture window, I pulled back the curtain and peered out toward the big house.

Two lights shone like cat's eyes in the otherwise darkened structure. One appeared to be downstairs, in the kitchen; the other upstairs, somewhere in the back of the house. My panic lessened. I had not been abandoned after all. The rest of the family, no doubt, were gathered at the big house. It was time for me to join them. In numbers lay comfort. I charged madly back through the trailer, toward the kitchen doorway.

I had negotiated the two hundred yards between the front door of the trailer and the Cooter house thousands of times in the past, but never in such a state of mind. The distance, as I gazed out across it, suddenly seemed much more imposing than before, a strip of no man's land, containing obstacles and traps for the unwary. The blackness, I knew, was a carnival of evil, crawling with freakish creatures, none of them cute or funny like those pictures that my father had drawn. If one was not quick enough one would be caught and then the party was over. The darkness took no prisoners.

Nothing was to be gained from dwelling on such thoughts. Perhaps I could outrun whatever was out there. My legs at least, thanks to my daily workouts, were up to the challenge. I opened the kitchen door and hurtled myself into the darkness in one motion.

My feet, once moving, flew over the grassy terrain. I was aware of a slight chill in the air. It felt good in my lungs, a reminder of vitality.

Nothing mattered but my breathing. In through the nose.

Out through the mouth. I did not look sideways for fear that a hand would reach out of the darkness and scoop me up. I did not look down for fear I would see a body lying limp and headless like discarded debris on the side of a road. I didn't look back for fear of finding something gaining on me.

Moments later I arrived unscathed and gasping for air at the front porch of the big house. Not bothering to knock, I pushed open the unlocked screen door and stumbled headfirst into the kitchen. It was empty.

Voices, soft and hurried, floated from the living room. A flickering gray light shone through the open doorway. The rest of the house was dark. I had let the front door slam before stumbling noisily into the kitchen. Why had no one heard me?

I moved quietly through the kitchen and peered around the doorframe into the living room. The window shades had all been tightly drawn. The only light came from the great black-and-white television set in the center of the room. Two figures in cowboy hats were standing over a body and arguing with one another. Someone was sitting in the lounge chair with his back to the doorway. He did not move as I stepped into the room.

"Hello?" I said to the back of the chair. There was no response, just the frantic voices coming from the television set.

"Hello?" I tried again. Louder this time.

The figure sprang from his seat and turned to face me. "Who goes there?" bellowed Father Cooter. "Stand and identify yourself or I will blow your fucking head off!"

He advanced toward me on his aged, wobbly legs. In his right hand he held a broom handle. He wielded it as if it were a saber, waving it pathetically in front of my face.

"It's Ollie."

"Who? Speak up and step into the light, Guddamn ya!"

"It's me, Grandpa," I said, politely pushing the broom handle out of my face. "Oliver."

"What! I thought all you bastards had hightailed it by now." He pulled the saber back slightly. "Ya ain't in disguise, are ya?"

"No sir."

"Well ya better get down less'n ya want your Guddamn brains blowed out."

He stepped quickly out of the light streaming through the doorway. Ambling over to the nearest window, he stood off to the side and carefully pulled the shade away from the glass. He peered outside before dropping the curtain back into position. "I tried ta tell the rest of 'em 'bout the big guns, but wouldn't none of 'em listen."

"Where is everybody, Grandpa?"

"Gone. Every one of 'em. Abandoned ship. The lily-livered cowards."

I switched on the overhead light. My grandfather covered his eyes and fell back into the lounge chair. He was dressed in his Army uniform. A pith helmet sat atop his scrambled old head. Seeing him that way reminded me of the picture that Scooter kept in his bedroom. Only my grandfather was younger then and his eyes, even in the photograph, were bright and sharp as lasers. "That's your grandfather, Ollie," my father had told me. "I wish you had known him."

"Gone. Gone. Everybody's gone. Left me all alone to defend the place," he blubbered, and the eyes, much duller now and permanently out of focus, still knew enough to cry. The tiny spit bubbles began to form between his lips, and as they popped, the saliva rolled slowly down his chin.

I wiped the tears and spit from the old man's face with a handkerchief and tried to figure out what to do next. Where, I wondered, was my grandmother? I could not recall her ever having left Father Cooter alone before. Especially after dark.

At night, his manner became more poignant, his skirmishes more sincere. A precursor, no doubt, to my own nocturnal anxieties.

"I had three boys, you know." Father Cooter had found his voice again.

"Yes, I know, Grandpa. Where are they? What happened to 'em?"

"Gone. Gone like shit through a goose. A battle zone ain't no place for womenfolk. I don't blame 'em for leavin' even armed as they was. But the boys. My boys shoulda never left me."

He began blubbering and crying again. He had imparted what information he had. Solutions were the bailiwick of others. There seemed nothing left to do but to reinstate him to the position in which I had found him. I put a pillow behind his head and gently removed the saber from his hands. Before leaving the room, I placed a blanket over his legs and shut out the light. On the television screen the two cowboys were arguing again. This time over a woman.

I probably would never have found the note if not for the Sheriff. I had returned to the kitchen with the intention of calling him. A stolen brother was one thing. A missing family was quite another. Sheriff Benson could hardly term such an occurrence a family squabble. I felt certain that he would have to respond to my request for help. It was when I reached for the phone book, that I found it.

It lay crumpled and wadded up on the tabletop as if someone had discarded it in a great hurry. I might not have read it at all if not for the dark print that it was written in. The letters had been carefully composed in black magic marker. Whoever had written them had pressed so hard that the stains were clearly visible from the blank side of the page. I smoothed out the wrinkles and placed the note on the countertop in front of me. Once I had finished reading it I changed my mind about calling the Sheriff.

I WAS THERE AT THE WINDOW. I SEEN IT ALL YOU
BUTCHER. IF YOU WANT TO SAVE YOUR WORTHLESS SOUL
BE AT THE HURLEY HOUSE AT 10:00 O'CLOCK TONIGHT. BE
THERE OR YOUR DEAD MEAT.

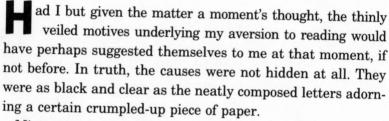

34

Had I but given the matter a moment's thought, the thinly veiled motives underlying my aversion to reading would have perhaps suggested themselves to me at that moment, if not before. In truth, the causes were not hidden at all. They were as black and clear as the neatly composed letters adorning a certain crumpled-up piece of paper.

Mine was an acquired distaste, the antithesis to Pavlov's dog's. The written word had not been kind to me. Each time I had been forced to confront it in my young life, it seemed I had come away slightly singed if not burned to a crisp. There were my father's scribbled farewells, as if on his way out the door to a new life he had suddenly remembered that he had forgotten to say goodbye to his old family. And of course Craig's untimely submissions to the *Anton Courier*. Then there was my mother's note, left with a middleman, in which she had offered to reopen negotiations on the finer points of my parents' marriage.

We had become a family who thrived on notes. Notes, unlike letters, are not mailed. They are deposited, left about like unfortunate accidents for someone else to find. They require neither addressing nor a stamp. Not even an envelope is necessary. A note needs nothing more than to be written and dropped somewhere.

It seemed a strange practice, this note leaving. We were, after all, a family living in close proximity to one another. An oral message, being more direct and certainly less prone to misinterpretation, would in most cases have been likely to suffice. Yet there was a uniqueness to these scribbled bombshells. As if to drop one was to impart to the reader a heartfelt sense of urgency in the composer's words.

It was, of course, the cowardly approach. The note, like a judge's proclamation, forecloses all discussion. By the time it is read, the writer has long since fled the scene, leaving his words to linger unchallenged in the minds of those left behind.

In this case, the writer had lacked even the courage to sign a name. Still, there could be but one possible composer, the only person besides myself who had witnessed firsthand the events so graphically alluded to. Who else could write with such bold assurance of those things? The certainty of this unveiled identity plunged into me like a dull knife.

Mary Jean had betrayed our oath of silence. Without so much as consulting me, she had decided to take matters into her own hands. Had our bond meant nothing? I remembered our blood merging and running in a river down the length of our naked arms. We had said we loved each other.

But why had she acted? Had she lost patience with the Power? Perhaps by luring Hooter up to the very doorstep of its abode, Mary Jean hoped to shame the formless ghost into action. I shivered as I thought of the last time these two evil behemoths had collided.

I looked at the wall clock. It was almost eight-thirty. Given the manner in which the note had been recklessly cast aside, there could be little doubt but that Uncle Hooter had read it—his face, in all likelihood, contorted in blown-up rage, as he did so. In a little more than an hour and a half he would be at the Hurley house. And so would Mary Jean. She couldn't possibly win.

A pathetic feeling of loneliness stirred within me. I lacked the will to fight it. My family had abandoned me. Mary Jean had forgotten me. I longed for a pith helmet and to join my grandfather in the living room; to dress up in a uniform so as to aid him in his lonely fight against the roar of the unseen enemy. The smack of reality had beaten me.

The answers did not present themselves. I was prepared to do nothing, simply because I did not know what else to do. It was, I felt, a meaningless pursuit to continue charging aimlessly about in search of my family. Whatever was to occur would do so regardless. The wheels had long since been set in motion. As had been the case from the beginning, I was to be nothing more than an observer. Howling at the moon. Better for me to crawl back into the confines of the darkened living room, to take up a position alongside my grandfather, behind the shaded windows, in a never-ending vigil against the big guns. At least I would not be alone.

It is the belief among certain religions that just before a dying man is to pass forever beyond the brink he will glimpse the clue that would unravel the mystery of life. At that point, with a final, heroic effort, it is said that he can fight off the clutches of death, thereby returning to life as a richer, more informed being. Few are able to do so. Those who do become holy men. They are blessed with strange powers. It is a metaphor of course.

I was all ready to arm myself with a saber, preparatory to taking up my position next to Father Cooter, when there appeared, as if in a vision, the cat's eyes. In all the excitement I had nearly forgotten them.

There had been two lights on when I left the trailer. That

could only mean that my grandfather and I were not alone in the house. Yet whoever was upstairs would certainly have heard the two of us talking. Unless for some reason they were unable to. Or it didn't matter. The idea formed slowly. It was no more than a passing thought, the first whiff of a foul stench. In seconds it had taken on terrifying proportions.

Suppose Uncle Hooter had found the note and read it. Would he have been able to figure out who had written it? And, if so, what would he do to that person? I remembered that night at Martha and Joe Wadkins's house. How, in the middle of the carnage, Hooter had turned and looked directly out the bedroom window, at where Mary Jean and I were crouched with our faces pressed against the glass. I was convinced he had seen us. "If he saw us he would hurt us," Mary Jean had said. "Bad."

I jammed the note into my pocket and tore up the stairs. Once at the top, I turned right and ran toward where the light had been. Toward Mary Jean's room.

I stopped. The bedroom door was shut. Light poured into the corridor from the space above the molding. I shrank against the wall as if the room had eyes and moved silently along its edge until I was just inches from the doorway. A million unpleasant pictures flashed through my head.

The closed door was fast developing into another Cooter trait. Dropped notes and closed doors. It seemed I was constantly crouching next to one or the other—crouching and listening for clues as to what might be occurring on the other side. Perhaps it explained my confusion over *Let's Make a Deal*. There were no deals behind closed doors. Opening them had caused me much pain in the past.

Pressing my ear against the paneled doorway, I listened for some sign of life within. There was something. A steady whirring, like the noise that skates make as their sharpened blades slide over the ice.

Noises, I had learned, could be deceptive, particularly in

relation to closed doors. I recalled the twittering laughter that had emanated from behind the living-room door at the trailer just prior to my discovery of Nora Anne and Mr. Groover in a game of peekaboo, and the busy mice that had been Mary Jean crying into her pillow.

I knocked loudly on the door. There was no answer. The whirring continued. Turning the doorknob, I pushed gently. The door swung slowly open. I stepped into the room.

She was there, lying face up on the bed, her hands clasped tightly behind her head. Her eyes were shut. Her head was enclosed in some type of leather brace. I sucked in my breath. I feared she was dead.

Then I saw her foot move. It was bouncing up and down on the mattress, keeping time to the music in her head. The whirring noise was an album spinning in shrinking circles on the turntable next to the bed. The leather brace was a pair of headphones fit snugly over her ears.

"Mary Jean!" I yelled, shaking her foot and feeling that perhaps there really was a God who watched over us. Had I at last picked the right door?

"What the hell! Ollie!" Her eyes popped open and her head snapped up as if the pillow had suddenly turned into hot coals. "Jesus Christ! You scared the hell out of me! Why didn't you knock? You ain't suppose to come into a lady's room without knocking first!"

"I did knock. You didn't hear me."

"What?" she said. "Speak up, will you?"

"I said I did knock."

"Oh, Jesus Christ!" she said, tearing the headphones off her ears. Smokey Robinson's voice poured from the speakers:

Take a good look at my face,
You'll see my smile looks out of place,

Look closer and you will see
The tracks of my tears. . . .

She got up and switched off the stereo. The needle scratched noisily over the surface of the record.

"You scared the shit out of me, you little bastard! And now you made me ruin my favorite album!"

"But . . . you're all right," I mumbled. "I thought you was . . ."

"Of course I'm all right! What in hell are you talking about?"

"I didn't think you'd be here. I mean, you ain't suppose to be."

"Where the hell else would I be?"

"Father Cooter, he . . ." Explanations failed me. I dropped my hands down to my sides and made no effort to hold back the tears. Mary Jean reached out with her long arms and pulled me in next to her. I felt the warmth immediately. It was the same heat that had oozed forth from my mother earlier. Perhaps, I thought, this warmth was a female trait; as if a great furnace burned within each of them. My fears melted and ran out of me.

"It's okay, Ollie. Jesus, it ain't like you're dead," she said, moving over and making room for me on the bed. "Take a load off'n your feet."

But she seemed so relaxed. As if her fast-approaching rendezvous with Uncle Hooter was the furthest thing from her mind. Was I imagining things? Moments ago I had been charging around in a house of horrors, death lurking at every corner. Now, amidst the warmth that was Mary Jean, it all suddenly seemed unreal; a product of my imagination. Had I slipped into the hazy wasteland occupied by my grandfather?

"All right, Ollie, now that ya got the faucets turned off why don't ya tell me what in hell all the fuss is about?"

I lifted my head from her shoulder and wiped my face on the back of my shirt sleeve. "Don't you know?" I asked.

"I know that Craig wrote some half-assed letter to the newspaper 'bout Hooter and Mrs. Wadkins and the like. And I know Hooter left here madder than a wet hen and drug Craig out to the woodshed on account of it." She reached behind her and fluffed up her pillow before lying back on the bed. "That what ya mean, Ollie?"

"That ain't all of it."

"Well, supposin' you tell me the rest."

I told her about Hooter beating up Nora Anne and stealing Craig, and about my father's telephone call, and about how Nora Anne had gone after Hooter with a shotgun and never come back. The only thing I left out was the note about meeting Hooter up at the Hurley house. I was hoping that she would tell me about that.

When I was done Mary Jean looked up at me unimpressed, reached under the mattress and pulled out a package of cigarettes.

"You know, Ollie," she said as she removed one of the cigarettes from the case and stuck it between her lips. "You gotta learn how to relax."

She held the pack out toward me.

"You want a smoke?"

I shook my head. She shrugged, shoved the pack back into its hiding place and reached for a book of matches sitting on the nightstand.

"I forgot. You're in training. I'd a thunk all that exercise would help you to relax." She smiled up at me. "You know what really mellows me out?"

"No," I shrugged, completely befuddled by her reaction to my story.

"Marywanna," she said. Lighting the cigarette, she inhaled deeply. It didn't smell like a normal cigarette. It had a bitter, funny smell. It looked different too. It was thin and lumpy. Mary Jean held the smoke in her mouth for several seconds as if she had suddenly forgotten how to breathe. At long last she opened her lips and blew a big puff of smoke into the air. It hovered there for a moment before coming apart and heading for the ceiling in confused columns. "I recommend it several times a day," she said and smiled.

She held the cigarette between her thumb and forefinger, looking at the burning ash. The acrid smell of the smoke filled the room. "The weed of the gods," she said.

"What?"

"Marywanna. That's what Lila calls it."

"Who?"

"Lila. You know. Looter's girlfriend from up Dead Creek." She took it in her mouth again and sucked, the burning paper crackling as it turned to ash. So this was marywanna. I had heard Looter talk about it before. He called it Smoky Joe and told Mary Jean and me that he couldn't make it through chores without a couple tokes of it.

"What I mean to say is this, Ollie." She exhaled again. The smoke bunched together at the ceiling and hung above us like storm clouds. "You got to learn how to accept things when you're a kid. Mellow out, Lila calls it. On account of we ain't the ones dealing the cards." She smiled and ran her fingers gently through her hair.

"Course once we get to where we're the ones doing the dealing there's some motherfuckers better watch out. Ya know what I mean?"

I shook my head, not having the vaguest idea of what she was talking about. Was it the marywanna that caused her to speak so strangely? I wanted her to explain things to me. Instead she was just making me more confused.

"Yeah," she sighed. "Hooter hauled Craig out to the woodshed and beat him up real good, even worse than that time he got you for stampeding the cows, from what I seen. Used an old conveyer belt on him. Craig took off somewheres. Reckon he ran into the woods. When Hooter come back to the house Nora Anne was there waitin' for him. She had an old shotgun leveled right on him. Woulda shot him too if'n Ma hadn't grabbed a hold of her and taken the gun. It was rich, Ollie. She was madder'n a wet hen. God love her for it."

She took another drag on the cigarette, laid her head back on the pillow, closed her eyes, and slowly blew the smoke out between her teeth. The smoke climbed lazily toward the ceiling.

"Course it didn't do her no good. Just like it never does none of us no good," she said, opening her eyes and turning her head back toward me.

"Hooter just stood there laughing and said he reckoned that maybe Nora Anne hadn't learned her lesson the first time. That if she had spent more time being a mother and less time humping school psychologists that maybe Craig woulda knowed better than to go and write somethin' stupid like that in the newspaper."

She stopped talking and crushed the burning end of the cigarette between her thumb and forefinger. Reaching under the mattress, she pulled out the package and stuck the half-smoked butt back into the cardboard box.

"So?" I asked. "What happened then?"

"Nothin' much. Me and the boys went and done the chores. Nora Anne said she weren't never gonna let you work in the barn no more on account of Hooter. Then Ma and Nora Anne went to look for Craig."

"But where is everybody?"

"They ain't back yet?"

"No. Ma never showed up. That's why I come over here."

"Well, I dunno. I guess they ain't found him yet."

Poor Craig. Stumbling around in the woods with welts as

big as tire tracks on his backside because he was too ashamed to let anyone see him cry. My brother hated the outdoors— "There's more to see in one book than in a hundred acres of forest," he told me once. In the dark and more than likely without his glasses—I remembered them hanging comically off one ear as Hooter carted him off—he was probably crashing blindly into trees by now.

"Nobody did nothin'?" I asked.

"Huh?"

"To keep Hooter from beatin' on Craig?"

"Sure," she snorted derisively. "Looter tried. Hooter shoved him outta the way and told him if'n he wanted worse than what Craig was gonna get to just try it again."

"That was it?"

Mary Jean turned on me, her nostrils flared. "What in hell did you do when he drug Craig outta the trailer?"

"I tried," I said, feeling weak and small. "I swear I tried to stop him!"

Mary Jean's face softened. She sat up on the bed, reached forward and touched my bruised cheek with her fingers. She ran them gently over the injured area. Bending forward she kissed the bruise lightly.

"So did I," she mumbled, more to the walls than to me or anyone in particular. "But it didn't do no good. It didn't ever do no good."

She reached into the headboard above her bed and pulled out a package of cigarettes. Real ones this time. She stuck one between her lips and lit it.

"What're we goin' to do, Mary Jean?"

" 'Bout what?"

"Hooter. Craig. Everything."

"Ain't nothing to do, Ollie. 'Cept wait."

"Wait for what?"

"The Power." She stood up and walked over to the window.

She gazed out through the glass into the darkness. "It's out there somewhere," she said. "Just bidin' its time."

Something didn't quite fit. It was skewed. A concealed bit of knowledge lay just out of reach. The thought of unearthing it made me uneasy. I gazed at Mary Jean's broad back and wished it wasn't so. Her backside was beautiful. Unrumpled and smooth.

"You didn't write the note?" I asked.

"What note?" she said without turning around. There was a halo of smoke around her head.

I reached into my pocket and pulled out the wad of paper. Smoothing out the wrinkles, I laid it face up on the pillow. Mary Jean turned slowly and walked over to the edge of the bed. She reached down and picked up the note. Silently, without looking up, she read through it.

"Where'd you get this?" she asked in a hoarse whisper.

"Off the kitchen table," I weakly replied. "You promised not to tell."

"I didn't." But of course I had already figured that out. It wasn't Mary Jean who had betrayed me. I was ashamed for having thought otherwise. We had always acted together.

She sat down on the edge of the bed and read through the message once more. When she was finished she looked up, the cigarette neglected and turning to ash between her lips.

"Has he seen this?"

"Who?"

"Hooter."

"How do I know? There weren't nobody downstairs 'cept for Grandpa. I don't know where anybody is."

"Then he's read it!"

"What?"

"He was suppose' to stay with the old man. Even Hooter wouldn't have left Father alone unless . . ."

Not bothering to finish the sentence she jumped up from

the bed and reached the closet in two giant steps. She began rummaging about on the floor.

"What're you doing?"

"Goin' to the Hurley place," she said as she bent over and began pulling her boots on over her pant legs. "What else?"

I watched, too stunned to speak, as she finished tying her boots and reached for her coat. She got her arms into the jacket and looked over at me.

"He's on his way up there right now," she said. "Sure as shit!"

"But if you didn't write the note," I asked, "who did?"

"The Power, Ollie! It had to be. No one else knows!" She buttoned up her jacket and reached for the doorknob. "The son of a bitch is going to die on the Power's front doorstep!"

35

Father Cooter had taken a respite from the siege. He was in the lounge chair eating Fritos and watching Gomer Pyle on television when Mary Jean and I walked into the living room. The front of his uniform was covered with fallen chips. His helmet and saber lay next to the chair, the enemy apparently withdrawn or defeated. His aged eyes were riveted to the set. They didn't move as we entered the room.

Mary Jean walked over and kissed him on the cheek. He turned his head and frowned.

"Clowns," he said, waving animatedly at the set. "Guddamn clowns is what they got in the Army today. Talk like friggin' sissies. Probably piss their pants when the shootin' starts." He reached down and picked up his weapon, tucking it into his shoulder as if it were a rifle. He sighted down the barrel at the television screen. Mary Jean took hold of the broomstick and laid it firmly across the old man's knees.

"What's the matter with you tonight?" she said. "How come you're making so damn much noise?"

"Ain't nothing wrong with me," sputtered the old man. "It's

the Guddamn world gone crazy. Let fruits into the Army, pretty soon ya live in a fruit bowl."

"Listen, Pop, I think you better get to bed."

"Yessir, that's what the world's a-come to. Whole bunch a' fruits living in a great big fruit bowl. Ha!"

"I'll help you get ready," said Mary Jean as if she hadn't heard him.

"Reckon it's time for bed," said Father Cooter. "Where's Ma? Ain't going to sleep without Ma. Must be in the kitchen."

"Yeah. She'll be in soon."

"Where's my boys?" he said, looking around as if they might be hidden under the furniture.

"They all went upstairs to bed, Pop."

"In bed, is they? Family shouldn't ought to go to bed without sayin' goodnight. Ain't nobody here to say goodnight?"

"I'm here, Pop."

"Reckon I'll see my boys in the morning for chores?"

"Yeah, Pop. I reckon," said Mary Jean as she helped the old man out of the chair. His arms, interwoven with knotted veins and used-up muscle, wobbled as he pushed against the arms of the recliner. He farted without effort, the muffled cough of a dying engine.

His daughter led him down the hallway and into the master bedroom. He plopped down on the bed without removing his uniform and immediately closed his eyes. His matted hair fell gently over his wrinkled forehead. Mary Jean brushed it aside with her hand, bent over, and planted a kiss on his cheek. "Goodnight, old man," she said. He sighed deeply without opening his eyes. She turned off the bedside lamp and tiptoed quietly from the room.

"He don't even know who I am," she said as we were walking down the hallway.

"Who don't?"

"My old man. He don't even know I'm his girl."

"What do you mean?"

"He don't know 'cause it was after the accident. No way he could know. Ma crawled up on top of him one night and worked like hell and all's he felt was a little tingling. Might just as well have been standing stud."

"Who's he think ya are?"

"I don't know. Maid or somethin', I guess." She walked over to the television set and turned up the volume. "Long as he hears voices he'll think somebody's home and he won't get scared."

"Didn't Grandma ever tell him?" I asked.

"Nah. Probably figured it would only mix him up more than he is now." She turned off the overhead light and faced me in the dark. "He knows his three boys sure enough though. Not one of 'em does what I do for him. Cleaning up for him, feeding him. Even changing his clothes when he pees his pants, but you don't never hear him ask where's his girl at, do ya?" She pushed by me into the kitchen. "I don't mind so much though. Know why?"

"Uh uh," I said.

"I figure he's a lot like me. Nobody pays no attention to him neither." She walked ahead of me through the darkened kitchen. "Shit, it ain't his fault he don't know me. Somebody jumps on ya in the middle of the night there ain't much you can do but go along with it."

Mary Jean opened up the kitchen door and we stepped into the night. The door slammed behind us. She started walking toward the garage, where the Jeep was parked. As if it were an afterthought, she spoke back over her shoulder. "Just the same, once in a while I kinda wish he knew." She quickened her pace, not waiting for a reply.

Mary Jean had convinced me that I had no choice but to accompany her to the Hurley house. We had started this together, she had said. It was the two of us who had brought it all about. Now it was ending and we were meant to be there.

Everything has a purpose, she had told me. The Power had intended for us to find the note. If we didn't show up there was no telling what havoc it might wreak. I believed her. Why not? She had convinced my grandfather that he was resting in a house full of sleeping people.

We rode in silence to the top of the hollow. The lights from the Jeep illuminated the road in front of us. It seemed different after dark, a road stretching out to nowhere. As if we weren't moving, but stuck forever in a golden puddle of light. I tried not to think of what might be awaiting us. I wanted only an ending. To awake in the morning with the specter of the Power gone forever.

At the end of the Hollow Road one had the option of continuing up a dirt driveway for another quarter of a mile or so to the Hurley place or of using the circular clearing just prior to it as a turnaround so as to head back in the direction from which one had come. The driveway had become overrun with weeds; fallen limbs and rocks lay buried within them like forgotten corpses. Few vehicles had passed over the drive in the last ten years. At its apex sat the highest point in Shenker Hollow.

As we approached the turnaround, the Jeep's headlights illuminated another vehicle. It was the Cooter pickup truck, the one that Uncle Hooter used around the farm. The truck was parked off to the left side of the road, under a stand of maple trees. Mary Jean pulled up directly next to it and switched off the Jeep's lights and ignition.

"You can't park here," I said.

"Why not?"

"Hooter will see it when he leaves."

"He ain't leavin'," she said as she opened the door and stepped out of the Jeep. "And if he does it won't make no difference to us."

Running adjacent to the driveway, a trail wound up through the woods to the house. In the wintertime, the Anton Highway Department plowed the Hollow Road only up to the turn-around. The driveway was too steep and too full of ruts to plow. According to my father, the Hurleys used to park their vehicles at the bottom of the driveway and showshoe the rest of the way up the trail to the house. Following a heavy snow-fall, he told me, the school bus would have to wait sometimes as long as twenty minutes while the Hurley kids made their way down through the woods. After appearing at the base of the trail, covered with snow and shivering in the dawn dark-ness, they would remove their snowshoes and stick them into a snowbank in preparation for the return trek at the end of the day.

There was the time, well documented amongst natives of the hollow, when Jeremiah arrived home late one winter's night with a full package on. Deciding he had neither the present ability nor the inclination to showshoe up the hill, he got a running start with the family station wagon and hit the driveway with a full head of steam. The car made it almost a quarter of the way to the top before becoming hopelessly mired in over three feet of show. Wrapped in several empty feed sacks, which he had located in the rear of the wagon, Jere-miah curled himself up on the backseat before falling fast asleep. In the morning, stiff and suffering the effects of a hangover, but thankfully not frozen to death, he walked the rest of the way up to the house. The station wagon was not so fortunate. It remained where it was until springtime, when the snow melted enough to permit it to be driven out. For the rest of that winter the Hurley family was without the ser-vices of a car. Jeremiah was forced to make his necessary forays into Anton wrapped up like an Eskimo atop a farm tractor, and Bonnie, on grocery days, accompanied her chil-dren in and out of town as a passenger on the school bus.

Mary Jean stepped onto the trail and was immediately swallowed up by the darkness. I followed suit. The sensation was like falling through a trapdoor into a sightless dungeon. A thick tangle of trees grew along both sides of the path, their limbs converging overhead to form a black tunnel through the forest. In my blind, flailing attempts to locate Mary Jean, I ran directly into her.

"Jesus, Ollie," she hissed. "Watch where you're goin', will ya?"

"I can't see nothin'! We'll never get noplace without a light!"

As if by magic, a thin beam of light lit up my face and the surrounding area. The trees appeared gigantic in their shadows. Branches dipped and swayed in the evening breeze like graceful dancers. My aunt stood in front of me, holding a flashlight in one hand, while the other rested haphazardly upon her hip.

"Happy now, nimblenuts?" She smiled that special smile— a jagged line of hidden warmth—that I imagined was reserved just for me. Her face was radiant in the light, filled with an undisguised zeal for our mission. At such times her beauty appeared to me to reach its full attainment, as if it were bubbling up from some hidden well in the fervor of the moment. Or perhaps it was only at such times that I took notice.

She took my hand and switched off the light. "We'll have to use it sparingly or somebody's sure to spot us," she explained. "Once our eyes get used to the dark it won't be so bad."

"Who else do you reckon's up there?"

"Who knows? But whoever it is you can bet your ass they ain't gonna be happy to see us."

The moon's light, refracted by the fusion of branches, found its way into the woods in eerie splinters. The trees slowly emerged as huge dusty shadows, the path as a winding rope through blackness. Our pupils grew to the limits of their capabilities.

Mary Jean, still holding my hand, started up the path. She gripped the unlit flashlight in her free hand, swinging it back and forth in front of her face, appearing like an Amazon hacking her way through untamed jungle. Upon making contact with a shrub or overhanging branch she would grunt in wordless fury before thrusting it savagely aside. Periodically she stopped and blinked on the light in order to reorient herself, before once again crashing off through the woods toward where just seconds before the trail had been briefly illuminated.

Sweat flew from her tangled hair. A wet spot formed in the center of her back, just below her shoulder blades. It darkened and spread out in a widening circle. I kept my eyes glued to it.

I followed along, pliable and unresisting, as if I had no will of my own. My mind wandered to the Great Plains of Africa; to an episode of *Wild Kingdom*. The show had featured a unique species of bird that spent its entire life being carted about on the backs of white rhinos. The rhinos didn't mind; the birds kept their hides free of insects.

The spot had encompassed Mary Jean's entire back. Her shirt clung damply to her skin. My eyes lost their point of focus. I looked down at my feet. Morosely, obediently they trudged one after the other through the underbrush. I felt certain that they were no longer controlled by my thoughts. I wished I were a bird on a rhino's back.

Something beyond fear prickled and burned on the fringes of my consciousness. It lacked a precise definition. It had something to do with blind allegiance and right and wrong, but the concepts kept merging together like two kinds of pudding into a nauseating mess.

My aunt, strong and determined, stalked the trail in front of me, her priorities clear. Her sense of purpose defined. She showed me the way. Hadn't we been here before? I was enveloped with a sickening aura of *déjà vu;* similar to seeing a movie for the second time, yet lacking a precise memory of where the scary parts occur until, that is, they suddenly jump out big as life in front of you.

"There it is." Mary Jean had stopped. As she turned back to face me, her voice was a hushed whisper. "From here on in we can't so much as fart."

The trail came out of the woods on the far side of the pond. In the distance, less than two hundred yards away, was the Hurley house. It loomed like a silent warning through the trees. Seeing it, I shivered inwardly.

Mary Jean crouched down, still under cover of the woods. Less than twenty feet away, the surface of the pond was barely visible through the tall grass that surrounded it. A gentle breeze rustled the grass, causing the moonlight on the pond to flash sporadically through the foliage like sparks from a distant fire.

I knelt down next to Mary Jean. A gentle splashing noise broke the silence of the night. It was followed immediately by a frantic crashing in the underbrush next to the pond.

The two of us jumped involuntarily. We grabbed onto each other and rolled onto the ground like a pair of Greco-Roman wrestlers. A large buck that had been drinking from the pond came bounding through the woods not ten feet from us. I heard Mary Jean's heart pound in her chest, just beneath where my head lay. The sound was like two rocks coming together.

"Jesus, Joseph, and Mary," she breathed. "You sure are jumpy, Ollie!"

"I seen its antlers, Mary Jean!" I whispered.

"Huh?"

"It was the biggest buck I ever seen!"

"Yeah. It was a big one allright. This here is a hell of a watering hole. I reckon every animal 'round these parts stops in here every once in a while for a quick one."

"You think he took off 'cause he heard us?"

"Yeah. They got damn smart ears. That's good though.

Means there ain't nobody else right around. Else that buck woulda heard 'em." The tenseness in her body lessened. "Whoever else come up musta taken the roadway."

We rolled onto our backs and looked up through the trees. The stars were like speckled bits of diamonds in the night sky. The moon was an evil face. I felt tiny and exposed. I laid my head on my aunt's chest.

"How far away's the stars, Mary Jean?"

"Thousands a' miles," she whispered. "Maybe millions."

Her chest as she breathed lifted and lowered my head. It was the steady, rhythmic motion of a gently swelling sea. She ran her fingers softly through my hair. I had my eyes on a certain star. Without warning, it flared like an exploding rocket, and dove silently for the earth. It disappeared long before it got there. It was as if it had never been.

"A shooting star," said Mary Jean.

"What makes 'em fall like that?"

"It died," she said. "They shine for thousands a' years and then all of a sudden they just die. They always shine brightest right 'fore they die."

"But what makes 'em die?"

"I don't know. Guess they just run outta energy." She sighed and ran her fingers across my forehead. "Bet ya can't remember where it was."

"Huh?"

"Bet you can't remember where'bouts that star was in the sky. Nobody ever can. Shines like that for thousands a years and when it's gone nobody can remember where it was."

I tried to picture it. But it was gone. I turned away, laying my face sideways across Mary Jean's chest. Her breasts cupped my head, holding it as if they were firm, loving hands. Hands without fingers. I felt warm and safe. Perhaps, I thought, we could lie there forever, or at least until morning. The thought calmed me.

"Mary Jean?"

"Yeah?"

"You reckon you'll really leave when you're sixteen?"

"Huh?"

"The farm. You really gonna take off like you said?"

"You bet your ass, kid."

"But s'posin' Hooter's gone. You won't have to leave then, will ya?"

"He'll always be here far's I'm concerned. Even after that fucker is six feet under he'll be here—a goofy fat ghost hanging 'round on account of he's got nowheres else to go. I don't want no goofy fat ghost leering down at me when I sleep." She stopped and took a deep gulp of the night air. "I see him even now in my dreams—even when he ain't there. Sometimes I think maybe he really ain't nothin' but a spirit already. Just a bad fuckin' dream."

She ran her fingers gently over my face and through my hair. Warm, human sounds gurgled in her chest. I couldn't imagine life without her.

"Mary Jean?"

"Yeah?"

"I love you."

"I love you too, kid."

Her hands lingered above my eyelids, before moving lower, down toward my chest. I felt her swallow, the sound like far-off, galloping horses. Her fingers played over the skin on my stomach. Sensations abounded. An army of soldiers charged through my bloodstream, all marching toward the same battlefield. I was consumed with a mysterious longing. A need for something.

"You've got a boner on," said Mary Jean. Her fingers gently prodded the thing as if it were a sleeping animal.

"I don't either." I quickly turned my head away, thankful that Mary Jean couldn't see my face.

"Don't be ashamed, Ollie. You ain't the first guy it ever happened to." The words were kind and gentle as she breathed them into my ear. "You just don't know it yet."

She leaned over and kissed me lightly on the cheek. Then her lips moved over to my own and her hand moved down below my belt to where the battle raged. Mary Jean unzipped my pants and reached beneath my underwear, taking my swollen penis into her hand. I suddenly knew what it was that I longed for; what all the turmoil had been about.

I lay quietly unmoving as she moved her hand slowly back and forth. The furthest thing from my mind was to do anything to stop her. In my head I saw her naked with me. Like Hooter and Mrs. Wadkins had been. She increased her speed, the sound of skin slapping against skin like a thousand divers hitting the water one after another. I felt my hips moving in a peculiar rhythm in the grass beneath her hand. The tingling, spasmodic explosion, when it finally occurred, produced pitifully little in comparison to its promise.

Mary Jean wordlessly cleaned up what there was with her own shirttails before lying down next to me. As quickly as it had come the frenzied need I had felt vanished. I was ashamed for the thoughts that had passed through my mind: the picture of Mary Jean beneath me like Mrs. Wadkins had been beneath Uncle Hooter. I turned my head away and made a ridiculous attempt to cover my shrinking genitals with my hands.

A pungent smell tickled my nostrils. It was the same smell that had covered Mary Jean's sheets that night so long ago in the big house. I remembered her limping painfully about, the backs of her legs covered in black and blue welts, her eyes as distant as the night sky. I saw Uncle Hooter tiptoeing down the darkened hallway like a thief in the night. I burned with shame. I wanted to cry.

Mary Jean's long fingers played over my face like dancing feathers.

"Someday you won't be embarrassed, Ollie," she whispered kindly. "You'll know just what you want and how to go about gettin' it. Then you'll be just like everybody else and then I won't love you no more."

36

Mary Jean rolled away from me. She sat up and switched on the flashlight, carefully shielding it with her coat. She directed the thin beam of light at her wristwatch. "It's a quarter to ten," she said as she blinked off the light. "We ought to be seein' some action soon."

I was still lying in the pine needles with my pants unhinged. My genitals, cold and abandoned, huddled like refugees at the crevasse in my legs. The right side of my face throbbed from the beating it had taken. My head was foggy with details.

I longed to speak with Mary Jean, to tell her something very important, yet I wasn't sure just what it was that was so urgent. I sensed that she had given me something and that it was far different from what she had given Uncle Hooter or even Billy Bates and his friends. She had given it of her own free will and it had come from her heart. I loved her, of that I was certain. I would love her forever. I wondered at the obstacles to marrying one's aunt.

She lit a cigarette and smoked it casually while peering

through the bushes at the Hurley house. In profile, she appeared suddenly much older, like a woman in an uncaptioned painting gazing out over a wheat field. I feared that I would never be as old as her.

I zipped up my trousers and propped myself up on one elbow. Mary Jean turned to face me. "At the first sign of life, we'll move in closer," she whispered as she motioned for me to crawl up next to her.

"What if there ain't one?" I asked.

"Ain't what?"

"A sign like you said. What if there ain't one?"

"Don't be a jackass, Ollie," she said, blowing smoke out of both sides of her mouth. "Of course there'll be a sign. People can't see without lights, can they?"

I simply wanted to talk to her. To lie in the grass with her, staring up at the sky while watching the stars fall. I cared nothing about the Hurley house or the Power. Her hand had held my cock! Incredible! It was like some kind of magic wand. Damn!

"I seen something!" she hissed.

"What?"

"I seen something in the house!" she said, motioning frantically with her arm. And then I saw it. A thin beam of light that flickered somewhere within the bowels of the building. It appeared to be on the first floor, bobbing up and down as if someone were carrying a flashlight as he moved through the house.

"Do you think it's Uncle Hooter?"

"I don't know," said Mary Jean. "Seems like we woulda seen him comin' 'cross the drive if'n it was."

The light moved steadily along the back of the house. Suddenly it stopped, jerking up and down a couple of times, before going out completely.

"What happened?"

"Jesus!" replied Mary Jean. "Whoever it is just went down cellar!"

"What? Why would they do that? There ain't nothing down there but . . ."

"Who the hell knows?" said Mary Jean cutting me off in midsentence. "But damn sure that's what they done. That's why the light went out on account of they're down below the level of the windows."

"But there ain't nothing down there but the Power!"

"Jesus, Ollie! Don't you think I know that?"

That settled it. My participation had come to an end. I would watch from a distance, but there was no way I would move a step closer to the house. Mary Jean could only expect so much out of a person and . . .

"Come on," she said. "Let's get a closer look."

"What! Now? Can't we watch from here?"

"Come on, Ollie. Don't be such a lily-livered coward. The Power's on our side!" She sprang quickly to her feet and began moving in a half-crouch through the high grass toward the house.

Damn! Would the choices never get easier? I could remain there by myself in the dark with who knows what or whom roaming about; or follow Mary Jean, more than likely into another living nightmare. Once again I found myself wishing that I were an adult, as if that would somehow make the choice easier.

"Wait up!" I hissed as I stumbled blindly into the weeds, deathly afraid of losing sight of my aunt. I was thrashing about on the edge of panic when she appeared out of nowhere at my right shoulder.

"Don't make so much noise, you dipstick!"

"Well, don't leave me like that!"

"Okay, okay. Here, for God's sake. You better take my hand," she said, grabbing hold of my arm and heading off into the grass again.

The abandoned weeds lashed out at our exposed skin like thousands of tiny daggers. Night creatures scurried about amidst the foliage, the sounds of their frantic movements like Christmas wrappings being torn from their contents. A chorus of peepers and crickets laughed in hideous delight as Mary Jean and I, blundering blindly about, ran roughshod over their nocturnal world.

A fox flushed from its hiding place jumped out directly at our feet. It bared its teeth in wide-eyed panic before diving back into the brush. My grip tightened upon Mary Jean's hand. To lose her now would mean certain death. This was a black, evil land that knew no mercy. Overhead, the moon watched in pale dominance.

We had made it to the edge of the thick weeds, no more than seventy-five feet from the edge of the house, when Mary Jean slung me brusquely to the ground and flattened herself on top of me like a blitzing linebacker. She pressed her hand tightly over my mouth. Through clenched teeth, she breathed into my ear: "There's someone out there!"

I grunted into her callused palm; it having effectively barricaded both my nose and throat, I feared I might never breathe again. Her hand tasted of salt and my own cum. I spat involuntarily.

Her breath, hot and close, beat in sporadic bursts against my neck. There was a misty fragrance to it that was not unpleasant. Women, I was discovering to my puzzlement, were a plethora of odors, emitting one or another depending upon the circumstances in which they found themselves.

"He must've come up the road!" She mouthed the words into my face. "He's walkin' across the lawn toward the front of the house!"

Putting a finger to her lips, she signaled for me to keep quiet before removing her hand from my mouth. I took a gluttonous gulp of night air. Straining to keep the panic from my voice, I asked the obvious question. "Who is it?"

"It's kinda far to tell, but I think it's Hooter!"

"But if Hooter's out there, then . . ."

"I don't know who's inside," she said, reading my thoughts.

Getting quietly to our knees, we peered through the dense foliage. He was halfway across the yard, less than fifty feet from the front of the building. There was no longer any doubt. It was Uncle Hooter, moving in choppy strides toward the front steps. He peered about confidently as if daring someone to jump out of the bushes at him.

"Ten o'clock," whispered Mary Jean as she studied her watch in the moonlight. "He's right on time."

He had apparently concealed himself somewhere along the driveway, hoping to surprise whoever came up after him. I was thankful that it had not been Mary Jean or me, shivering as I thought of what the outcome might have been. Obviously no one else had showed up either or else my uncle would not then be walking in the direction of the Hurley house. But why was he coming up to the house? Something did not quite fit. It gnawed fitfully at the edge of my consciousness. If no one aside from Uncle Hooter had come up the roadway then whoever was in the house must have arrived some time ago or else been there all along. . . .

"Holy shit!" hissed Mary Jean. "It's leavin'!"

"What's leavin'?"

"The light," she whispered. "Look there! In the back of the house!"

It was there again, the thin shaft of light that we had seen earlier. It was outside, moving away from the rear of the house toward the shelter of the woods. Whoever, or whatever it was, must have left the cellar through the same broken window that Mary Jean and I had climbed in and out of so many times in the past. It might have been moving around down in the basement since we had first spotted it and we would not have known. Because of the level of the windows it was impossible to see into the cellar from outside the house unless one was right up next to the building, peering down into it.

From the front of the house, Uncle Hooter could not see the light as it moved rapidly toward the cover of the woods; likewise, whoever held the light, his vision blocked by the building, was oblivious to anything occurring at its front. Mary Jean and I had the only full-vision seats in the house. Her body, wet with sweat and fear, pressed against me. Beneath my stomach, something slithered through the grass. I clenched my teeth, not daring to move.

Uncle Hooter stopped at the front of the house. Instead of opening the door, he crouched down under the window on the hinged side of the doorway, out of sight to anyone who might have been inside. The light at the rear of the house had disappeared into the woods. Above the sounds of the night I heard Mary Jean's heavy breathing and the monotonous pounding of my heart. The slithering beneath my stomach ceased.

My uncle reached into his coat. It was a studied, deliberate movement as if he were reaching for a fresh chaw of tobacco. When his hand reappeared it contained a long, solid object. The moon's light reflected eerily off its surface.

"Holy shit!" said Mary Jean. "He's got a pistol!"

"He means business, don't he, Mary Jean?"

"He always did, Ollie. Don't you know that?" Her voice was surprisingly kind and gentle, as if the difference in our ages was thirty years instead of three. "But here's where it ends."

"The Power?" I asked.

"Of course. You believe it, don't you, Ollie?" She squeezed my leg. "With all of your heart?"

"Yes." And I did; for both of us.

He reached out with the pistol and rapped sharply on the door, the sound echoing into the night like angry laughter. The rest of the night turned suddenly quiet.

Hooter leaped back out of sight, exhibiting the same quickness he had shown when eluding the fedoraed stranger. There's no one in there, I wanted to yell out. It's all a big misunderstanding. Everyone can come out of hiding now. Allee! Allee! Umphree!

I had a strange urge to laugh out loud at the ridiculous sight of Uncle Hooter squatting outside an empty house with a pistol in his hand. Then the door swung slowly open on its rusty hinges and suddenly it didn't seem so funny anymore.

"Ollie." Mary Jean was whispering into my ear. "No matter what happens you stay right here! Do you understand?"

"Don't leave me," I pleaded.

"Sometimes the Power needs help," she said and then she was gone. Before I could say more she was off her haunches and moving quietly through the grass like a great cat stalking its prey. At the edge of the thick brush she stood up and ran across the open field, her long arms flopping madly about, her ponytail beating rhythmically against her shoulders.

I watched from the safety of the high grass as she reached the side of the house closest to me and flattened herself out against its wall. She was directly around the corner from where Hooter still crouched, silent and lethal, in front of the now-open doorway. The door banged noisily against the decaying wood on the inside wall of the house.

It is that scene, with but one small addition, that remains frozen in my mind like a snapshot on someone's mantel, glazed over with varnish and embedded in stone. The one addition being a trickle of smoke in the upper left-hand corner of the frame, barely visible to the naked eye and curling upward from the back of the house as if it were a rope lowered from Heaven.

I glanced briefly at the moon. It seemed to smile. "Whatever it is," I heard it say, "will soon be over." I wanted to throw back my head and howl. Something stopped me. In the corner of my eye, a star suddenly dropped from the sky.

Uncle Hooter must have heard the noise a split second before I did. In one motion he came up out of his crouch and rolled headfirst through the open doorway, into the unlit confines of the house. And not a moment too soon.

In that same instant the sound that had registered only seconds before as a faint rumbling turned into a full-fledged roar. A lumpy monster, eyes bulging in yellow hunger, came barreling around the curve at the top of the driveway. A deformed cretin, its pathetic mouth agape, it bore down upon the house.

I recognized the truck as being one of our own. It stopped some fifty feet in front of the building, its headlights illuminating the front yard as if it were part of a movie set.

My uncle had purchased the truck at a foreclosure sale several years before, despite the fact that he could not think of any particular reason why we might then need a dump truck. He had gotten a good price on it, he said. Every farm could always use another truck. The problem was that it had a funny-shaped bed. It was too small to haul hay in, too high off the ground to shovel shit out of, and too shallow to carry grain in. The only person who had derived much use from the vehicle was Looter, and that was only when he was forced to take it on one of his evening forays when the pickup was for some reason unavailable.

The engine popped and farted and then shut off entirely. The headlights blinked off. The night was momentarily silent.

"Hello, house!" came a voice from inside the cab.

"Who's out there?" Hooter's voice boomed forth from the house like the roar of a caged lion.

"Your loving brother! Who else?"

"Looter!" My uncle's voice was incredulous. "Jesus Christ! Was that your note?"

"Fucking-A!"

"Hoo! Hoo! Hoo!" His laughter burst into the night in great gasps. It was hollow, devoid of humor. It hung, suspended in the night air, like mist above a graveyard.

"So? What the hell do you want?"

"Your fat ass on a platter!" Looter's words were slurred, as if he had been drinking. He opened the door of the truck and stepped out. He held a shotgun in his hands.

A lantern came on in the lower window of the house. Where had that come from? I wondered. My uncle had not arrived with it. Was someone else inside?

"Them's mighty big words for a two-bit punk," came Hooter's voice from inside the house.

"This here punk has got you by the nuts, Big Brother!" He brought the shotgun up to chest level. "Now step on outta there!"

There was no immediate answer. Nothing seemed to move, as if the night had called timeout. At the edge of my vision, Mary Jean was a spidery spot on the side of the house. Looter fidgeted with his feet. The front door swung slowly open.

"Here I am," Hooter appeared as a shadow in the open doorway. "Now who you got by the nuts?"

"You don't even Goddamn get it, do ya? That's the worst part. You don't even fucking-A understand why I'm here!"

"So tell me, genius. What's eatin' ya?"

"I seen it all," replied Looter, his voice shaky, drained of some of its earlier confidence. "And it's all writ down ready to go to the Sheriff!"

"You weren't there," Hooter's voice was sure as ever. "You didn't see shit."

"That don't matter none. Bobo's just waitin' for somebody to give him just a fuckin' morsel and your ass'll be grass!" He waved the gun in the air as if at a fly.

"I'm the one called old Joe Wadkins and put a bug in his

ear 'bout your Friday-night fuck-a-thons with Martha!" He giggled like a child. "I told him if'n he was to stop by his place he might get hisself a real surprise."

"You Goddamn fool!" bellowed Hooter. Along with his chaw, he spat out a long string of juice. "You're the one killed 'em! What in hell did you do that for?"

"Knowing what old Joe's temper was I figured he'd plug ya sure as shit! No questions asked and he woulda been doing the rest of us a big favor!"

In the corner of my eye the smoking rope was getting thicker. I was vaguely aware of some other activity occurring in the woods behind the house. Still, I could not remove my eyes from the drama occurring directly in front of me. Hooter still stood in the doorway, his brother some fifty feet away, the shotgun now drooping in his hands.

"So you think ya got somethin' on me! Is that it?"

"Huh?"

"What is it you want to keep your Goddamn mouth shut? That's why you're here, ain't it?"

"I don't want nothin' but to see you beg! I didn't have the balls to say nothin' to the Sheriff before, but what you done to Craig tonight was the last straw. I writ it all down so's I couldn't back out, and tomorrow I'm meeting with Sheriff Benson." He took a step toward the house and stumbled. "I'm doin' it for the whole family and I wanted to tell ya face to face. That's the reason I'm here!"

The noise at the back of the house could no longer be ignored. Someone was running through the bushes, frantically waving his arms. He was halfway down the length of the house when he screamed: "Get away! Get away!"

Looter wheeled about in drunken fear, the shotgun coming up to his shoulder and pointing in the general direction of the unseen voice. Hooter raised his own arm and leveled it at his brother. Mary Jean appeared from around the corner of the house, reaching the doorway in two steps of her long legs and lunging toward Uncle Hooter.

"Look out!" she yelled. "He's got a gun!"

It will never be known who or what Looter was aiming at, or whether he even intended to pull the trigger at all. Perhaps as he reeled about in inebriated confusion at the sudden sound of so many voices, the gun simply discharged by itself. What is known is that the shotgun went off and the load of birdshot it contained shattered the window and the lamp behind it.

Mary Jean and Hooter went rolling into the suddenly darkened confines of the house, entwined like two human snakes. There was the sound of a single gunshot from somewhere and then the whole place went up. In that instant, above everything else, I heard but one word. It came not from inside the house and not from Looter, but from the madman crashing through the underbrush at the back of the house. "Noooo!" he wailed.

37

It was magnificent, in the way that distant bombs exploding in the night must appear magnificent to the pilot flying overhead. A thing of abstract beauty. A display of awesome brilliance, as if someone had torched a discarded Christmas tree. Sparks screamed angrily into the night. Flames stretched in orange tentacles toward the sky. The house was engulfed within seconds.

I came out of hiding and charged toward the house with but one thought in mind; Mary Jean was somewhere within that inferno. It was up to me to get her out. Nothing else mattered.

Vaguely I sensed someone bearing down on me from behind. I sensed, as one senses a punch moments before it lands, that this person was after me. It was a race to determine whether he would catch me before I could reach what was left of the Hurley house. It was a race I wanted more than anything to win—the race I had been training for ever since my father and I had embarked on our first predawn run over a year and a half earlier. I was ready. My legs were fire-driven pistons. I could not be beat.

My sole purpose was to make it there. Never mind what might occur afterward, that everything in the house was already close to charcoal and that I would likely be in the same condition moments after plunging headlong into the blaze.

The important thing was to act. The idea had appeared suddenly like a lost diamond in the sand after hours of hopeless sifting. I grabbed hold of it as if it were life itself. We had been observers, Mary Jean and I, back-scene peeping toms who had opened the gates of Hell before sitting back to watch as the Devil threw a party. Wide-eyed and aghast, we had feigned innocence. Yet, it seemed now, the ending must never have been in doubt.

It was this need to act that sent me on my mad dash across the field. That and an indescribable sense of loss, as if a hole had been bored into my soul that could never be filled.

Whoever it was, he too was in shape. He was running as if the outcome were of some consequence to him as well. He was closing fast. I heard his labored breathing at my back. The air being expelled through his lungs was like the sound of cars rushing through a tunnel. He was yelling something, but the words meant nothing. He was wasting precious energy. I did not look back.

I reached the bottom of the front steps. Sparks flew from the front doorway, singeing the skin on my face. The fire lashed out from within like an evil warning. The finish line was a lunge away.

Without pause, I charged up the steps. I had made it. Once inside, it would be up to some greater power to guide me.

My lungs filled with thick, heavy smoke. My chest felt as if it would explode. Orange devils reached out from everywhere. A stench rose above it all. Death. It was Death that smelled, worse than anything in life. And then he had me.

He pulled me away from the front doorway. I struggled, but it was not to be. The bastard would not let go. He was, I realized, much stronger than I. It seemed terribly unfair. To have run my best race and to have lost.

He threw me rudely to the ground. We were in the grass together, rolling over and over like Mary Jean and I used to do when we were much younger. Starting at the top of the knoll behind the Cooter house we would roll down the hill together in each other's arms, laughing and gasping for air, until we reached the bottom, dizzy and out of synch with the world.

Only he wasn't letting go. He was wrapping me up in a blanket and talking all the while as if he had forgotten how to stop. The words were not registering. They disappeared into the night like snatches from a neighbor's television set floating through an open window. The blanket smelled old and mildewed, as if someone had pissed on it and left it in a closet to dry. I fought against it, in mortal fear of suffocating, my last taste of life being someone else's stale piss.

I was entombed. The son of a bitch was kneading the outside of the blanket, slapping at it as if he were preparing pizza dough for the oven. He seemed determined to reshape me, to mold me into something aside from what I was. I wished he would stop. There was nothing else I would ever be. I craved only a breath of fresh air; to be free from the darkness of the tomb he had embalmed me in. The blackness was unbearable.

After much struggling, my head popped loose, protruding grotesquely from one end of the blanket like an emerging embryo. I opened my eyes. The sky was bright, emblazoned with a pinkish-red glow. Behind me, I was vaguely aware of the fire crackling and popping, noisily gorging itself upon the remains of the Hurley house and all that was in it.

I was suddenly sick. Rolling over, face down in the dirt, I coughed and retched. My insides felt as if they would be torn loose from whatever secured them. I had a sudden vision of

Billy Bates throwing up his intestines on his mother's kitchen floor, and prepared for the worst.

What came up was a greenish, syrupy liquid. It seemed, when I saw it, to be pitifully meager. It had felt like a pool of refuse as it surged upward through my throat. Now, out in the world, it seemed merely a puddle. It was immediately absorbed into the already piss-stained blanket.

There is a cleansing aspect to the process of vomiting, something beyond the internal cleansing of one's stomach. Heaving up and then lying amidst one's own filth lends to the rest of the world a polished look. It's as if what was inside of you was the worst of it. Nothing in the sudden clarity of the outside world would ever be uglier than that which was within you.

He was patting my back and still talking incessantly. The words began to make sense. One word was repeated over and over—"Ollie! Ollie! Ollie!"—as if he were a matador at a bullfight. Of course the voice was familiar to me. The speaker, no matter how hard I wished for it, was no stranger. I would have to face him sooner or later. Either that or lie forever face down in the dirt choking upon my own vomit. I rolled over to confront him.

"What?" I said, staring up into my father's face. It was black, coated with a glistening veneer of soot. His eyes bulged from within like swollen onion bulbs.

"I told you to stay away," he said, sobbing. Tears rolled down his cheeks, plowing fresh tracks through the soot. "You should have stayed away!"

"I couldn't."

"Why? Why did you have to come here tonight? Why did anyone have to come here tonight of all nights?"

"The Power," I said, feeling that the answer was obvious. "The Power brought us all here."

"What have I done? What have I done!" He began to sob

uncontrollably. His athlete's body rocked in earth-shattering tremors. I cradled his head next to my chest as my mother had done to me when I was younger. I ran my hands gently through his hair and made cooing noises as if he were a child. "It's all right, Daddy. It's all right. No one is to blame. The Power used us all."

"But I killed them." He sputtered the words into my chest. "It's me. I'm the one to blame!"

"Killed who?"

"Mary Jean and Hooter."

His words made no sense. He was speaking gibberish. I could not imagine why he had been at the house. Surely he must have known by then of the Power. It was too much of an effort to think. I patted his head and gazed upward, watching sparks explode like fireworks into the night sky.

"Our house is burning," he said.

"What?"

"I burned down our house!"

And then everything fell sickeningly into place. I fell upon him with a gut-wrenching scream and began beating on his head with my fists, trying my best to kill him. I thought of Mary Jean and Mrs. Wadkins; of Uncle Hooter and Craig; of good and evil; of love and hate; of four gusts of wind rising up together from a sealed tomb in a dark cellar, and of my father, with his perfect body and soot-stained face, as all four of them at once.

Then Looter was there, grabbing hold of me, trying desperately to pull me away. But still I would not stop. My father was the Power. He lived in the tank.

Epilogue

Peter Pond was a tremendous man. His body jiggled like a salad mold as he labored to cross the kitchen floor without respite. His breath escaped in dying gasps. His legs shook beneath their tremendous burden. As he approached the kitchen table, he glanced warily at the frailness of the assembled chairs. With a mountainous heave of his great shoulders, he pushed the two sturdiest-appearing ones together, before lowering himself onto them as if reclining into the soothing comforts of a warm bath.

My mother had prepared tea for the occasion. A cup of the steaming brew sat in front of Mr. Pond on the table. He picked it up, dwarfing the mug in his hand, and took a sip. It was a dainty sip, the type of sip one would expect to see from a blue-haired schoolmarm, certainly not from this mountain of a man.

He placed the cup gingerly into its saucer, smacking his lips as he did so, and looked across the table at my parents. His gaze moved unhurriedly from one to the other as if it were a powerful beam of light.

It paused momentarily upon my father, perched like some petulant bird upon his seat. Facing the wall, head cocked, Scooter studied his hands with apparent interest. He had not looked up since Mr. Pond's arrival.

The beam moved on. Sweeping the wall behind my father, it came to rest finally upon Nora Anne. She leaned carelessly back in her chair, legs slightly opened, pointed at the big man's vitals. Her skin, bereft of hair, shone like plated armor. She returned Mr. Pond's gaze with one of her own.

The air was charged, the room quiet, save for the tinkling of the teacups in their saucers. Craig and I huddled together in the doorway to the living room, friends of the bereaved come a-calling and uncertain as to the amenities upon entering. The big man spoke.

"You understand, Mr. and Mrs. Cooter, that the waters are fraught with suspicion." The slits containing his eyes opened slightly wider. A ridge of tiny mountains appeared amongst the skin on his forehead. "Great suspicion indeed."

He cleared his throat, the ensuing sound like that of an approaching helicopter as it reverberated throughout the confines of the tiny kitchen. Mr. Pond shook his great head, seeming surprised at the power contained within his own vocal cords. My parents said nothing.

"At the present time we can, of course, substantiate nothing. We have at our disposal, however, an army of trained investigators who will leave no stone unturned in their quest to uncover the truth." He smiled, the skin on his face rearranging itself, his forehead, like a wave of flesh, falling over his eyes once again.

My father picked up a salt shaker from the kitchen table. Still facing the wall, he tossed it lightly up and down in his hand, the shaker landing in a cadence of muffled thuds.

"We are not without sentiment. We understand that there has been a grave loss, the matter of the building aside for the moment."

He was one of those truly large people with a voice to match his girth. The type of voice that, regardless of the content of its words, thunders about a room as if being delivered from Heaven itself; its effect being, more often than not, to leave the more timid amongst its listeners cowering like newborn birds fallen from the nest.

"The Sheriff seems satisfied that the young girl apparently started the fire by accident. It seems plausible, given the fact that she was known to use the place as a sort of hideout. Of course there were also the scattered matches and burned candles found in the general vicinity. Still and all . . . at that hour of the night, and then too, the matter of the gasoline . . ."

"Cut through the bullshit, Pond." It was Nora Anne who dared silence the big man. "Say what it is that you came to say."

Mr. Pond cleared his throat once more, the sound not quite so voluminous this time. "I was merely suggesting that there are substantial holes in the various accounts of the evening's activities. The matter of Mr. Cooter, for example."

"We have been through this before," said my mother. "All of us were sitting in the kitchen when we noticed a red glow on the horizon. The menfolk drove up to see what it was all about. When they heard Mary Jean holler for help, Hooter went in after her. It was too late. Neither of them came out."

"Frankly," said Mr. Pond, "your stories don't add up."

"The Sheriff seems to buy them."

"Sheriff Benson does not represent the interests of Northeastern Mutual, Mrs. Cooter. We are entitled to conduct our own investigation. You must admit that the timing of Mr. Cooter's purchase and the suspicious nature of the fire leave us all a bit . . . curious, shall I say?"

Mr. Pond nodded toward Scooter as if my father were a part of the kitchen décor. Had the nod been intended as a cue, then my father failed to acknowledge it as such.

He had taken up a new position. Having turned to face the room, his hands now rested flat upon the table, his chin perched delicately atop them. The salt shaker had been returned to its holder. His eyes were open. He peered wordlessly up at Peter Pond, seemingly stunned into silence by the sheer enormity of the man.

No doubt there were things beyond Mr. Pond's girth on my father's mind, although in Scooter's case it was often difficult to tell. He was, after all, a creature of instinct. Or so he had proclaimed to the remainder of the family, immediately following the tragedy at the Hurley house.

The meeting had been arranged for the dual purpose of assessing our losses and solidifying our various accounts of the night's events for the edification of Sheriff Benson. My father's sudden pronouncement had followed a long silence and, once uttered, had paved the way for the remainder of his confession. It was this instinctual nature, he said, that had caused him to purchase the Hurley house in the first place.

Upon discovering through the Devon County Clerk's office that there were some five thousand dollars in back taxes due on the property and that the farm could be purchased simply by paying off what was owed, he acted upon the prompting of some divine intervention. The matter of where he was to come up with the money he left for some later sign.

It was the opportunity he had been waiting for. A chance for the big score, to return, victorious and brimming with spoils, to the family nest. He wasn't exactly sure of how the pieces would all fit together, but this would be the beginning. Of that he was certain. It was a message dropped like manna from Heaven—"More like birdshit from a migrating goose," interjected Mother Cooter, but at least we were spared Uncle Hooter's accompanying laughter.

Being anxious to get the property back onto the tax rolls, the county agreed to accept a five-hundred-dollar down payment against the arrears. My father received the deed and gave the county a sixty-day note for the balance. The fact that, after sixty days, the taxing authorities could have seized our trailer, the pickup truck, and anything else we then owned to cover the amount due had apparently not concerned him. "I knew something would come up," he said. "I was on a roll."

In fact the pickup truck could not have been seized. This portion of the story Scooter revealed as if it were a long-lost family heirloom suddenly stumbled upon by him just prior to his unveiling it to the rest of us with a grand flourish. The truck was safe from the authorities, my father assured us, because it had already been sold in order to raise the funds necessary for purchasing a fire-insurance policy on our new home.

There was an existing appraisal of the house for thirty-five thousand dollars. No one from the insurance company had bothered to update it. Scooter purchased the full coverage for a three-hundred-dollar premium, feeling secure in the knowledge that he had exchanged his only means of transportation for a year's worth of protection on his new investment.

"I might also add," said Mr. Pond, "that anything which our people uncover will immediately be turned over to the Sheriff as well as to the District Attorney's office to aid them in any possible criminal prosecution."

"What are you suggesting?" asked Nora Anne. "That one of us would kill two members of our own family for the purpose of collecting insurance money?"

"I am suggesting nothing, other than that there are a multitude of possiblities, Mrs. Cooter." The adjuster's smile broadened. He took a deep breath, filling his lungs with air as if they were a pair of great bellows. "And you may rest assured that wherever the truth lies our people will uncover it. It's their job."

"And the Sheriff's report?"

"I am not belittling Sheriff Benson's capabilities. His resources are limited. We, on the other hand, are used to dealing with such matters."

"Okay, Pond." My mother leaned forward in her chair. Moving the empty teacups aside, she faced the big man across the table. "What's the bottom line? If you had any concrete evidence you wouldn't be here."

"Unlike some of the larger companies we do not keep investigators on retainer. They cost money. Investigations also take time, Mrs. Cooter. Even if we were to come up with a clean slate, your claim might be held up for several years."

"The bottom line, Pond."

He shifted his great weight, his body resettling into its new position like the earth after a storm. A tiny bead of sweat formed just below his hairline. It dangled precariously as he spoke. "We feel that fifteen thousand dollars is more than an adequate compromise."

"Twenty-five."

"Seventeen."

"Twenty."

"Eighteen-five. Firm.

"Done," said Nora Anne. The bead of sweat dropped from Mr. Pond's head, landing with a quiet splash upon the table's surface. My father's eyes blinked shut.

The idea for the fire had come much later. The precise moment, according to Scooter's account, occurring while his right arm was inserted up to its elbow in the moist vaginal tunnel of a Holstein in heat.

"My brother's barn burned," said the owner of the receptive, if not totally ecstatic, heifer. "Lucky bastard."

"Ain't he gonna rebuild?"

"Hell, no," said the farmer. "He never could farm for shit nohow. He's takin' the insurance money and retirin' to Florida. Six years younger than me too."

"How'd it happen?" Inquired Scooter at the same instant that his hand released its potent load.

"Says it was an accident," scoffed the farmer. "Huh! Some lucky accident, says I. He'd been tryin' to sell out for years."

The heifer lowed softly. The seed had been planted in more ways than one. A double whammy had been achieved, the Divine One demonstrating not only an appreciation of symbolism but perfect timing as well. My father grasped onto the message with both hands, determined to carry it in for the big score.

As it turned out, of course, the message was a bit garbled and Scooter's timing could not have been worse. He had scored in triplicate and was left with nothing but the bitter taste of ashes in his victory cup, along with the knowledge that to reveal what he knew would only serve to tear further asunder a family already gutted in number and spirit.

Once again, despite his noble intentions, it seemed that my father had fumbled on the goal line. A royal fuckup. If Uncle Hooter were alive he would be Hoo! Hoo! Hooing! until he was blue in the face. But, of course, Uncle Hooter was no longer. As Scooter finished his tale of woe the room was encased in a deathly silence, enlivened only by my grandfather's occasional gurglings, sprinkled like bell peppers throughout an otherwise bland salad. We were, it seemed, not only laughless but leaderless. Like a grouping of formless algae, we awaited someone's gentle prodding.

"Fuck it!" said Looter at long last. "The damage has been done. Ain't no sense makin' things worse. Let's take the fucking money and keep quiet about it."

"What about justice?" asked Craig, perhaps already forming the idea for another ball-buster submission to the *Anton Courier*. He had been more aloof than ever since the night of the fire. He was the last member of the family to learn of the tragedy, having wandered out of the woods by himself early the following morning.

"Justice!" raged Looter. "That bastard licked you to within an inch of your life. You call that justice?"

"Keep quiet!" said Mother Cooter. "I won't have you talkin' about my son that way. He was the one who kept this farm afloat."

"Yeah. And it was fuckin' hell for the rest of us!" said Looter in a tone of voice he would never have used in Uncle Hooter's presence.

What about Mary Jean? I wanted to ask. How about justice for her? Everyone seemed to have forgotten that she had been lost as well. In fact no one seemed to remember her at all. I thought again of the dying star. I promised myself I would never forget.

None of them knew what the fire was all about. None of them knew what any of it was about. I wished that Mary Jean and I were playing basketball or lying in the tall grass next to Hurley's Pond. If only the night could have ended there. Her words came back to me and took on new meaning: "Someday you'll know just what you want and how to go about gettin' it. Then you'll be just like everybody else and then I won't love you no more."

"I would hope," said my mother, "that there would be enough money from the insurance to enroll Craig in a decent private school."

"Away from this hellhole?" asked my brother with new hope in his voice.

"Well, there certainly aren't many educational institutions of note in Devon County, dear."

"How's that for justice, kid?" asked Looter as if he had just produced a rabbit from his hat.

"Sakes alive!" said Craig. "There's a God at last!"

Perhaps my brother, in his zeal, should be forgiven for overstating the facts. Not God, but Northeastern Mutual had come to save him from the drudgery of Devon County. His eyes lit up like gilded nuggets. His body quivered in tremulous anticipation. Justice momentarily forgotten, he quickly regained his composure, before glancing nervously about the room and resuming his place next to Nora Anne.

"My main concern is what's best for the family," interjected Mother Cooter. "How we all goin' to survive?"

"I figured with the insurance money I could buy us a couple of really good breed bulls, Ma." Scooter came suddenly to life. He popped up off the couch as if he had sat on a cattle prod. This was it. The big dream, born to fruition. "We could start our own insemination service! Century's the only other one in Devon County and it does most of its work in the southern part of the county. We'd be the first in Anton!"

"What about the farm? Gonna just leave it rot?"

"This place is farmed out, Ma." His voice lowered with respect. "There ain't no room for a small farmer no more, leastwise not one tryin' to till a mountain a' rocks."

"It's been plenty good enough for me and your father for over forty years, and his'n for a lot longer than that."

"I know, Ma, but times change and we got to change with 'em."

"Nothin' wrong with change, I reckon, but a man's got to have some idea of where it's headin'."

"I got it all planned out," said Scooter.

My grandmother's wrinkled face appeared for a moment as if it might crack. She shoved a stray wisp of hair from her eyes and gazed wistfully up at her son. "Are you dreamin' again, Harold?"

"No, Ma. I ain't dreamin'." He glanced quickly at Nora Anne and then back to my grandmother. "I done wrong. I know that. Nobody feels worse about it than me. But I was trying to do right . . . for my family. And I still am."

"It's got to work for all of us," said Mother Cooter. "That's the important thing."

"I know that. I figure with the money we get for sellin' the herd and what's left a' the insurance we'll have plenty to get started. And I already learned enough to handle the business end of it." He was wound up, a kid at Christmas with visions of bulls' nuts dancing in his head.

The morning following the fire, he had tiptoed gingerly into my room, dressed in his THE sweatshirt and running shorts. He stood silently in the doorway, gazing toward my bed. I had spent the evening awake, staring intently up at the ceiling; there were the plaster and the cracks within, spreading out like echoes from a deep cave; and the cave itself—a deep, dark hole in the center of my vision. It was a great cave—ominous in its dimensions, yet alluring in its hidden possibilities. It seemed of vast importance that I not look away from it, that I probe it deeply with my eyes. Thus, when I was forced to look elsewhere, I did so very slowly and with a great deal of pain. When, at long last, I moved my eyes from the ceiling to the doorway, I discovered that the darkness had moved as well. It was there, black and foreboding, in the middle of my father's chest. It was, I realized with a start, no longer a part of the ceiling. It had become a part of me.

"It sure beats milking sixty head a day," said Looter. "And we wouldn't have to hire nobody neither. It'd be a family business."

Scooter turned to my mother. She sat silently on the couch, her hands intertwined in her lap like fighting vines. She looked suddenly beautiful, in the way that a caged animal appears beautiful without choice.

"But everyone's got to agree," said my father, gently placing his hand on Nora Anne's leg. "I want my family to be together."

"Where would we live?" my mother asked. "The children need stability."

"Here. For now." He squeezed the fleshy part of her leg. "But once the money starts comin' in we'll move into town if'n you want."

"In a house?"

"Yes, N'Anne. In a house. And there won't be no cowshit to track inside. I promise." He smiled down at her, shuffling his feet like a nervous child. He wore the THE sweatshirt. If it hadn't been for the wrinkled lines of age embedded in his face he might have looked like the track star whose picture adorned my mother's bedside table.

He had walked from my room that first morning without saying a word. I heard the front door open and shut, and then his footsteps pound rhythmically over the packed dirt of the driveway—whoomp whoomp whoomp—as he ran off down the Hollow Road. Later, I had heard him in the backyard doing his calisthenics, the air being pushed from his lungs in distorted grunts. In my room, the tunnel of darkness would not disappear. I knew somehow that it never would; that, in time, its pitch-black clarity might fade, but the hole would remain always, if only as a spot.

The next morning, he had showed up again, once more dressed in his running attire. Once again, he had stood in the doorway, staring wordlessly into my room. Once more I lay without moving, returning his silent gaze with one of my own. That scene was repeated the next day. And the next. And the next. Not once during those five days did a word pass between us. He would not linger long in the doorway—five minutes at the most before leaving for his run. Upon his return, he would complete his workout in the backyard, walk back inside, shower quickly, and then leave for the day. I did not hear him speak to anyone.

Nora Anne gazed up into his face, her mouth quivering, a dusting of wrinkles showing beneath her eyes. "How's your health, Harold?"

"Never better," replied my father.

The room was silent. Everyone looked at my mother. The

weight of the Cooter Farm rested heavily upon her shoulders. She fussed with her hair, took a deep breath. She reached out for Scooter's hand, slowly blowing the air from her lungs as she did so. "I'm willing to try," she said.

"It's agreed then," interjected Mother Cooter.

"Fucking-A!" said Looter.

My grandfather gurgled and dribbled spittle down his chin, actions we all took as an indication of his consent.

Thus the deal was consummated; the ruse memorialized forever. Everyone, it seemed, was to receive a piece of the pie. Everyone, that is, with the exception of me; and what I longed for most had been burnt to a crisp in the Hurley house. Amongst the spoils, I could see nothing for me—save for a spirit that would never burn, a spirit that would dance forever atop the meadow's grass, singing softly in my dreams, caressing gently while I cried.

On the fifth day, I stood at my window, gazing out as my father went through his calisthenics. His movements were precise, technically perfect—"It's better to do a couple of right ones than a whole bunch of wrong ones," he had once told me in regard to push-ups. His body appeared tight and perfectly coordinated. His skin shone with a healthy glow. How, I wondered, could a person appear so perfect on the outside and yet be so out of synch on the inside? That at least was the gist of what I was thinking. Still, he was my father. I sensed in him something wholesome—as if he were, I suppose, a loaf of natural bread, no artificial preservatives added. I got down on the floor of my room, placing my hands flat on the rug, sticking my legs straight out behind me. Slowly, I brought my chin down and touched it to the floor, being careful to move my lower body as well. I did ten of them. Perfectly.

There were details, of course. The deception itself had to pass muster. Since we were a family grown accustomed to secrets, that did not seem to present an insurmountable obstacle. Practice breeds confidence. Our studied roles were drilled to perfection. In the end, however, it was something quite apart from our consistent accounts of the night's events that swayed Sheriff Benson.

"A family don't take its own on no account," he said. "Least-wise not in Anton." Perhaps if Sheriff Benson had been with Mary Jean and me over a year earlier, when we had witnessed the fedoraed stranger behead his wife, he would have taken a different viewpoint. But then the Sheriff did not know about the Power either, or understand the ways in which it could enter a person's blood. He knew nothing about how it could get hold of a person and make him do things that he would never believe possible.

There was nobody to blame. I knew that. Mary Jean had told me that the Power acted in strange ways. My father had warned me that willing things was dangerous, that it could explode in one's face. They were both right. There was nobody to point a finger at. Nobody to hate.

The Power had been in all of us for a while. That's the way it operates. It was in Craig when he sent his last letter to the *Anton Courier;* it was inside of Looter when he had come up with his murderous scheme; and it was in my father when he lit the rags near all of that gasoline.

On the sixth day, with my father watching from the doorway, I got up from my bed. Wordlessly, I moved over to the closet and took out my running shoes. I walked over to the dresser and opened the top drawer; inside, perfectly folded, were my running shorts and the sweatshirt with the word COOTERS emblazoned across the back. Naked, in front of the mirror, I felt flabby and weak, as if I had been sick for a period of time. I slipped on the shorts and sweatshirt, before bending over to quickly lace up my shoes. Nodding—the corners of his mouth moving slightly upward—my father turned and walked from the room. Outside, he moved quickly to the front, setting the pace without looking back. I fell in behind him, my legs feeling stiff and unused. I found a slow but steady pace and stuck with it. It would, I knew, be a long and tortuous run.

The fire had done quite a job. All that remained of the house was a charred skeleton of what had been. Scooter had brought two cans of gasoline with him. After pouring some of the gas onto the cellar floor, he lit a couple of rags toward the back of the house. The rest of the gas he sprinkled throughout the upstairs. He had figured on the fire spreading slowly from the basement up, he told the rest of us. He did not, of course, count on Uncle Hooter's finding the gas lantern he had left behind. By the time Looter shot the lantern out of the window where Hooter had placed it, there were enough fumes and petrol in the house to cause a miniature explosion. The old dry house went up like kindling.

After the ashes had cooled down, a few members of the Anton Volunteer Fire Department were rummaging through the debris when they discovered the tank. It had not been touched. The varnished wood and metal were black and charred but still intact. Some of the firemen hauled it out. Looter, with the aid of a wire brush, spent several hours cleaning and polishing it. A lady from the *Anton Courier* came out to the house one morning and took a picture of it for the newspaper. Beneath the picture was a caption that posed the question "Protected by Spirits?" The article went on to explain how the tank, as a result of some miracle, had made it through the fire when nothing else in the house had.

An antique dealer from the city offered us a couple of hundred dollars for it. Folks in the city, he said, would plant flowers in it, or maybe just use it for decoration. Looter told him it wasn't for sale. "Fucking thing has protective powers," he claimed. He carted it down to the Cooter house on the back of the Chevy. He and Scooter spent the better part of one afternoon getting it down the stairs and into the cellar, where, as far as I know, it still sits.

Saving the tank didn't bother me. I knew it wasn't the cause of anything. It was what lived inside of it that had wreaked so much destruction. With that in mind, one night I snuck down to the basement and secured the lid. I snapped the padlock shut. The next morning I went up and threw the key into Hurley's Pond, just in case the Power was still lurking about, searching for a nice dark place to move into.